Readers love
SCOTTY CADE

An Unconventional Courtship

"This is a very nice story with interesting characters."
—On Top Down Under Reviews

"Mr. Cade had all the right ingredients for an amazing story… Cade's novels are for the grown and sexy group."
—Mrs. Condit & Friends Read Books

An Unconventional Union

"Scotty Cade has a sweet and easy style that is highly enjoyable to read… I will be reading more of Scotty Cade's work in the future."
—Hearts on Fire

"Beautifully written with characters that live and breathe off of the written page, *An Unconventional Union* is one of my favorite books I've read this year… Highly Recommended!"
—Top 2 Bottom Reviews

The Mystery of Ruby Lode

"This is a great read… Felt the author's ghost story was refreshingly different and its resolution was satisfying and fit the story well."
—Gay List Book Reviews

"Scotty Cade delivers a wonderful, slightly spooky story that has a wonderful mix of past and present."
—MM Good Book Reviews

By Scotty Cade

Acting Out
Final Encore
The Mystery of Ruby Lode
The Royal Street Heist

Sunrise Over Savannah • Chasing the Horizon

An Unconventional Courtship
An Unconventional Union

LOVE SERIES
Bounty of Love
Foundation of Love
Treasure of Love
Wings of Love

Published by DREAMSPINNER PRESS
http://www.dreamspinnerpress.com

THE ROYAL STREET HEIST

SCOTTY CADE

Dreamspinner Press

Published by
DREAMSPINNER PRESS

5032 Capital Circle SW, Suite 2, PMB# 279, Tallahassee, FL 32305-7886 USA
http://www.dreamspinnerpress.com/

The Royal Street Heist
© 2014 Scotty Cade.

ISBN: 978-1-63216-421-6
Digital ISBN: 978-1-63216-422-3
Library of Congress Control Number: 2014945923
First Edition November 2014

Printed in the United States of America

This paper meets the requirements of
ANSI/NISO Z39.48-1992 (Permanence of Paper).

To Kell, my husband and life partner for seventeen years, and the same man who tells me how handsome I am each and every morning of my life. His love and support make me the person I am today, and I would be lost without him. I love you, Skeeter!

And to my niece-in-law and manager of The Charleston Renaissance Gallery in Charleston, SC, Jane Harper Hicklin-Dollason. Thank you for answering my endless and sometimes stupid questions about the world of Southern art. Your knowledge and expertise made this fictional story as true and accurate as possible. Kell and I love you very much.

ONE

CRYMES VILLERIE stood beside his Chevrolet Suburban in the New Orleans Garden District, looking up at a grand but ailing St. Charles Avenue manor. He squinted against the bright July sunshine, trying to read the street numbers above the door, and turned away when his vision became blurry and his eyes started watering.

Silently cursing the sun and the stifling midsummer heat, he retrieved a white linen handkerchief from his inside coat pocket and pressed the neatly folded square against each of his eyes. He shook out the handkerchief, wiped the sweat from his brow, and dabbed at his face and neck before folding it again and sticking it back in his pocket.

Holding up his hand to block the sun's rays, Crymes gave it one more attempt, and this time he was able to read the first three numbers of the address before his eyes started watering again. He looked down at the scribbled numbers on the back of one of his business cards and felt reasonably satisfied he was at the right place. He smoothed the front of his navy blue blazer and opened the wrought-iron gate. The screeching sound of metal on metal filled his ears. Crymes cringed when the gate slammed shut behind him with a thud.

The day before, Crymes had received an anonymous cold call from someone organizing an estate sale, inviting him to preview the artwork before the sale officially began. Being an art dealer himself and the owner of a gallery on Royal Street in the heart of the French Quarter, he couldn't pass up an opportunity to discover a rare find or simply add to his collection. The Royal Renaissance focused on southern historical art, mostly surrounding the Civil War, and with forty years of experience under his belt, Crymes knew this was exactly the sort of place where he would be more than likely to find his cup of tea.

Crymes walked up to the house, took the four steps onto the wraparound porch, and knocked on the door. When the door opened, a portly man who looked to be in his midsixties stuck his hand out.

"Good afternoon, I'm Dudley Robinette. Would you be Mr. Villerie?"

"Yes. And please call me Crymes," he said, shaking the man's hand.

Dudley nodded. "Please do come in, Crymes," he said with a thick Southern drawl.

Crymes wiped his feet out of habit and stepped through the front door. The distinctive air of old money instantly overwhelmed his senses, and his heart raced with anticipation. *Stay cool, Crymes. Don't look too excited.*

Casually glancing around while his eyes slowly adjusted to the dimly lit foyer, he had to stifle a gasp of delight when he saw oil paintings hanging gallery style end to end up and down the hallway, as well as up the stairway. Determined to keep his composure and remain nonchalant, Crymes cleared his throat and looked to his left and right. Much to his surprise, the rooms to either side were more of the same.

He noticed a few people moving about and perusing the artwork on display, and was suddenly anxious to get started.

"Everything is priced, but, of course, negotiable," Dudley said. "Please wander around freely and let me know if you have any questions." Dudley looked at his watch. "Oh. I've booked appointments for four dealers at a time, and you have about forty minutes before the next round arrive."

"Thank you," Crymes said, and Dudley turned and disappeared to the back of the house.

He felt like a kid in a candy store as he previewed the gallery walls, studying each painting very closely, determining the artist, the quality of the work and frames. Although he saw excellent art, he was disappointed none fit within his specialty.

Another dealer walked up and admired a piece Crymes was studying. "Very nice," he said.

"Indeed," Crymes agreed. And then the man moved on.

Crymes ended up in the foyer again and decided to head upstairs and take in the second floor before he tackled the first. He climbed the stairs and stopped dead in his tracks midway up. Hanging in front of him was a painting he'd seen before, either in an art magazine or online somewhere. He thought the painting was called *The Tiny Soldier* or something along those lines. The price was marked at $71,500.

Crymes took out his cell phone and called the gallery.

"The Royal Renaissance."

"Harper! I need you to research the provenance of a painting."

Harper Villerie Hayes was Crymes's gallery manager, as well as his only child. She'd graduated from Tulane University with a major in art history and, after graduation, had spent some time in New York City dabbling in the art scene. She'd inherited her love for the arts from her father and, after her short stay in New York, had come back to New Orleans to follow in his footsteps.

"Hey, Crymes," she said. "Hold on. Let me get something to write with."

Crymes frowned at the use of his first name, but soon after Harper had started working beside him in the gallery, she'd dropped the Daddy thing and started calling him Crymes, forcing the issue that she wanted to make her own way without being referred to as "Daddy's little girl" or "the owner's daughter." He still wasn't used to her calling him by his first name, but he understood her reasoning and accepted it.

"Okay. I'm back," Harper said. "Shoot."

"See what you can find about a painting by Eastman Johnson. I think it's called *The Tiny Soldier*. The painting is signed by E. Johnson and dated 1864 on the bottom left corner."

"What's the approximate size?" Harper asked.

"Hold on," Crymes said as he dug into his pants pocket and pulled out the little tape measure he always kept with him. He measured the visible face of the painting and then the overall size, including the frame. "The painting itself is about fourteen and a half by eleven and a half. When you add the frame, it's twenty and three quarters by seventeen and three quarters."

"Got it. I'll get right on this."

"Oh, and Harper. I've only got about thirty-five minutes before the next set of dealers are scheduled to arrive, so call me as soon as you get something."

"Will do."

Crymes continued up the stairs and wandered through every room on the second floor. The collection there was as impressive as that in the downstairs hallway, but he found nothing that would fit in his wheelhouse. He went back down to the first floor and turned left into the formal dining room. There were three or four artists he recognized and a few scenes of New Orleans and Canal Street, but nothing he considered of any real value.

Crymes heard footsteps and an occasional hushed voice as the other dealers milled about on the first floor. He stepped through the swinging door into the kitchen and found Dudley seated at the little table flipping through a magazine. When Dudley saw Crymes, he immediately closed the magazine and jumped to his feet.

"Oh, Mr. Villerie?" Dudley asked nervously. "Is there something I can help you with?"

"Oh no, not really," Crymes said. "I'm still looking around, but I did see something I may be interested in. I have my gallery manager looking up its origin as we speak."

"Oh? Which one would that be?" Dudley asked.

Crymes pointed over his shoulder. "The Eastman Johnson hanging in the stairway."

Dudley smiled. "Oh yes, that's a lovely reproduction. One of only a few, I'm told."

Crymes cleared his throat. "Yes, but it will need some restoration work done to it before it can be resold," he said, doing his best to remain calm and looking around for a way out of the kitchen.

"Right this way," Dudley said, gesturing to another door. "There's a maid's quarters through that door," he added, looking over his shoulder, "but it's empty. However, through this door is a study, a music room, and a parlor, and then you're back to the foyer."

"Thanks," Crymes said. "I'll call you if I have any questions."

Dudley smiled again. "Very well."

Crymes walked through the study, paying special attention to every piece of art as well as the fixtures, but again saw nothing that fit his specialty. He thought about picking up a few pieces to resell to other dealers, which would turn a small profit, but he didn't want to tie up his money in something out of his comfort zone that might take a while to sell.

He proceeded to the music room and saw it was adorned with paintings from various artists depicting Mardi Gras at the turn of the century. There were colorful paintings of horse-drawn floats from the Krewes of Rex, Momus, and Proteus, all with various themes such as Robin Hood, Pinocchio, and the World of Magic. But the most impressive piece he saw was an excellent reproduction of *Le Bal Masqué* or *The Masked Ball* by the Peruvian painter Albert Lynch. He stood and gazed at it for a few minutes.

"Lovely, isn't it?" a gentleman said, walking up and then stopping next to him, folding his arms across his chest.

"It is," Crymes replied. "It's not my specialty, but I'm debating on whether to try and negotiate the price down and try to turn a quick profit."

"I'm Emanuel Della Penna, by the way," the man said, unfolding his arms and extending his hand. "Are you a dealer?"

"Crymes Villerie," Crymes replied. "I own The Royal Renaissance gallery on Royal Street."

"Ah yes. I know it well," Mr. Della Penna said. "Very nice gallery."

"Thank you," Crymes said, looking back up at the painting. "Then you know it's not really my specialty," he added.

"Your emphasis is on Southern and Civil War art, if I'm not mistaken."

Crymes nodded. "Very good. Are you a dealer?"

"Not really," Della Penna replied. "But I do dabble here and there."

"I see," Crymes replied, handing him one of his cards. "If you ever come across anything you think I might be interested in, please feel free to give me a call."

Della Pena nodded. "Surely."

"It was very nice chatting with you, but if you'll excuse me, I'd like to preview the rest of the collection before the other dealers get here."

"Understood. Good day, Mr. Villerie," Della Penna said as he walked in the opposite direction.

Crymes stepped into the parlor and grabbed the doorframe to steady himself when he saw what was staring back at him from above the mantel. It was a very old painting of Robert E. Lee at the Battle of Chancellorsville. From experience, he knew a French painter named Louis Mathieu Didier Guillaume had painted the original, and he held his breath as he tried to make out the signature at the bottom of the painting. Guillaume always signed his paintings as L.M.D. Guillaume, and Crymes ran his finger gently over the oil, which was starting to flake just a bit, and squinted to make out what he thought was a *L* and then an *M*, and then his heart started pounding when he saw a *D* and what he thought was a *G*, but it was hard to tell as the painting was deteriorating badly.

"Oh my God," Crymes mumbled under his breath. "This couldn't be the original. Could it?"

His phone rang and startled him out of his thoughts. He glanced at the caller ID and saw it was Harper. "Harper! You won't believe this," Crymes said in a shaky voice, covering his mouth as he spoke.

"What?" she asked.

"I'm looking at what I think is the original of *General Robert E. Lee at the Battle of Chancellorsville* by Guillaume."

"No way," Harper replied.

Crymes heard fingers frantically typing away at a keyboard. "Can you look up the origin and size and see if there are any reports about the original and its location?"

"I'm already on it," Harper said, mumbling as she read.

Crymes reached for his tape measure again.

"Crymes," Harper said.

"I'm here."

"The original is forty-one and three quarter inches by thirty-four inches."

Harper started mumbling again as she continued to read whatever document she'd found.

Crymes climbed on a chair and held his tape measure against the canvas horizontally. Goose bumps formed all over his body. *Oh my God!* Then he got up on his tiptoes and did the same vertically, and he felt weak in the knees.

The canvas was a hair smaller than the measurements Harper had just given him, but he had no idea how much of the canvas was actually hidden behind the frame. The gold-leaf rococo frame was at a least a foot in width, and it was in better condition than the painting.

He stepped down off of the chair on shaky legs and gave Harper the details. The price on the painting was $195,000, and Crymes was confident enough in his abilities to know that even if this wasn't the original, it was still worth a shitload more than two hundred grand.

"Crymes," Harper asked again.

"Yeah."

"According to this document from the Museum of the Confederacy, the original is rumored to have been stolen by Union soldiers just before the war ended, presented to Grant as a gift, and hasn't been seen since."

"Until now," Crymes whispered into the phone.

"Oh my God," Harper said. "How much?"

Crymes looked at the price tag again. "A couple hundred grand."

"That's a steal," Harper said. "Oh, I almost forgot. The painting you called about earlier is called *The Little Soldier*, and the last record of sale was in 1903 for seventy-five hundred dollars. It is currently valued at between six hundred and eight hundred and fifty grand."

"That's all I need to know," Crymes said. "I'll call you in a bit."

Crymes again wiped the sweat from his brow with his handkerchief and tried to put on his poker face before he found Dudley.

When he walked back into the kitchen, Dudley was just where he'd left him, looking through the same magazine. "Mr. Robinette?" Crymes said.

Dudley jumped to his feet. "Yes, sir."

"I do believe I'm interested in the Eastman Johnson in the hallway and the *Robert E. Lee* hanging in the parlor."

"I see," Dudley said.

"I'll give you two hundred thousand for both," Crymes said in the calmest voice he could muster.

"Let's see," Dudley said, picking up his calculator and punching in numbers. "I believe the Johnson is priced at $71,500 and the Lee is $195,000. That's $266,500."

He frowned. "I'm afraid I can't go that high."

Dudley punched his calculator a few more times. "The lowest I can go is $247,500."

"I'm afraid that won't work," Crymes said. "The *Lee* needs a lot of restoration, and the Johnson will need some work as well. The best I can do is $210,000."

"I'm sorry, Mr. Villerie, I'm just not authorized to go any lower. And I still have eight other dealers to consider." Dudley looked at his watch. "Four in about ten minutes, to be exact, and the other four about forty-five minutes later."

"Do you really think that between eight dealers, they are going to buy all of this artwork?" Crymes asked. "I do believe that's being very shortsighted on your part. In fact," Crymes added, "they may buy a few pieces, but you're going to have to take nickels on the dollar if you have to rely on the general public to buy this stuff."

Dudley chewed on his bottom lip, and Crymes saw his opportunity. "Good day, Mr. Robinette. And thanks for the call."

Crymes turned on his heels and was halfway down the hall when he heard Dudley scream his name. "Mr. Villerie. Wait! Give me five minutes to make a call."

Crymes smiled and turned. "Certainly, Mr. Robinette. You do that."

A few minutes later, Dudley reappeared in the foyer, smiling broadly. "We will accept your offer, Mr. Villerie."

"Wonderful," Crymes said. "I knew you were a very smart man."

Crymes asked for the required bank-routing and account numbers, called Harper, and had her wire the money directly to the law firm handling the estate before anyone could change their minds.

"I'll wait, and as soon as you can verify the bank wire, I'll take both paintings with me," Crymes said.

"Are you sure?" Dudley asked. "I can certainly have them delivered later today or tomorrow."

"That won't be necessary," Crymes said. "I'm headed to my restoration expert right now, so it will save me a second trip."

The Eastman Johnson was easy enough to handle, but it took both men, because of the frame, to get Lee down from over the mantle. By the time Crymes was closing the back of his Suburban, both men were sweating and breathing heavily. Crymes stuck out his hand. "Thank you very much, Mr. Robinette, and please keep my number if you have more artwork from future estate sales."

"I'll do that," Dudley replied. "And thank you."

Crymes got in his car and pulled away from the curb. He felt a little twinge of guilt, but the estate got nearly asking price for the paintings, although they really didn't know what they had. "That's the art business," he said out loud.

Besides, he wasn't even sure the *Lee* was an original, and if it wasn't he might very well lose money on it after restoration. The Eastman Johnson he knew was a sure thing.

TWO

A LITTLE over six months later, Crymes and his wife Charmaine were dressed to kill just minutes before The Royal Renaissance's opening of their latest exhibit, featuring the fully conserved original Louis Mathieu Didier Guillaume of *General Robert E. Lee at the Battle of Chancellorsville* and *The Little Soldier* by Eastman Johnson.

As Crymes and Charmaine gazed at the two paintings displayed proudly front and center in the gallery's main parlor, Harper and her husband Jamie walked up and joined them.

Crymes chuckled as Harper looked her mother up and down and smiled. Charmaine was in a platinum shimmer-knit floor-length gown that hugged her shapely five-foot-eleven-inch frame.

"You two look fantastic. Mom, is that a St. John?" Harper asked, hugging her mother.

"You have a great eye," Charmaine replied though a smile.

"Hey, Crymes," Harper added over her mother's shoulder. "Wow, you pulled out the tuxedo and everything?"

Crymes smirked and winked at Harper as he turned to his son-in-law. "Jamison," he said, calling him by his formal name and shaking his hand.

"Good to see you, Crymes," Jamie said as he placed a kiss on Charmaine's cheek. "Harper's right, Char. You look incredible."

"Aren't you sweet?" Charmaine said, batting her eyelashes.

"What y'all looking at?" Harper asked teasingly.

"They're beautiful, aren't they?" Charmaine said, turning back to the two paintings.

"Crymes, I must say," Harper admitted, folding her arms and tapping her foot as she looked around. "You did a fantastic job with the lighting and the backdrop. The paintings look stunning."

Crymes nodded.

"He did, didn't he?" Charmaine agreed.

Jamie leaned in and whistled when he saw the little gold-framed price tags on the paintings. "Wow," he said. The completely restored and newly appraised Guillaume came in at just under a million dollars and the Eastman at $850,000.

"Crymes," Jamie said. "You really made out like a bandit on these. Harper told me what you paid for them."

Crymes smiled. "Yeah, I'd say we got a pretty good deal on both of them."

Harper chuckled. "That's an understatement," she said under her breath.

A server walked up with a tray of crystal flutes. "Champagne?"

Crymes handed a flute to his wife and took one for himself. He glanced at his watch. "It's about show time," he said, kissing Charmaine on the cheek and scanning the room to make sure everything was ready.

Jamie took a glass from the tray and handed another to Harper. "To *The Little Soldier* and *Robert E. Lee*," he said, holding up his glass. They tapped their flutes together, and all turned in unison when the little bell on the door chimed, signaling the arrival of their first guests.

Crymes stood off in the corner, as he often did, trying to gauge the expressions and interest of the guests studying the art on exhibit. As he scanned the room, he saw Charmaine mingling and smiled to himself. She floated with ease from guest to guest, tossing her shimmering silver hair back while she chatted and then moving on to the next group. Her tall, thin form flowed easily through the crowd, and when she smiled, her blue-gray eyes sparkled. Her high cheekbones and chiseled features commanded attention and admiration. *Man, did I get lucky or what!*

Harper walked up and slid her arm inside his. "She's amazing, isn't she?"

"That she is," Crymes agreed. He squeezed Harper's arm. "I don't know how I ever got so lucky. With either of you," he added. "You know, I probably don't tell you often enough, but you're doing a great job with the gallery."

"Why, thank you—" She paused and then rose to her tiptoes and whispered in his ear. "—Daddy."

Crymes smiled and kissed her cheek. Just then a door slammed, and the gallery went silent. A man in a disheveled suit stood just inside the door, swaying back and forth.

"Where is Crymes Villerie?" the man shouted.

Crymes released Harper's hand and walked up to the man. "I'm Crymes Villerie. I don't think I've had the pleasure."

"I'm Anthony Le Moyne," the man slurred.

"Have we met?" Crymes asked, searching his brain for any connection to the boisterous man while at the same time trying to ignore the increasing buzz in the room.

"We have not." Le Moyne nabbed a champagne flute as a server passed by with a tray and then crossed the room to the Guillaume and the Johnson. "You mean you don't recognize my name?" he shouted over his shoulder.

Le Moyne? Crymes did a quick scan of his brain again, and for the life of him, he didn't. He joined Le Moyne at the paintings. "No, I'm sorry, I just can't place you."

"Well, isn't that just peachy," Le Moyne said, waving his glass around, champagne flying dangerously close to *Robert E. Lee.* "I'm the man you stole these two paintings from."

"Why don't we step into my office," Crymes said, wanting to get the man as far away from his paintings as possible.

"I don't think so," Mr. Le Moyne slurred. "I'd rather stay right here." The man then turned to the crowd. "Can I have your attention," he yelled. "You see these two paintings?" He paused for a second as the crowd quieted again. "Your gracious hosts stole these paintings from my family's estate."

"That's preposterous," Crymes said, seeing Jamie step up behind the man. Jamie was slight of build, and Crymes knew this man could crush him with one blow, so he held up a hand to stop him. "I have a bill of sale proving I bought these painting legally from an estate sale on St. Charles Avenue."

"Oh!" the man rambled almost inaudibly. "You bought them all right, from my mother's house. But you basically stole them for pennies on the dollar."

Before Crymes could respond, the front door opened, and two uniformed policemen walked into the gallery. *Oh, thank God!* He looked around and found Harper, and when she nodded, he knew she'd called them.

"This way, officers," Crymes waved. "This gentleman is intoxicated and disorderly, and I would appreciate it if you would see him out of my gallery."

The officers took Mr. Le Moyne by each of his arms and escorted him to the door. But before they could get him to the street, he yelled over his shoulder, "This is not over, Villerie. You haven't heard the last from me. I'll get those paintings back. They belong to my family!"

Before the man could say anything else, the officers pulled him away into the crowd on Royal Street and out of sight.

"I'm sorry for the intrusion," Crymes said, raising his hands and bringing them together. "Everyone, please! Have more champagne and enjoy yourself."

Charmaine and Harper got to him at the same time, with Jamie right on their heels. "Who was that man, Crymes?" Charmaine asked.

"Apparently, it was his mother's estate from which I bought these paintings," he said, gesturing over his shoulder to the Johnson and the Guillaume. "I guess he's upset because of how little I paid for them. But he needs to take that up with the manager of his estate. I made an offer, and they accepted. That's how business is done."

"Excuse me. Mr. Villerie?"

Crymes turned around to see a man in a dark business suit. "Yes?"

"May I have a word with you in private?"

"Certainly," Crymes said, hoping this was about interest in one of the paintings. "Right this way."

"If you'll excuse me," Crymes said to his family and added a wink. "I'll be right back."

Charmaine, Harper, and Jamie nodded as the two men walked away.

"Please have a seat," Crymes said when they reached his office. "What can I do for you?"

"I'm Robert Boudreaux, senior vice president at First Citizens Bank of New Orleans."

Crymes felt the blood literally draining out of his face. He cleared his throat. "Ah yes, Mr. Boudreaux. I know you've left me several messages, and I've been meaning to call you."

"Please call me Bob, and I'm sure you have," Mr. Boudreaux said. "I've been trying to get a hold of you for the last three weeks by phone, and I even came by the gallery several times, but you're weren't in."

"Yes," Crymes said. "I'm sorry about that. I've been very busy lately acquiring new artwork for the gallery."

"Unfortunately, Mr. Villerie, I hate to be the bearer of bad news," Bob said, "but I'm here to inform you that as of tomorrow, you will be served with formal foreclosure notices for the gallery here on Royal Street, your residence on Esplanade Avenue, and your property on Sullivan's Island in Charleston, South Carolina."

"But," Crymes said, "where is John Jacobs? I've dealt with him for years. Why isn't he here?"

"I'm sorry, Mr. Villerie, but Mr. Jacobs asked that I handle things from here. But believe me, he's gone to bat for you many times, and frankly, he is the only reason all of this hasn't happened any sooner. And since I know you are personal friends as well, I assured him I would handle things as gently as possible."

"I've been doing business with your bank for over twenty years. Your bank and I... we have always worked through issues, and I've *always* handled my debt."

Bob nodded. "We are well aware of that, Mr. Villerie, but your debt has been continually increasing over the last year, and as of yesterday you are now over seven months behind on both of your New Orleans mortgages and six months behind on your Charleston property. In addition, you've maxed out all of your credit and equity lines. I'm sorry, but you've given us no other choice."

Crymes leaned back in his chair and closed his eyes. He'd been hoping his two latest acquisitions would bail him out before any of this got out of hand, but the restoration had taken much longer than anticipated, and now it looked like it was going to be too late.

"Bob," he said calmly. "We're both reasonable men. I have two paintings hanging in the gallery right now for which I paid just over two hundred thousand dollars, and including restoration, I have less than a half of million invested. Both of those paintings are originals and combined are priced at just under two million dollars. When these paintings sell, I will be able to catch up on all my debt and still have money left over. Please! Can you just give me another thirty days?"

"I'm sorry, Mr. Villerie, but the process has already started. Because we've had such a long history of working together, I've been trying to catch up with you to inform you of the foreclosures in person before you received the papers. Tonight was my last attempt."

Defeated and exhausted, Crymes said, "I appreciate the gesture. I just kept hoping I could sell the paintings before all this came to a head. How much time do I have?"

"You'll be served a formal notice of foreclosure tomorrow for all three properties, and as the laws vary from state to state, next you will receive a foreclosure judgment for the Charleston property and a writ of seizure for each of the Louisiana properties. After you receive either of these, you have from ten to thirty days to vacate the property."

"I see," Crymes said. "Is there a way to serve my attorney instead of my home and my business? I have not informed my family of any of this."

"Unfortunately, that's not possible. Legally, we must serve the contact address on the mortgages."

"How about I come by the bank tomorrow morning and pick them up?" Crymes asked. "Will that work?"

"I think we can manage that as long as you sign a notice of receipt."

"I'll do that," Crymes agreed. "Say, ten o'clock?"

"I think that will be fine."

Crymes stood and extended his hand. "Thank you for coming by."

"You're welcome," Mr. Boudreaux replied. "I wish it had been under better circumstances. By the way, John speaks very highly of you."

"John is a good man." Crymes walked around his desk. "Come on, Bob. I'll show you out."

Crymes held his hand out, and Bob walked through the door and ran right into Charmaine. "Oh God," he said. "I'm so sorry."

"Oh, Charmaine," Crymes said. "Bob, this is my wife, Charmaine. Charmaine, this is Bob Boudreaux."

"Again, I'm so sorry, Mrs. Villerie."

Charmaine waved him off. "Nonsense. It was my fault. Pleased to meet you, Mr. Boudreaux."

She turned to Crymes. "I'm so sorry to bother you, darling, but I was checking to see if I could get you gentlemen anything from the bar."

"Not necessary, Char," Crymes said. "I was just showing Bob out."

"Oh!" Charmaine said. "Then it was a pleasure, Mr. Boudreaux."

Bob nodded and stepped through the door.

"I'll see you in the gallery, Char," Crymes said.

LATER THAT night, when Crymes crawled into bed, he was mentally and physically exhausted. When he sighed heavily, Charmaine looked up from her novel. "Is everything all right, Crymes?"

He lay on his back with his hands folded across his chest and his fingers linked together. He was having an internal debate with himself on whether he should tell her they were about to lose their houses and their business.

"Crymes?" she said again.

He looked in her direction. "Yes, honey?"

"I asked if everything is all right."

"I'm sorry, I didn't hear you. I must have dozed off," he lied.

"Well?" she asked again.

He figured it would just keep her up all night, and he wanted her to get one last good night's sleep before he broke the news to her. He decided tomorrow would be soon enough. "Everything's fine, Char. Why do you ask?"

"You seemed very distant after your meeting with Mr. Boudreaux this evening."

Crymes didn't want to lie to his wife outright, so he had to think quickly on his feet. "I was just disappointed. I thought I might have had a sale for one or even both of the paintings." *There. That wasn't a lie.*

"What happened?" she asked.

"We just couldn't come to an agreement."

"Was it because that man said you stole the paintings from his family?"

"I have no idea," Crymes said, giving her a peck on the cheek. "Good night, Char. I'm really exhausted."

"Good night, darling. Tomorrow's another day."

Don't remind me!

CRYMES GLANCED at the clock for what felt like the hundredth time since he'd gone to bed. It was four fifteen. He decided he just couldn't take the tossing and turning anymore, so he quietly slipped out of bed, careful not to wake Charmaine, went downstairs, and started his coffee regimen. With his first cup in hand, he wandered around the darkened living room of their eighteenth-century Esplanade Avenue home and smiled weakly as he looked at all the photographs of the years of memories created here. Each photograph painfully reminded him of the life he'd shared here with Charmaine, Harper, and now Jamison. *How am I going to tell them we're about to lose it all?*

He'd already decided on the drive home they could certainly live without their Charleston property. The Sullivan's Island beach house had been a gift he'd given Charmaine twenty years ago, and although they'd used it a lot when Harper was younger, it sat mostly empty now except for a week or two in the summer or when Harper and Jamie occasionally brought friends there for a long weekend.

But this house and the Royal Street gallery, how could they bear to lose either of them? They'd bought the house when Harper was just a baby, and they'd celebrated every birthday and holiday together right in this very room. He and Charmaine had painstakingly renovated their French Quarter home from the ground up, and she'd decorated it and redecorated at least ten times over the years and had put her heart and soul into it every time. And the gallery? Next to Harper and Charmaine, it was the thing he was the most proud of. He'd gutted the historic building and worked very closely with the Vieux Carré Commission at every turn, reviewing every known photograph and artist rendering to make sure the building was an exact replica of itself when it was first built.

Crymes blinked a few times, trying to hold back the tears stinging the backs of his eyes. "I just can't spring this on them. It'll break their hearts," he said to himself. "I've got to find another way."

Sitting in the wingback chair in front of the window, holding a half-full cup of cold coffee, Crymes watched the hopeless night turn into an even more hopeless day. He jumped when Charmaine rested a hand on his shoulder. "How long have you been up?" she asked.

"A few hours," Crymes said, resting his hand over hers.

"Crymes, I'm worried about you," Charmaine said, sitting on the ottoman across from him and taking his hand into hers. "You haven't had a good night's sleep in months."

"I'm fine, sugar," Crymes said, standing and kissing the top of her head. "You don't give it another thought. You know I'd love to sit here and share a cup of coffee with you, but I've got an appointment downtown, so I need to shower and get ready."

CHARMAINE BENOIT Villerie offered her husband a weak smile. After thirty-seven years of marriage, she knew him very well and realized he would never burden her with whatever it was that was bothering him, but she could clearly see his distress. She remained seated after he walked out of the room and dropped her head in frustration. She was fiercely protective of her family, and she wasn't going to sit by and watch any of them suffer.

Charmaine stood and walked over to the fireplace. She ran her hand along the side of a photograph of a young couple on their wedding day, full of hope and their entire lives ahead of them. She in a flowing white gown, and Crymes, with his dashing good looks, in a black tuxedo, standing in front of the St. Louis Cathedral with their parents flanking them on either side.

Where have all the years gone, she wondered silently. Now that their parents were deceased, Charmaine, an only child, had just Crymes, Harper, and Jamie to take care of. Like most strong Southern women, she was determined to do whatever it took to protect them. She straightened her shoulders with resolve and walked to the kitchen. After pouring herself a cup of coffee, she met her husband, who was at the base of the stairs, dressed and ready to go.

He kissed her cheek. "I'll call you later, sugar," he said. "You have a nice day now."

Charmaine smiled. "I have some errands to run this morning, but I'll stop by the gallery later," she said, climbing the stairs, her silk robe flowing behind her.

CRYMES PICKED up his foreclosure papers from the bank and went straight to his attorney's office. He confirmed his suspicion that bankruptcy was indeed an option and would certainly buy him some time, but ultimately, unless he could find a way to catch up on his debt, he would still lose all three properties. Selling off his inventory was also an option, but would take a great deal of time he just didn't have. The only decent news he received during his meeting was when his attorney told him under no circumstances was he to vacate any of his properties, no matter how many notices he received, until he had written proof the property had actually sold. And he knew that would take some time, so the urgency to tell Harper and Charmaine waned a bit.

His attorney explained that as of late, banks were starting foreclosure proceedings and forcing owners out of the property, then not completing the process, resulting in the owners being sued for back taxes for property they thought they no longer owned.

His only hope to get out of this was his two latest acquisitions.

When Crymes got to the gallery a little after noon, Harper and Charmaine were in his office with a spread of food covering his desk. "What a pleasant surprise," he said.

Harper looked at her mother and smiled. "Mom picked up lunch. Wasn't that sweet?"

"It was indeed," Crymes said, bending down and kissing his wife.

She offered him a warm smile. "You're going to waste away to nothing," she teased.

"Hardly," he replied, patting his stomach. "But it all looks delicious, sugar. Thank you."

"Oh, Crymes," Harper said, holding her sandwich up to her mouth. "I almost forgot. The Museum of the Confederacy called about *Robert E. Lee* and *The Little Soldier*. I guess the press release I put on the newswire got their attention."

Crymes perked up. "And?"

Harper chewed her food and swallowed. "They're sending someone to take a look at them, and they also want to authenticate."

"That's great news, Harper," Crymes said excitedly. "I was planning on calling them today anyway to discuss the very same."

"They did say that, according to their estimations, the prices were a bit high," Harper added.

Crymes smiled. "Of course they did, darling. Oh, and speaking of, did you call Lloyd's of London to make sure the paintings were insured for the proper value since the restoration?"

"Yes, sir," Harper assured him.

"Good job," he said. "How much did you insure them for?"

"Two point two million," Harper said. "The difference in premiums between insuring them at their actual value or upping it a bit was so minimal, it was worth the extra expense."

Charmaine chimed in. "Can we shelve the business talk long enough to have a nice lunch?" she asked.

"Why, certainly, sugar," Crymes said. "Harper. You heard your mother. No more business talk for the next thirty minutes."

"Yes, sir!"

Charmaine waved a hand through the air. "Oh stop it, Crymes. Now you're just making fun of me."

"Never, sugar," he said, winking at Harper.

THREE

CRYMES HEADED north on Chartres Street and turned left on Esplanade Avenue. He and Charmaine had been to a private fund-raiser at the gallery, and he'd done his best to be charming and engaging, but he'd been completely preoccupied with the events of late. The last few days had gone by with little activity, at least regarding the foreclosures. There was no word from the bank on any of the properties, and although Crymes knew not to expect anything so soon, he kept waiting for the other shoe to drop.

On a good note, the fund-raiser had brought a great deal of well-to-do patrons into the gallery, which in turn brought some much-needed attention to *Robert E. Lee* and *The Little Solider*.

"Have you heard from the Museum of the Confederacy?" Charmaine asked as they made their way down Esplanade Avenue.

"Not since the preview," Crymes said, driving past their home and taking note of how beautifully lit the gardens were. The flames from the gas lanterns flanking the front door were dancing with the slight breeze coming in off the mighty Mississippi River. Even from across the avenue, the house was stunning, and its surroundings were very impressive.

"Is that normal?" she asked.

"Not really," Crymes said. "If they see something they want, they usually go after it right away."

Crymes made a U-turn and pressed a button on his console. The wrought-iron gate slowly opened, and he pulled the car into the driveway and around to the parking pad at the rear of the house.

"That makes sense," Charmaine said. "I guess it would only cost them more to acquire the art if they added another owner to the mix."

"Precisely," Crymes replied, getting out of the car and walking around to open Charmaine's door.

When she stuck her shapely leg and high-heeled foot out of the car and offered him her hand, Crymes was reminded of just how sexy his wife still was, even after all these years. He took her hand and helped her to her feet. "You're still as stunning as the day I married you, sugar," he said.

"Thank you, darling," she whispered as she kissed his cheek. "And I'm sure you'll hear from the museum very soon."

WHEN THE phone rang, interrupting his fitful sleep, Crymes sat bolt upright in bed. His heart was racing, and he was trembling. He could hear Charmaine's soft voice and feel her hand patting his arm. "It's okay, Crymes. It's just the phone, darling." He looked over at the clock. *Three twenty-five.*

"Hello," Crymes said into the phone.

"Mr. Villerie?"

"Yes, this is Crymes Villerie."

"This is Roger Ellis from French Quarter Sound and Security. The motion detectors at 622 Royal Street have been triggered and the alarm is sounding. We have no indication of any exterior breaches, but the police have been dispatched and are on their way."

"Thank you. I'm on my way as well," Crymes said.

"Yes, sir."

Crymes jumped out of bed and dressed, insisting Charmaine go back to sleep. "It's probably just a false alarm. No use both of us losing sleep."

He drove the ten minutes to the gallery, and when he arrived, there were two police cars parked in front with flashing blue lights. Four officers stood on the sidewalk, and the security alarm was still blaring.

Crymes walked up to the group of uniformed policeman "Officers, I'm Crymes Villerie," he yelled over the wailing alarm. "I'm the owner of the gallery."

Before the officers could speak, a very clean-cut and nice-looking man walked up in plainclothes and flashed a badge. "Yes, Mr. Villerie. I'm Detective Jenkins with the NOPD. We've done a preliminary search of the alley, the courtyard, and the rear of the gallery, and we see no open doors or windows. If you'll let us in, we'll take a look around the interior."

"Certainly," Crymes said, opening the front door and entering a code on the keypad to disarm the alarm.

"What's upstairs?" Detective Jenkins asked.

"Mine and my daughter's offices, as well as a two-story guest apartment."

"You mind if we check everything out up there as well?"

"Please do," Crymes said as he flipped on the gallery lights and turned around. He instantly went weak in the knees and felt the blood drain out of his face when he saw two empty gold picture frames leaning against the wall and both of his prized paintings gone. He stumbled back against the door, and the only thing that kept him from hitting the ground was Detective Jenkins.

"Bring me a chair," Jenkins yelled.

FORTY-FIVE MINUTES later, Crymes was seated in his office with Harper, Charmaine, and Jamie standing over him.

"My God, Crymes," Harper said. "You're white as a ghost." She looked at Charmaine and Jamie. "Should we call an EMT?"

"No!" Crymes said. "I'm fine. It was just a shock to see the paintings gone. Just give me a few minutes to wrap my head around all this."

"Call homicide," an officer yelled.

"Homicide?" Crymes asked, jumping to his feet and heading for the door. "When did this turn into a homicide?"

Uniformed officers were suddenly running past his office door, into the apartment, and up the stairs to the third floor. Crymes ran up the stairs behind the officers with Harper, Charmaine, and Jamie right behind him, the women pleading with him to stop.

When he got to the third floor, someone was stretching yellow crime-scene tape across the door to the bathroom. Crymes slowly approached the bathroom door and stopped. He gasped when he saw Anthony Le Moyne lying in the bathtub with a bullet hole right in the middle of his forehead. He grabbed the doorframe to steady himself as his daughter, wife, and son-in-law came up behind him.

"No!" he said. "Stay back." But he was too late. Charmaine screamed and covered her mouth with her hand, and Harper shrieked and turned and buried her face in Jamie's chest.

"What in the hell?" Crymes said. "Anthony Le Moyne?"

"You know this man?" Detective Jenkins asked.

"WHAT DO we have?" Lead Detective Montgomery Beaumont Bissonet asked, walking up to the bathroom door with his partner, Detective August Hebert, right behind him. Bissonet looked at his partner and frowned when he saw the investigating detective already at work on the crime scene.

Detective Bruce Jenkins offered him a weak smile. "Meet Anthony Le Moyne, Esquire," Jenkins said. "A two-bit attorney. No. More like an ambulance chaser than an attorney."

"Looks like he lost one too many cases," Detective Hebert said.

"Any idea why this happened?" Bissonet asked.

"My guess is he walked in on another crime being committed here tonight."

Bissonet gave Jenkins a questioning glance.

"Follow me," Jenkins said as he led the two detectives down the stairs and into the main parlor. He walked up and stood in front of the empty wall where the two paintings had previously hung.

"A couple of hours ago, two original paintings from the Civil War era hung in this very spot. They were called *General Robert E. Lee at the Battle of Chancellorsville* and *The Little Solider*."

"Anyone checked Ulysses S. Grant's house?" Hebert teased.

"How much were they worth?" Bissonet asked.

"Combined, a little under two million," Jenkins replied.

Hebert raised an eyebrow.

"Yep," Jenkins said. "The kid was worth about eight fifty and Lee about a million," Jenkins explained. "The gallery owner acquired them about six months ago from the estate of Le Moyne's late mother. He apparently got them for a steal, and Le Moyne wasn't happy about that. He showed up intoxicated at the gallery a few days ago during the opening, caused a scene, and even threatened the gallery owner."

Bissonet looked around. "It appears this place has motion detectors. Did the alarm sound?"

"Yes," Jenkins said. "But only motion detectors. No exterior sensors were disturbed."

"How did the thief get in?" Hebert asked.

"There was a gala fund-raiser event here earlier this evening. The thief could have been a guest who snuck upstairs and hid until the event was over."

"And how did he get out with the paintings?" Bissonet asked.

"We think through a rooftop deck and the fire escape of the adjoining building."

"And the alarm didn't sound?" Bissonet asked.

"Apparently the first floor is the only area secured by the alarm system," Jenkins explained.

"That's odd," Hebert said.

"Not according to the owners," Jenkins explained. "The owner said there is only one way to the second and third floors, and that's the route up the main stairs you used earlier."

Detective Bissonet looked back over his shoulder in the direction of the stairwell. "Apparently they were wrong."

"Apparently," Hebert agreed.

"I'd like to talk to the owner," Bissonet said.

"He's upstairs in his office with his wife, daughter, and son-in-law. They all seem to be in shock, so you might want to take it easy on them."

Bissonet looked Jenkins directly in the eye. "Don't tell me how to do my job, Bruce."

"Come on, Beau," Jenkins said. "Have things deteriorated so badly between us we can't even work together?"

"Oh, I don't know, Bruce," Bissonet said wryly. "Why don't you ask the teenager you cheated on me with?"

Jenkins cringed and Bissonet smiled.

"He wasn't a teenager and you know it, Beau," Bruce said. "And maybe if you would have spent a little more time at home, I wouldn't have turned to someone else."

"Fuck it, Bruce. We've been over this a million times," Bissonet said. "I'm tired of beating a dead horse. Now tell me where the owner is again?"

"Upstairs in his office with his family," Bruce said in a defeated tone.

Bissonet turned and headed for the stairs with Hebert by his side. "Sorry you had to witness that, Auggie," Beau said. "I still can't stand to look at the guy."

"I get it, man," Auggie said. "If my wife cheated on me, I'd be in prison for murder."

"Yeah, but I've gotta get over it. I still have to work with him."

Auggie raised a hand to Beau's shoulder. "Just give it a little more time, man."

Bissonet approached the door to Crymes's office. *In shock seems to be an understatement*, he thought, glancing at Hebert. The two women were crying openly, and the older woman was also trembling and white as a sheet. The men were doing their best to console the women, but they didn't appear to be succeeding.

Bissonet knocked lightly. "Excuse me," he said. "I'm sorry to intrude, but I have some questions."

"Can this wait?" one of the men said.

Bissonet shook his head. "I'm sorry, it really can't. Which one of you is Mr. Villerie?"

"I'm Crymes Villerie," the older gentleman said.

"I'm Lead Detective Bissonet, and this is my partner, Detective Hebert."

Mr. Villerie nodded. "This is my wife, Charmaine Villerie, my daughter, Harper Villerie Hayes, and her husband, Jamison Hayes." He paused and then asked, "Detectives? What in the hell happened in there?"

"For starters," Bissonet said, "we think the victim interrupted a robbery in progress."

Crymes put his hands on his hips. "So let me get this straight. You think Le Moyne was attempting to steal my paintings, but someone beat him to it and then killed him?"

"That's what the evidence is showing so far," Hebert said.

"But who?" Harper asked. "After the way Le Moyne acted when he was here, I would have bet my life if anyone attempted to steal the paintings, it would have been him."

Bissonet made a few notes and then looked up. "You would have probably been right if he'd been a couple of hours earlier."

"I understand he came into your gallery and threatened you?" Hebert asked.

"That's right," Harper said. "He threatened my father on opening night."

Bissonet looked at his partner. "Mr. Villerie. Can you tell me the circumstances surrounding your interactions with Mr. Le Moyne?"

The detectives listened as Crymes explained how he'd received the anonymous call, how he'd come to purchase the paintings, and Mr. Le Moyne's actions and threats when he came to the gallery. "I purchased those paintings fair and square from an estate manager," he said. "I made the man an offer and he accepted. At the time I had not confirmed the origin of the paintings, nor had I determined if they were even originals or just very good reproductions."

"Of course, we'll need the name of that estate manager," Bissonet said.

"And I assume by the price they were indeed both originals?" Hebert asked.

Crymes nodded.

"Do any of you have an idea who might have stolen the paintings? Enemies? Competitors? Etcetera?"

They all seemed to be contemplating the question. "I'm afraid not," Crymes said. "But they were worth a lot of money. It could have been anyone."

Bissonet looked at Harper. "No. Not that I can think of," she replied.

Charmaine and Jamie both shook their heads.

"What about a gun? Do you have a gun on-site?"

Crymes opened his desk drawer and froze. "It's gone," he said. "I always keep my .45 right here in case of an emergency. This *is* the French Quarter, after all."

Bissonet nodded and looked at Hebert. "Get CSI in here to check for prints."

"One last question," Bissonet said. "Detective Jenkins tells me there was no security system on the second and third floors. Is that correct?"

"Yes," Harper said. "All of the artwork is kept in our vault or downstairs on display. Our offices are up here, as well as a guest suite we use for customers who come into town to preview artwork."

"It appears the thief exited through a rooftop deck with the paintings in hand," Hebert informed them. "And… escaped by hopping onto the adjoining building and down the fire escape. I don't think your building is as secure as you thought."

"Evidently," Crymes said.

"Before you leave," Bissonet said. "I'll need all of you to give statements to Detective Jenkins about the night Mr. Le Moyne came to the gallery."

"And… we'll need a list of everyone who attended the gala this evening," Hebert added.

"I'll send Detective Jenkins right up. And thank you for your time. I'll be in touch."

Bissonet and Hebert turned to leave, but Bissonet stopped. "Oh, and I almost forgot. Are the paintings insured?"

"Yes," Harper said. "By Lloyd's of London."

"And for how much?"

"Two point two million," Harper replied.

"I see," Bissonet said. "Has the insurer been notified?"

"As a matter of fact, they have," Harper said. "As soon as I arrived, I reported the stolen paintings."

"Good," Bissonet said. "Is it common to insure artwork for more than the retail value?"

"Detective," Harper explained, "with paintings as rare as these are, the value can increase on a daily basis, and also because of the value, they may not sell overnight. We just want to make sure we're protected. And besides...."

Bissonet listened as Mrs. Hayes explained the very small rate difference between the actual value and the policy amount and her rationale for overinsuring.

"Thank you very much for your time. Detective Jenkins will be up shortly."

Beau and Auggie walked down the stairs and into the parlor. Auggie found Jenkins and told him the owners were ready to give their statements, and Beau paced back and forth in the gallery in front of the blank wall.

"What gives, Beau?" Auggie asked.

"I don't know, but I've got a stinking suspicion something is not adding up here."

"Let's go over it," Auggie said. "The owner gets a mysterious call and buys two paintings from an estate for a couple of hundred grand, and the paintings turn out to be originals worth a couple million dollars. The owner has them restored or conserved, whatever they call it, hangs them in his gallery, and attempts to sell them at the appraised value."

Beau took over. "And somehow the heir to the estate finds out they were originals, is majorly pissed off, and shows up drunk, threatens the owners, and promises revenge."

"Meanwhile," Auggie added, "the owners overinsure the paintings by a couple hundred grand, and three days later they are stolen and someone is dead."

"Stolen just after a gala where someone sneaks upstairs," Beau said, "hides until the gallery is closed, and then steals both paintings. Gets surprised by the heir to the estate, also intending to steal the paintings, but instead, the original thief kills the heir and escapes through a rooftop deck and down a fire escape with the paintings."

"But...," Auggie said. "There wasn't enough time after the alarm sounded for the thief to kill Le Moyne, drag him into the bathroom, and still get the paintings out before we show up."

"Which means," Beau explained, "the thief must have killed Le Moyne before he came downstairs and set off the motion detectors."

"Exactly," Auggie said.

"None of that is likely! This was an invitation-only gala, and all guests were business associates or personal friends of the board of directors for the charity," a strange voice said.

Bissonet turned to see an extremely handsome, tall, dark-haired man snapping a rubber glove onto his right hand. *Damn, he's hot* was Beau's first thought. *Wait! Who in the fuck does this guy think he is?*

"Excuse me?" Bissonet said.

"Odds are the thief came in through the french doors leading to the rooftop deck."

"I'm sorry?" Bissonet asked. "Who in the hell are you?"

"I'm Tollison Cruz. I'm the insurance investigator for Lloyd's of London, the gallery's insurance company."

Bissonet frowned. "So just for shits and giggles, if he got in through the rooftop, how did he get out?"

"Either through the courtyard or the same way he came in," Cruz said.

"But none of the exterior sensors were disturbed," Hebert objected.

"As I understand it," Cruz explained, examining the display wall and running his fingers along the wall's edge, "the security alarm was set off by the motion detectors, and that's what the security system reported. The courtyard door could have been disabled after the alarm was already sounding, at which point the security company would have already done their job by calling the account contact and/or the police."

"That's all well and good, but what about proof?" Bissonet asked.

Cruz stopped and pulled off his rubber glove. "I don't need proof to know I'm right. It's my job. And if you like, I can help you with yours."

"How so?" Bissonet asked.

"I get a twenty percent finder's fee for recovering stolen objects in addition to my already exorbitant salary. I want that money, and you want your murderer. We have common goals. I could consult on your case and share my insight and years of experience."

"Sounds like a great idea," Hebert said. "We can always use––"

"No," Bissonet said. "That won't be necessary."

"Can't blame a guy for trying," Cruz said, looking Bissonet up and down and smiling. "Good to meet you, detectives," Cruz said over his shoulder, walking up the stairs.

Beau wiped the drool at the corner of his mouth as he watched Cruz take the stairs two at a time, the muscles in his ass flexing with every step and his round cheeks filling every millimeter of his black wool slacks. He shook his head. *It's been way too long. I need to get laid.*

"What gives?" Auggie asked. "We could have used him."

Beau waved his hand through the air. "He'd just get in the way."

"Really?" Auggie asked. "And what if he's onto something?"

Beau rolled his eyes when he saw Bruce coming down the stairs.

"Jenkins!" he yelled.

"What?"

"Check the courtyard door and see if the security sensor has been tampered with, and also see if there's an escape route from the courtyard to the alley and beyond," Bissonet instructed. "I know this guy wasn't brazen enough to carry two stolen paintings down Chartres Street at three thirty in the morning."

Auggie smiled at him. "Now, was that so hard?"

Beau smirked and looked at Auggie. "Are you coming with me, or are you gonna stay here and investigate with Mr. Cruz?"

BACK AT the precinct, Auggie was on the phone getting more details from Jenkins while Beau talked through the case again out loud.

"So," Beau said, "Le Moyne breaks into the gallery and attempts to steal the paintings he feels were stolen from him. But… he interrupts someone who beat him to it, either on the way down to steal the paintings or on the way up with the paintings in his hand. More than likely, from the location of Le Moyne's body, on the way down. Then he brings the paintings back up two flights of stairs and then carries them down the fire escape of the adjoining building."

"Except, as it turns out, that's not how it happened," Auggie said, hanging up the phone. "It appears the courtyard door sensor was tampered with, just like Cruz said." Auggie smiled.

"A very lucky guess," Beau mumbled, looking shocked.

"It appears the two screws securing the top sensor to the doorjamb were unscrewed, and the sensor was simply placed on top of the sensor on the door. That way when the door opened and closed, the connection wasn't broken, and the security company didn't see any exterior entrances breached. And... that's how the thief exited the building."

"And what about his escape?" Beau asked.

"There is a straight shot through the courtyard, down the alley, and onto Chartres Street, where Jenkins found tire marks, quite possibly when the getaway car burned rubber when they left."

"Damn," Beau hissed. "I want all the neighbors interviewed to see if they saw or heard anything, and see if you get your hands on any surveillance camera footage."

"Jenkins is already on it," Auggie said.

"Bissonet?" Captain Trenchard yelled. "In my office. Now."

"Yes, sir," Beau said, jumping to his feet and rolling his eyes at Auggie.

Beau crossed the precinct, stepped into the captain's office, and almost spit when he saw Tollison Cruz sipping on a cup of coffee.

"Detective. I believe you've already met Tollison Cruz," the captain said.

"Hiya," Cruz said with a nod and a coy smile, his leg casually crossed at the knee.

"What the f—" Beau mumbled. "What are you doing here?"

Captain Trenchard interjected. "I received a call from the mayor earlier, and apparently this has turned into a very high-profile case. Mr. Villerie is a personal friend of the mayor's, and he wants this crime solved as soon as possible. And... by using every available asset," the captain explained. "To that end, Mr. Cruz has presented me with a very compelling proposal."

"Yeah," Beau said. "I've already heard one proposal, so I can't wait to hear this one."

Cruz smirked.

"Well, I like what I heard," the captain said.

"Captain Trenchard, please tell me you're not putting him on this—"

The captain cut Beau off. "He has expertise that can help us solve this case. I'm putting him on as a consultant."

"Sir," Beau said. "With all due respect, I prefer working with my team."

"I believe Mr. Cruz will be an asset to this case."

"But—"

The captain held up a finger. "This is no longer up for discussion."

Beau cursed under his breath, but smiled and nodded.

"I look forward to working with you," Cruz said wryly, offering his hand.

Beau hesitated, then accepted. The big, tanned hand was warm, and Cruz's grip was extremely strong. Beau cursed himself for where his thoughts went from there.

He turned and walked out of the captain's office with Cruz on his heels.

"I'll give you this," Beau said when they were out of earshot of the captain. "You've got some gigantic balls."

"Thank you," Cruz said with a raised eyebrow. "I didn't think you'd noticed. But let's save the bedroom talk for later. Over a drink, maybe?"

Beau ignored the comment and poured himself a cup of coffee, not offering Cruz one.

"My theories about the thief?" Cruz asked. "Was I right?"

Beau took a sip of his coffee and smirked without answering.

"I do my job very well, Detective Bissonet," Cruz said. "This is the quickest way for both of us to get what we want. Think of it as a merger of sorts."

"More like a hostile takeover," Beau grumbled. "I'll have Detective Hebert bring you up to speed."

"AND THAT'S about where we are," Detective Hebert told Cruz while Beau looked on with a scowl covering his face.

"So what's our next move?" Cruz asked.

Bissonet stepped up. "The Major Case squad sent in a list of collectors who might be interested in Civil War history, and so we are looking into that now to see if anyone has tried to contact them regarding the paintings."

"These paintings are too hot to handle now that's there's a dead body on them," Cruz said. "The thief knows that and won't do business with anyone on your list for fear of being discovered."

"Okaaay?" Bissonet asked. "Do you have a better idea?"

"From my standpoint," Cruz said. "I'm only interested in recovering the missing paintings, so my plan is to start with the gallery owner and his family."

"Insurance fraud?" Hebert asked.

Cruz nodded. "Accounts for about fifty percent of my investigations."

"What about the estate manager?" Hebert asked. "Something doesn't seem right to me there. And Villerie's wife? She seemed overly upset over the death of someone she'd only seen once and who, while in an intoxicated state, embarrassed her husband."

"I didn't see the wife, but I agree with your summation of the estate manager," Cruz said. "If this guy even suspected he had originals, he wouldn't have let them go for such a small amount of money. And normally these estate companies do their homework."

Beau sipped his coffee and listened. Now Auggie was conversing with Cruz like he was one of the team, and Beau was getting more and more pissed by the minute.

Before he could put a stop to it, Jenkins walked up with a folder. "Yo! Guys. I think I found something."

Beau watched as Bruce stopped and did a double take when he saw the tall, dark, and handsome stranger sitting on the corner of Beau's desk.

"Bruce, meet Tollison Cruz," Auggie said. "He's working with us on this case."

Bruce nodded and smiled.

Beau gave Auggie a nasty look and then looked up at Jenkins. "Let's hear it."

"It appears our Mr. Crymes Villerie is in debt up to his eyeballs. The bank has already started foreclosure proceedings on his home, gallery, and vacation property in Charleston, South Carolina, and he's sinking fast."

"Bingo," Cruz said. "If I'm lucky, I might be able to wrap up my end of this case by dinnertime."

"You mean if *I'm* lucky," Beau said under his breath.

Cruz looked down at Beau and smiled. "Am I that hard on the eyes?"

Cocky fucker! Beau stood, ignoring the question. "Let's go and pay Mr. Villerie a visit."

"Wait," Bruce said. "That's not all."

Bruce shuffled folders and opened a second one. "It also appears that Jamison Hayes, Mr. Villerie's son-in-law, has quite a gambling problem. Horses, to be exact, and he's in deep to a couple of very ruthless bookies."

"Well, well," Beau said. "In a matter of a few minutes, we now have a person of interest and two suspects."

"And I'm still working on their phone records," Bruce added. "Should have those by late this afternoon."

FOUR

CRYMES WAS seated at his desk in the gallery, still in a daze. He and Charmaine hadn't slept a wink when they'd finally made it back home, and she'd been an absolute wreck, hysterical almost. He'd done his best to try and comfort her, but Harper finally managed to slip a Xanax in her tea, and that had settled her down a good bit before he and Harper left the house.

His phone buzzed, startling him out of his thoughts. "Yes, Harper," he said into the receiver.

"Detectives Bissonet and Hebert are here to see you."

"I'll be right down," Crymes said.

Crymes walked down the stairs and saw Harper talking to a stranger while Bissonet and Hebert were standing off to the side.

"Detective Bissonet," Crymes said as he stepped off the landing. "Please tell me you've found my paintings."

"I wish I could," Bissonet said. "But we do have a few questions. May we speak in private?"

Before Crymes could respond, Harper walked up. "Crymes, this is Tollison Cruz. He's the insurance investigator Lloyd's of London sent over."

"Nice to meet you, Mr. Cruz," Crymes said, shaking the man's hand.

"I'll be working with Detectives Bissonet and Hebert to try and recover your paintings," Cruz explained. "Is there some place private we can talk?"

Bissonet rolled his eyes. "I've already asked that question, Mr. Cruz."

"Oh, I'm sorry," Cruz replied.

"Yes," Crymes said. "Let's go up to my office."

Crymes led the way with Hebert, Cruz, and Bissonet pulling up the rear.

The three men took seats on the couch in Crymes's office while he sat on the corner of his desk.

"I'll get right to the point, Mr. Villerie," Bissonet said. "It has come to our attention that you are in quite a bit of debt and the bank is foreclosing on this very property, as well as your home and vacation home. Is that correct?"

Crymes felt his knees weaken. He gripped the ends of his desk for support, sighed, and dropped his head. "I'm afraid so."

"Mr. Villerie," Cruz said. "I'm sure you can imagine how this looks to me and my insurance company. It reeks of insurance fraud."

Crymes thought about what Cruz was saying. It had never occurred to him before now he might be a suspect. He stood. "You aren't actually insinuating I may have been the one to steal my own paintings?"

"It's a definite possibility," Cruz said. "You would be the one who stands to profit the most from the insurance settlement, as well as the sale of the paintings."

Crymes straightened his shoulders and tried to stand as tall as possible. "Well, gentlemen, I can assure you your suspicions couldn't be further from the truth," he said adamantly. "I was here at the gallery until the fund-raiser was over. I then took my wife home and went to bed. You can check my phone records and anything else you want. I assure you I did not arrange for those paintings to be stolen."

"What about your daughter?" Detective Hebert asked.

Crymes felt the hairs on the back of his neck stand at attention. "I can also assure you Harper had nothing to do with this crime either."

"How can you be so sure?" Bissonet asked. "The way I see it, if you lose the gallery, she loses her job and her legacy."

"First of all," Crymes pointed out, "she has no idea we are about to lose the gallery, and secondly, I know my daughter, and she would never get involved in anything illegal. Foreclosure or no foreclosure."

"Desperate times call for desperate measures," Cruz said.

"Mr. Villerie?" Bissonet asked. "What about your son-in-law?"

"Jamison?" Crymes asked. "Out of the question. He's a fine young man from an upstanding New Orleans family, and he's about to make partner in his father's law firm. He wouldn't chance being disbarred and embarrassing his family for something so ridiculous."

"He stands to lose as much as your daughter does," Cruz pointed out.

"Yes, gentlemen," Crymes argued. "That might all make sense if I thought either of them knew about the foreclosures. But they had no way of knowing. I… I was just notified myself a few days ago. I picked up the foreclosure papers from the bank personally to avoid being served here at the gallery so I could tell them when I found the right time."

"Are you aware your son-in-law likes the ponies?" Hebert asked.

"I'm aware he goes to the track occasionally," Crymes said. "Hell! I've even gone with him a few times."

"And what about his bookies?" Hebert asked. "Our sources tell us he's in pretty deep."

Bookies? "What bookies?" Crymes asked, unable to hide the shock in his voice.

"Mr. Hayes is very heavily indebted to two well-known and fairly ruthless bookies."

Crymes felt like all the oxygen had been sucked out of the room, and he could no longer breathe. His throat was closing up, and his vision was fading in and out. He felt his way around the edge of his desk and collapsed in his chair, unable to support his own weight. He rubbed at his eyes and covered his face with his hands. "I had no idea," he forced out when he could finally speak. "I had no idea."

"Just so you'll know," Bissonet said. "We'll be looking closely at your daughter and son-in-law, as well as your wife, as we proceed with our investigation."

"Charmaine?" Crymes asked, feeling weaker by the minute. "But she knows nothing about the foreclosures either."

"That may very well be," Hebert said. "But we're not as convinced about all this as you are."

"Thank you for your time, Mr. Villerie," Bissonet said. "We'll be in touch."

Crymes nodded and leaned forward in an attempt to stand.

Hebert held his hand up. "Please don't get up. We'll show ourselves out."

Mentally and physically exhausted, Crymes leaned back and closed his eyes. *Harper, Jamie, and now Charmaine. What is going on around here?*

BISSONET GESTURED for Hebert and Cruz to go ahead of him, and he watched Cruz's broad, muscular shoulders and tight little ass as the man walked down the stairs in front of him. The guy was a pain, all right, but he was a good-looking pain just the same! If Beau had to guess a nationality, he would go with Latin American. Cruz's mocha-colored skin, rich brown eyes, and jet black hair were dead giveaways. Combine that with the slightest bit of an accent, and he figured Cruz was from Brazil or maybe Portugal.

When they got to the bottom of the stairs, Cruz looked over his shoulder, smiled, and winked at Beau, which pissed him off immensely. "Fucker!" he said under his breath as he passed him by.

"Now, now, Beau," Cruz said wryly. "No need for obscenities."

Beau smirked and stepped out onto Royal Street, letting the door shut behind him. The heat and humidity hit him like a ton of bricks, and he crossed the street to get out of the direct sunlight. Cruz and Hebert caught up to him just as his cell phone rang. Beau looked at his phone and frowned when a picture of Jenkins's smiling face filled his screen.

Beau flashed back to the day he'd taken that picture—on the balcony at the Bourbon Pub during Mardi Gras a little over four years ago. It had been his and Bruce's second anniversary, and his heart hurt a little, seeing the twinkle in Bruce's eyes and remembering how happy they were then.

They'd broken up a year and a half ago, and he was still so angry at Bruce for cheating on him and fucking it all up that he had a hard time dealing with him. He'd had to maintain a certain amount of professionalism because they still had to work together, but he'd be damned if he was going to forgive and forget and make the whole thing easy on Bruce.

Both of them had been uniformed officers when they'd met, and after their shifts they'd had lots of time to spend together, in and out of bed. But everything had changed when Beau was offered a detective position. Their time together started to lessen, and after a year, when Beau had been promoted to lead detective, everything started to fall apart.

His caseload had been extremely heavy, and Beau had been working eighteen-hour days. In Beau's mind, though, he'd been trying to prove himself and secure his job to ultimately make a better life for the both of them, but Bruce hadn't exactly seen it that way.

In an attempt to save his relationship, Beau had called in a favor, unbeknownst to Bruce, and Bruce had been offered a detective position. Not that Bruce needed his help. He was a damned good detective and would have been promoted eventually, but their relationship wouldn't have made it until then. Things started to get better, and Beau thought they were going to make it until he found out about the affair.

Once Bruce fessed up, there was no way Beau could go back. He couldn't be with a man he couldn't trust, and everything had ended right then and there. Beau knew he shared some of the blame by neglecting Bruce, but it was his job, and if the shoe had been on the other foot, he would have never cheated. Auggie and his wife, Jenny, had been his saving graces; they had been his shoulders to lean on and had literally coaxed him back to the land of the living.

So here they were. A year and a half later, they were still working together because of a promotion Beau had arranged, and both of them were miserable doing it.

The phone rang again, startling Beau out of his thoughts, and he accepted the call. "Bissonet."

"Beau, it's Bruce."

"I'm listening," Beau said with no emotion in his voice.

Beau heard Bruce sigh and momentarily felt sorry for the guy, but it didn't take him long to recover. "Talk?" he said.

"I got the phone records back for Harper Hayes, Jamison Hayes, Crymes Villerie, and Charmaine Villerie," Bruce explained.

"And?"

"Besides the bookies," Bruce said, "Jamison's phone records are clean, and so are Mr. Villerie's and Harper Hayes's."

"And Charmaine Villerie?" Beau asked.

Bruce cleared his throat. "That's a very different story."

"I'm still listening."

"Her phone records show that the day after the paintings were first displayed at the opening, and in the days leading up to the robbery, Mrs. Villerie placed a half-dozen or so calls to a number we traced back through our database to a convicted felon named Emanuel Della Penna, who served time for that heist at the New Orleans Museum of Art ten years ago. He got five years, did his time, and up until now, he hasn't resurfaced."

Beau smiled and wiped his forehead with his coat sleeve. "I think it's time we pay Mrs. Villerie a visit. And bring Della Penna in for questioning. We'll be there as soon as we can. Is that it?" Bissonet asked.

"For now," Bruce said, disconnecting the call.

Beau looked at his phone just as Bruce's smiling face disappeared and the call was ended. "Cheater."

"Are you always that rude to your coworkers?" Cruz asked.

"Stay out of it," Bissonet said.

Hebert gave Cruz a sympathetic look. "Long story."

Beau glared at Auggie as he shared the information about the phone records with him and Cruz. They got in Beau's car and headed to Esplanade Avenue.

Bissonet parked on the street and walked up to the house. He leaned on the intercom at the gate until an unsteady voice finally answered. "Yes?"

"This is Detective Bissonet with the NOPD," Beau said. "I'd like a few words with Mrs. Villerie, please."

"This is not a good time," the voice said.

Bissonet sighed. "I apologize for the intrusion, ma'am, but I must insist."

There was silence for a few seconds. "Fine, then," the voice said rather curtly. They all grabbed their ears when a screeching sound escaped the intercom speaker and the gate started to open. "I'll meet you at the front door."

When they walked up the steps to the porch, the door opened, and an exhausted-looking Charmaine Villerie appeared in the doorway.

"How may I help you, Detective?"

"I have a few questions for you Mrs. Villerie," Beau said. "May we come in?"

Charmaine stepped back and opened the door farther, inviting them in.

"This is Detective Hebert and Tollison Cruz," Beau said, gesturing between the two men. "Mr. Cruz is the insurance investigator sent over by Lloyd's of London."

Charmaine nodded. "Can we get this over with, gentlemen? I'm a bit under the weather today."

"I can only imagine," Bissonet said. "I'm sure it is quite a shock to have your husband's paintings stolen and someone murdered in your gallery all in the same night."

"Indeed," Mrs. Villerie agreed.

"I'll get right down to it, Mrs. Villerie," Hebert said. "What was your relationship with Mr. Emanuel Della Penna?"

Beau watched the blood drain out of Mrs. Villerie's face, and she became ghostly white. Her head rolled to the side, she stumbled back, and Cruz caught her right before she hit the ground.

A few minutes later, when Mrs. Villerie came to and opened her eyes, Beau was sitting at the foot of the fainting couch on which Cruz had laid her. *Appropriately named piece of furniture*, he thought wryly.

Mrs. Villerie looked very disoriented. "Can I get you a glass of water?" Beau asked.

She shook her head from side to side, but she didn't speak.

"Do you know who I am?" Beau asked.

Mrs. Villerie nodded, covered her face with her hands, and started crying hysterically. Beau gave her a box of tissues he found in the foyer and let her cry until the sobs stopped.

"All I wanted to do is help my husband," she said through the remaining tears. "We were about to lose everything. I never meant for anyone to get hurt."

"Your husband was under the impression you knew nothing about your financial situation," Beau said.

"I overheard him talking with the bank representative the night of the opening," Charmaine said. "I never let on that I knew."

"Did you have an agreement with Mr. Della Penna?" Cruz asked.

"Yes," she said. "I cleaned out our safe and gave him ten thousand dollars in cash. But he was only supposed to steal the paintings, not kill anyone. I swear."

"How and where did you pay him?"

"Someone dropped directions to a post office box, along with a key, in my mailbox," Charmaine said. "I drove to the post office, placed the envelope of money in the box, and as instructed, tossed the key and the note in the trash."

"Do you remember the post office and box number?" Cruz asked.

Charmaine rubbed her temples. "It was a post office on Metairie Road," she said. "In the seven hundred block, I believe."

"And the box number?" Cruz asked.

"Box number four twenty... four. No! Five. Four twenty-five. That's it."

Bissonet looked at Hebert.

"I'm on it," Hebert said as he whipped out his phone.

Bissonet stood. "Charmaine Villerie. You're under arrest for conspiracy to commit grand larceny and conspiracy to commit insurance fraud. You have the right to remain silent...."

"Nooo! Please," Charmaine begged. "I didn't mean for any of this to happen."

Bissonet raised his voice and spoke over Charmaine's pleading as he continued to recite her Miranda rights. When Bissonet was finished, Hebert handcuffed her and walked her to the door.

"Don't I... don't I get a phone call or *something*?" Charmaine pleaded through sobs.

Bissonet actually felt bad for the woman, but this was a high-profile case, and the mayor was involved. He wanted to make sure they went strictly by the book.

"You'll be able to call your husband or attorney once you've been booked," Hebert explained.

"Booked?" she screamed.

"Yes. Booked," Hebert said.

"Mrs. Villerie," Bissonet said as kindly as he could, "the charges against you are very serious, and you confessed to me in front of two witnesses."

"Please? At least call my husband," Charmaine begged as Hebert escorted her out the front door.

Bissonet looked at Cruz, and Cruz offered him a weak smile.

"What the fuck," Beau said as he whipped out his phone.

Cruz laid his hand on Beau's arm before he could dial. "No. Let me," he said. "That way if there's any backlash, you had no knowledge of the call, and you can stay in the clear."

Bissonet's first thought was that Cruz was trying to set him up, and he eyed the man warily. *What's this guy's angle?*

Cruz gave him a quizzical look. "What?"

"Why should I trust *you*?" Beau asked.

"Come on, Bissonet. What could I possibly gain by making one phone call? We're supposed to be working together. Remember? And besides, I feel as badly about Mrs. Villerie as you do. She's obviously not the sharpest tool in the shed."

Bissonet decided Cruz had a point. "Fine. Make the call."

Cruz walked outside and came back a few minutes later. "He'll meet us at the precinct."

Beau nodded and looked into Cruz's honey-brown eyes. "Thanks for doing that."

"No problem, man," Cruz said with a smile warm enough to melt Antarctica in a day. "I'll go tell Mrs. Villerie he's gonna meet her there."

Beau watched Cruz walk away and tried to avoid licking his chops like a hungry wolf. The man's swagger was confident and smooth, and he was built like a brick shithouse. Of course, Beau was sure Cruz knew that and used it to his benefit whenever possible.

"You coming?" Auggie asked. "Or are you gonna stare at the guy's ass all day."

"Fuck you," Beau said to Auggie.

"In your dreams, man," Auggie teased. "How many times do I have to tell you that?"

"And how many times are you going to use that tired old joke?" Beau asked. "It wasn't even funny the first hundred times you said it. Let's just go." Beau sighed, wondering if he sounded as exhausted as he felt.

WHEN THEY reached the precinct, Emanuel Della Penna had already been picked up and was in the interrogation room, waiting to be questioned and demanding he be allowed to call his lawyer.

Bissonet let Hebert handle booking Mrs. Villerie, and he and Cruz went straight in to question Della Penna.

"Mr. Della Penna. I'm Detective Bissonet, and this is Insurance Investigator Cruz," Bissonet said.

Della Penna narrowed his eyes at Cruz and smiled coyly.

"Mr. Della Penna," Bissonet said. "It has come to our attention that Mrs. Charmaine Villerie paid you ten thousand dollars to steal two paintings from her husband's Royal Street gallery. Anything you care to tell us about that?"

"I've never met the woman, nor do I have any idea what you're talking about," Della Penna said.

"Come on, Emanuel. Is it okay if I call you Emanuel?" Cruz asked.

Della Penna just glared at Cruz.

"I guess not." Cruz glanced at Bissonet. "How long are we gonna play these games, *Mr. Della Penna*?" Cruz asked dragging out the "Penna."

"I never met the woman," Della Penna insisted.

"That may very well be true, but you did have an agreement with her," Bissonet said. "We have her testimony. Her telephone records confirm conversations between the two of you, and we know the drop-off point for the money. We have someone on the way to the post office to check it all out."

"Are all those coincidences?" Cruz asked before Della Penna could answer, apparently trying to tag team the guy.

"Let's try another route," Bissonet said. "How did you know Anthony Le Moyne?"

"Who?" Della Penna asked.

"The man you shot and killed when he interrupted your robbery already in progress," Cruz said.

"What!" Della Penna said. "That's preposterous. I didn't kill anyone!"

"We believe otherwise," Bissonet said. "Therefore, we obtained a warrant, and officers are searching your residence right now looking for the murder weapon or any more evidence that might link you to this case."

"I demand to see my lawyer," Della Penna yelled, slamming his fist down on the table.

"All in good time," Bissonet said.

"You want to tell us where you were last evening, Mr. Della Penna?"

"I had a late dinner engagement," he said, eying Cruz. "And then I went to Harrah's Casino on the river for a friendly game of blackjack. I got home a little after one in the morning."

"Were you alone?" Cruz asked.

"As a matter of fact, I was not," Della Penna added with a smirk.

"You know we will review surveillance videos from the casino and check your alibi as well?" Cruz promised.

Della Penna linked his fingers and eyed Cruz again, resting his hands on his knees. "You go right ahead and do that."

"Look," Bissonet said. "You can keep denying all of this, but like I said, we have Mrs. Villerie's confession, drop-off instructions, and the key to a post office box, as well as the telephone records. That's more than enough for an indictment for conspiracy."

Bissonet looked at Cruz because he knew he was stretching the truth, but Cruz seemed willing to play along.

"He's right," Cruz said. "I've seen people convicted on a hell of a lot less."

Della Penna was starting to perspire and fidget, a sign Bissonet knew all too well. Their tag-team approach was working, and he was getting close to cracking.

"So, Mr. Della Penna," Cruz asked, "are you ready to tell us your version of the story?"

"Fine," Della Penna said. "She called me, okay. And she begged me to do the job and wouldn't take no for an answer. I didn't commit and never intended to do it, but even if I would have, I never got the chance. I saw the news report this morning on the Royal Street heist. And… I know nothing about any post office box."

"Come on, Della Penna," Cruz said. "Are you really going to play it like this?"

Before Della Penna could answer, there was a knock at the door. Cruz turned to Bissonet, who opened the door and frowned when he saw Jenkins standing outside. He shook his head vaguely at Cruz and then moved into the hall and closed the door behind him. "What?" he asked.

Jenkins handed him a brown paper bag. "Here's your money. It was in the post office box where Villerie said it was."

"And the post office box?" Bissonet asked.

"New," Jenkins said. "Registered to a Matthew Davis. The address on the paperwork was an abandoned storefront on Aris Avenue in Old Metairie."

Bissonet opened his mouth to ask his last question, but Jenkins held his hand up to stop him. "Our database search turned up nothing."

"Fuck," Bissonet hissed. "Della Penna never retrieved the money."

Beau glared at Jenkins. He hated interacting with the guy now, but he had to admit the man knew how to do his job. He'd come a long way since his promotion, infidelity or not.

"Get someone to take a photo of Della Penna over to Brennan's and verify that he was there for dinner last night and then check out the surveillance video from the blackjack tables at Harrah's Casino between ten o'clock and 1:00 a.m. I want to see if Della Penna was gambling there, and more importantly, if he left with someone."

Without a word, Bissonet turned and headed for the interrogation room. He placed his hand on the doorknob and then looked over his shoulder. The pain and sadness on Bruce's face was obvious. Beau had lived with him. Slept with him. And he'd seen that same lost look once before when Bruce's mother had died suddenly. He had the sudden urge to wrap Bruce in his arms and make it all better.

"Fuck," he cursed under his breath. *What the fuck, Beau? No! Stop it!*

Beau straightened his shoulders and quickly buried the onslaught of emotions that, if left unattended, might just be his demise. *I am not wasting my time feeling sorry for him.*

"Oh, and I want a tail on Della Penna the minute I release him," he managed to say before he reentered the room and shut the door on Bruce.

Bissonet walked around the table, leaned on his hands, and glowered at Della Penna. "Mr. Della Penna," he said, "you're free to go. For now! Do not leave the state, and if we can't verify your alibi, you'll be sitting in this chair again very soon."

"What?" Cruz said, glaring at Bissonet.

Della Penna smiled coyly and stood.

"You're letting him walk?" Cruz asked.

Bissonet ignored Cruz's question. "We'll be in touch."

As soon as Della Penna was out of the door, Cruz slammed his fist down on the table. "What the fuck, Bissonet?"

Beau narrowed his eyes and held up a finger. "Don't you ever question my decisions in front of a suspect again? Got it?"

"Fuck you," Cruz said. "I thought we were working together. And pretty efficiently, I might add."

"There's no magic here, Cruz," Bissonet said sarcastically. "If Hebert would have been here instead of you, we would have been doing the same good cop, bad cop tag-team routine we do during every interrogation like this. So don't go patting yourself on the back so soon."

Cruz's eyes narrowed and his face got beet red. He clenched his fists, mumbling something under his breath Beau couldn't make out. Beau braced himself. He thought for certain Cruz was going to lunge over the table and come at him with full force. But to the man's credit, he started taking deep breaths and attempting to calm himself. "Why did he walk?" he said through clenched teeth.

"He didn't take the money," Bissonet said. "It was in the post office box right where Villerie said she'd left it."

Cruz just shook his head.

"And," Bissonet added, "if his alibi checks out, which should be relatively easy to verify, we have nothing to hold him on."

"We know he agreed to do the job for Villerie," Cruz said, now pacing.

Bissonet shook his head. "But we can't prove it yet. Right now it's his word against hers."

Cruz stopped and ran his fingers through his thick coal black hair.

"Look!" Bissonet said. "I've got a tail on him, so we'll know his every move, and if we get something solid, we'll bring him in again. It's that simple."

"Fine," Cruz said, heading for the door. "I've had enough of your pleasantries for one day."

Bissonet smirked and followed him out of the interrogation room and down the hall. "The sooner we get this over with, the sooner you can get back to your cushy little insurance job," he finally said to his temporary partner.

Cruz stopped short, and Bissonet had to step to the side to avoid running into the back of him. The man folded his arms over his chest. "Before I leave today, I sure would like to know who rammed something up your ass and pissed you off at the same time. You are one bitter, angry motherfucker."

In Beau's mind, he staggered back and struggled to remove the dagger Cruz had stabbed right through his heart. In actuality, he knew he'd simply frozen in place with his mouth slightly agape.

But Cruz was right. Since things had gone south with Bruce, he *had* turned into a bitter, angry motherfucker. The problem was no one had ever called him on it before now. Most of his close friends on the force knew about him and Bruce and what had gone down between them, so they just left it all alone and took whatever anger he dished out. The sad truth was when his relationship with Bruce ended, Beau had felt furious, disconnected, and totally adrift. And things hadn't gotten any better. He didn't want to feel this way, but he didn't know how not to. *Fuck Cruz*, he thought. *This is none of his fucking business.*

Beau really wanted to let Cruz have it, but at the moment, he was just too tired to fight, so he decided to let the comment go for now. He sighed, shook his head, and started to walk away.

"I'd bet my life Detective Jenkins did the ramming, though," Cruz said sarcastically.

Beau stopped when he heard Cruz's words. He turned and glared at the man, who was still standing with his arms folded across his chest. But now he had an all-knowing smirk on his face to match his stance.

Beau closed his eyes and took a deep breath. Decking his short-term associate wouldn't get him many brownie points with the captain—or with the mayor, for that matter—so he chose his words carefully. "Listen up, Cruz, 'cause I'm only going to say this once," he muttered as they stood face-to-face in the hallway. "My demeanor and my personal life are not up for *discussion*. We're not going to be buddies. I don't want to know how many times your heart's been broken or how many times you wet your pants. Frankly, I don't want to know anything about you. I want to solve this case and get you out of my hair as soon as possible. Is that clear?"

Cruz smiled like he knew he'd hit the nail on the head. Beau had the sudden urge to throttle him right there, but wouldn't his captain just love that? He quickly decided the guy wasn't worth the effort.

"Seven a.m. sharp," Beau hissed.

On the way out of the building, Beau ran into Auggie. "How did it go with Mrs. Villerie?" he asked.

"We booked her," Auggie said. "Her attorney, who just happens to be her son-in-law, came in and arranged for her bail hearing. What about Della Penna?"

As they walked to their cars, Beau filled Auggie in on what went down with Della Penna, the money, and how they were still checking his alibi.

"Tomorrow's another day," Auggie said as they approached his car.

"Hey, Aug?" Beau said. "Can I ask you something?"

"Sure," Auggie said.

"Am I a son of a bitch to work with?"

"To me? Noooo," Auggie said hesitantly.

Beau cocked an eyebrow. "And to others?"

Auggie sighed. "Okay, sometimes, maybe. Especially to Bruce."

Before Beau could say anything, Auggie held up a hand. "And I know why. But man, you're gonna have to let go of that sometime soon."

Beau looked down and kicked a piece of gravel around with the toe of his shoe. When he looked up, their eyes met, and Auggie offered him a weak smile.

"You're right," Beau said. "But I'm just so damned angry at him for ruining our lives."

"Look, man," Auggie said. "Don't hit me or anything, but if things were so perfect between you, Bruce would have never gone outside of your relationship. I know him, remember, and I think he's a good guy who made a stupid mistake. We all make them."

"If it were Jenny who'd cheated on you, would you be able to work with her every day and not let it get in the way of your job?"

"Oh hell no," Auggie said. "But I'm a forty-seven-year-old Neanderthal who has the 'little woman always obeys' and 'a man's home is his castle' mentality. You're a thirty-four-year-old homosexual who is supposed to be more modern, open-minded, and forgiving."

Beau chuckled. "Don't let Jenny hear you say that."

"Tell me about it," Auggie said nervously as he opened his car door.

Beau slapped the hood of Auggie's black Crown Vic. "Thanks, man," he said. "I'll give this some thought."

Auggie leaned over, threw his leg into the car, and froze. "Jesus," he screamed, bracing himself on the car door. "Beau?"

Beau was around the door in seconds and by his side. "Is it your back again?" Beau asked.

"Yeah," Auggie said. "I can't straighten up."

"What do you mean, you can't straighten up?" Beau said.

Auggie huffed. "What part of that statement didn't you understand?"

"Really?" Beau asked.

Auggie tried to straighten again and almost dropped to his knees. "Please tell me you have your SUV today?"

"Yeah. Why?"

"The only way I'm gonna get home is lying flat on my back in the back of that thing."

Beau looked around. "I'm on the next level up. Are you gonna be okay while I get the car?"

Auggie nodded. "Just hurry, man."

Beau took off running and headed for the stairwell. He took the stairs two at a time, bolted across the parking garage, and was behind the wheel of his SUV in minutes. He screeched to a halt in front of Auggie's car, opened his hatch, and threw his racquetball gear and gym bag into the front passenger seat. He folded down the back seat and then went over to help Auggie.

They slowly made it to the back of the SUV by taking very small, deliberate steps. Auggie crawled into the back on all fours and stretched out. Beau walked over and shut Auggie's car door and locked it before he closed the hatch to his SUV.

"ARE YOU purposely trying to hit every bump on Rampart Street?" Auggie yelled.

"I'm doing the best I can," Beau said. "New Orleans is the home of the potholes."

"Damn, man," Auggie hissed. "Take it easy before I end up in traction."

Beau whistled. "Anybody ever tell you you're a difficult patient?"

"Just shut up and drive."

Beau hit the hands-free button on his steering wheel. "Call Auggie at home."

The female voice quickly responded, "Calling Auggie at home."

The phone rang a few times, and then Jenny answered. "What's wrong, Beau?" she asked nervously.

"Hello to you too. Why do you always assume the worst?" he asked with a chuckle.

"You didn't answer my question," Jenny said.

"Auggie threw his back out again."

Jenny sighed. "What crazy thing did you have him doing this time?"

"Nothing. I swear," Beau muttered. "He was just getting into his car."

"Jesus," Jenny replied. "Where is he?"

"He's sprawled out in the back of my SUV. We'll be there in five minutes."

"I'll be ready."

Beau heard the computerized female voice again. "Call ended."

"Bye to you too," Beau said into the silence.

An hour later, with Auggie in good hands, Beau headed uptown to his Prytania and Broadway neighborhood. He recounted his conversation with Auggie about his moods of late and the way he treated his coworkers, especially Bruce. He concluded Auggie was probably right. Bruce *was* a good guy who'd made a big mistake. But that realization wouldn't help him get over it any quicker.

He resented the hell out of Bruce for ruining their lives, but Bruce wasn't solely to blame. The more he thought, the more he realized he must nevertheless care for the guy if he was still letting all this get to him. But Beau also knew himself well enough to know no matter how much he cared for Bruce, he could never trust him again, and he could never be with someone he couldn't trust.

"We're never going to be in a relationship again, so maybe it's time I give the guy a break," he said to himself. "There's no use holding on to the past." Then suddenly, Tollison Cruz's handsome face came to mind. "That asshole is a totally different story, though. No fucking breaks for him."

FIVE

BEAU WAS seated at his desk, going over the paperwork for the case, when Cruz walked in with one cup of coffee and sat in the chair opposite him. Beau glanced at his watch but didn't look up. "I knew you'd be late."

"And I knew you'd still have a stick up your ass."

Beau continued reading but stifled a smile. "I just got a lead that one of the paintings may have surfaced in Charleston."

"Which one?" Cruz asked.

"*Robert E. Lee*," Beau replied. "I've booked a flight that leaves in a couple of hours."

"I'm going with you," Cruz said.

"I figured as much," Beau said. "I booked you a ticket as well and had our travel department book us a hotel for the night."

"Thank you," Cruz said with a surprised tone in his voice. "What about your partner?"

Beau bounced the eraser of his pencil on the surface of his desk. "He's out for a couple of weeks with a back injury."

"Jesus," Cruz cursed. "You mean I've got to deal with you all by myself until I solve this case?"

Arrogant bastard, Beau thought, but let the comment slide. "Looks that way," he said, gesturing to the door. "You better head home and pack a bag."

Cruz stood. "How long will we be gone?"

"Probably just overnight, but you never know."

Beau looked up when he heard a knock at his door. He fought the urge to scowl when he saw Bruce waving a folder in his hand.

"May I come in?" Bruce asked.

Beau gestured to the other chair, and Cruz sat down again.

"Do you have any news?" Cruz asked.

"Yeah," Bruce said without hesitation and went right into his report. "It appears that Della Penna was indeed at Brennan's night before last, dining with an attractive guy in his thirties, according to their waitress. He said they seemed to be having a pretty intense conversation. We're working to identify him right now. Della Penna was also at a blackjack table at Harrah's for approximately three hours and was joined at the table by a short, attractive brunette about an hour into his game, and according to outdoor and parking garage cameras, they left together just before one a.m."

"Damn," Beau said. "Not what I wanted to hear."

"Is that it?" Cruz asked.

Bruce nodded. "For now."

Cruz stood again. "If you'll excuse me, I have some packing to do." He turned to Bissonet. "I'll be back in an hour."

Beau nodded.

Bruce looked extremely nervous and stood.

"Wait," Beau said. "Before you go, I just… I just wanted to say I'm sorry for the way I've been treating you."

Bruce's eyes widened and his mouth hung open.

Beau held up a hand. "Don't get me wrong," he said. "I'm still extremely pissed off at you for… for what you did, but I realize I had a part to play in it as well. But that was our personal life, and this is business, and we do have to work together. And besides, I think it's time I let it all go."

Bruce stood up and closed the door. "I made a mistake, Beau," he admitted, his eyes starting to tear up. "The worst mistake of my life, and if I could, I would have taken it back the minute it happened, but I can't. And I know it cost me you, and I'll have to live with that consequence for the rest of my life. I'm sorry for hurting you."

"There's no need to rehash any of this," Beau said. "We've been over it all hundreds of times, and talking about is not going to change any of the facts."

Bruce wiped a tear from his cheek. "Thank you for saying what you did. But you can cut yourself some slack because you haven't been any harder on me than I have been on myself. I deserve everything you gave me and probably more."

Beau got up and walked around his desk. He stood in front of Bruce and wrapped his arms around him. It felt good to hold him. Beau inhaled, and Bruce's familiar scent filled his nostrils. For a moment he was encompassed with the easy feeling of home, but it felt different now. The need and anticipation were no longer there, and in the end it was just sad and empty. Beau felt Bruce holding on for dear life, and when Bruce buried his head in Beau's neck, Beau released his hold and stepped away.

Bruce smoothed the front of his shirt and wiped at his eyes. "Thank you for that."

Beau nodded, opened the door, and stepped to the side.

Bruce walked past him and then stopped and looked back. "I'll let you know as soon as we find out the identity of the guy Della Penna had dinner with."

"Thanks, Bruce."

THE TRAFFIC on I-10 westbound was stop and go all the way from Causeway Boulevard to the airport exit, and the drive was stressful at best. Beau tried to make small talk a couple of times, but apparently Cruz had heard him loud and clear the night before. *We're not going to be buddies. I don't want to know how many times your heart's been broken or how many times you wet your pants. Frankly, I don't want to know anything about you. I want to solve this case and get you out of my hair as soon as possible. Is that clear?*

When Cruz did grace him with an answer that was something other than a grunt, it was regarding the case and right to the point. Beau was relieved when they finally parked at the airport and headed to the Delta counter to pay for their tickets.

Beau smirked when he overheard Cruz, who must have just realized they were sitting together, asking the attendant to relocate him to another seat. He smiled to himself when the attendant said both legs of the flight were heavily booked and all she had was a center seat in the exit row on the New Orleans-Atlanta leg and nothing available from Atlanta to Charleston. With this news, he heard Cruz agree to stay where he was. But Beau quickly realized he must have really pissed the guy off if he didn't even want to sit next to him on an airplane.

Beau flashed his badge and alerted the attendant that he had a weapon and ammunition in his baggage, which he knew had to be checked. He overheard Cruz arguing with the attendant next to him when they wouldn't accept his permit to carry a concealed weapon and allow him to check his carry-on bag with his weapon inside.

Beau walked over and smiled at the attendant. He glanced at her nametag as he held out his badge again. "Excuse me, Ms. Tisdale. Tisdale? What a lovely name."

"Thank you," the attendant said.

"I couldn't help overhearing your conversation, and let me just say I think you're doing an excellent job of enforcing security regulations."

The woman smiled and batted her eyes at him. "Thank you again"—she looked down at the badge—"Detective. And thanks for all you do as well."

Beau flashed her his million-dollar smile. "My pleasure, ma'am. And this man is accompanying me to Charleston on a very important case. I can vouch for him, and if you like, I'll even allow him to put his weapon in my checked baggage with mine. Would that be easier for you?"

"It would indeed."

"Okay, then. Let's do that."

Cruz rolled his eyes when Beau winked at him, unzipped his duffel bag, and held it open for Cruz to drop in his .45, along with a box of ammunition.

Beau stepped back over to his attendant and placed his bag on the scale. After it was weighed, his attendant picked it up and put it on the conveyor belt behind her and handed him his boarding pass. Cruz was already walking toward security when Beau caught up to him.

"You're welcome," Beau said, slowing his pace.

"Fuck you, Bissonet. Are all you lily white sliced-bread Caucasians the same?"

Beau saw the fire burning in Cruz's dark Latin eyes and decided it might be best if he didn't respond with his normal sarcastic humor.

"Just because my passport says Tollison Eduardo Braga Cruz and I'm a Portuguese-American, do I look like some kind of drug lord or terrorist to you? That back there," Cruz said, gesturing over his shoulder, "was nothing more than racial profiling at its best. Who does she think she is? Just because Ms. Tisdale is a blonde with blue eyes, lives in the suburbs with her husband, two point five kids, and a damn dog doesn't make her any better than me."

"Suck it up, Cruz," Beau said. "I'm sure you're not the first person to be racially profiled."

Cruz glared at him, which was quickly becoming a normal occurrence, but he kept walking and didn't respond.

By the time they got through security, their flight was already boarding. Luckily they had a window and aisle on the two-seat side of the plane, and Cruz, without asking, slid into the window seat. "I think I have the window seat," Beau said.

"Suck it up, Bissonet. I'm sure you're not the first person to have someone take your seat on an airplane."

Beau stood in the aisle and shook his head. Although Cruz rubbed him the wrong way at every turn, he was pretty quick-witted. Beau had to give him that much.

After Beau removed the case file from his satchel and shoved the leather bag in the overhead compartment, he took the aisle seat, which he preferred anyway, and held the file on his lap, looking straight ahead.

Cruz pulled down the shade and leaned against the window, folding his arms over his chest and closing his eyes.

"Night," Beau mumbled sarcastically.

TOLLISON WAS fuming in his seat. His heart was pumping blood through his veins at breakneck speeds, and it took everything he had to not let Bissonet see how pissed off he really was. How pissed he'd been since he'd arrived in New Orleans and was paired with the not-so-dynamic duo.

He couldn't remember the last time he'd been so angry with anyone, let alone someone with whom he was working. But then again, no one he'd ever worked with before had been such an asshole.

Who does this guy think he is? Tollison thought. *I'm just trying to do my job.*

Once they were airborne, the jet engines whined and the vibration lulled Tollison into a calmer state. He slowed his breathing and willed himself to let go and finally relax. *Don't let the fucker get to you,* he said to himself.

By the time the plane had climbed to its final cruising altitude and leveled out, Tollison had calmed himself down enough to think rationally. With no other distractions, he was finally able to see things from Bissonet's perspective. The man was used to working with his partner and having no one question his authority. All of a sudden, Tollison showed up and threw a monkey wrench into his routine. But Tollison had had no way of knowing the mayor was going to get involved and actually put him on the case with Bissonet and Hebert. That had come as a total surprise to him as well.

Although Tollison fought the urge to deck Bissonet at every turn, he had to admit the man was hotter than shit. He was very handsome and built like a big buff gymnast. *The guy must work out for hours every day.* But based on their current schedule, Tollison couldn't imagine when he found the time.

When Bissonet let his guard down, which wasn't often, he had this childlike quality that tugged at Tollison's heartstrings. When a piece of the case fell into place, before he caught himself, his silvery blue-gray eyes sparkled and his smile dripped with satisfaction and pride. In addition, when he dropped the attitude and relaxed, his voice was warm and velvety and clung to Tollison like a soft, silky skin. But those instances were few and far between. Ninety-nine percent of the time, Bissonet was a hardass, motherfucking know-it-all who wanted no part of anyone's opinions except his own.

The man was intimidating, no doubt, and although they were about the same height, Tollison had tried to make himself appear to be taller when the opportunity presented itself, just to have that little bit of an edge. On the few occasions when they had stood close to each other, Tollison had had to fight the urge to imagine how they would line up in bed and how Bissonet would feel in his arms.

Just before Tollison dozed off, his last thought was of the way Bissonet treated Detective Jenkins. Tollison would bet his life there was a story there, and he felt certain it went way beyond the NOPD.

BEAU SLOWLY read and reread the paperwork surrounding the case one page at a time. It was a habit he'd picked up a long time ago to see if he could identify anything he might have missed in an earlier pass. But no matter how hard he tried, he just couldn't focus. Every so often he caught himself glancing at Cruz out of the corner of his eye, and something about the man sleeping next to him held his attention.

Finally giving up on the quick glances and the case, Beau watched Cruz intently as his breathing eventually evened out and the stress and worry lines disappeared from his face. Every now and then, Cruz made the softest little whimpering noise, and for some reason, the sound made Beau smile. Intrigued by the guy, Beau rested his head on the back of the seat facing Cruz and studied him further. In his current position, to the other passengers and crew, it would simply look like Beau was napping, so he took full advantage of the time, not knowing if he would ever get the opportunity again.

Cruz's dark hair was disheveled and falling across his forehead. Beau pictured the rich, caramel-colored eyes hiding behind the closed lids and admired the long black eyelashes lying flat against his naturally tanned skin. Cruz's nose, lips, and chin were perfectly shaped for his slender face and head, which sat atop broad shoulders. His handsome silk necktie was tied loosely around his thick neck, and his arms were still folded across his chest. Beau could clearly see his broad upper body and massive arms stretching the fabric of his obviously expensive and well-tailored white dress shirt.

Finally, his upper body tapered down to a small waist and flat stomach that led to long legs stretched out in front of him, crossed at the ankles with highly polished black dress shoes tied tightly on his feet. Cruz was no doubt a sight to behold, even if he was an arrogant and oh-so-annoying asshole.

Studying the guy, Beau realized that, however annoying, Cruz was the first man he'd even looked at twice since the demise of his relationship with Bruce.

After letting go of some of his anger and cutting Bruce a little slack earlier today, Beau thought he might finally be making progress in his quest to escape the emotional maze in which he'd been living and therefore preparing to move on with his life.

He closed his eyes and, for a second, wished for happier times with Bruce, but deep down he knew those days were gone forever. Realizing he was tired of being hurt and angry, Beau decided he needed to start putting the pieces of his life back together. No more escaping to the gym for hours at a time to attack that leather punching bag with the mental picture of Bruce's face smiling back at him. No more lifting weights to work out his frustrations and anger day after day for hours on end until he was too exhausted to think. He wanted to laugh again and do normal things like normal people. If he was being honest with himself, he could see that although the pain had subsided some and the anger had softened around the edges a bit, he'd chosen to hold on to it all, as opposed to letting it go and moving on with his life.

It was time to stop.

He was startled out of his thoughts by the familiar ding and announcement that they were starting their initial descent into Atlanta and to prepare the cabin for landing. Cruz was still sound asleep, so Beau reached over and touched his arm gently.

"Cruz?"

The sleeping giant didn't move.

"Cruz? Wake up. We're almost to Atlanta."

TOLLISON HEARD that soft, velvety-smooth voice and rolled over to his side, laid his head on a solid shoulder, and draped his arm across the chest of the man sitting beside him.

"Cruz? What are you doing?"

Tollison opened his eyes and panicked. He saw Bissonet staring at him with amusement. He withdrew his arm, straightened in his seat, and cleared his throat. "Uh, sorry. I was asleep."

"Uh-huh," Bissonet replied in a sarcastic tone. "Can't keep your hands off of me, can ya, Cruz?"

"Fuck you," Cruz whispered for the umpteenth time today. "There you go flattering yourself again."

Tollison raised his arms over his head and stretched. He covered his mouth and tried to stifle a yawn. As the plane touched down, he elevated the window shade and squinted against the bright sunshine.

He looked at his watch. *Right on time*, he thought. *I hope the next leg goes as smoothly.*

And it did. They changed planes, and an hour later they touched down in Charleston.

Bissonet and Cruz made their way through the unusually crowded airport to baggage claim, where they stood at the carousel and waited for their bags. As Beau looked around, he noticed the baggage claim area was crowded with very fit men and women, all sporting runner's bodies.

"Oh dear lord," he said. "I hope this isn't the weekend for the Cooper River Bridge Race. If so, we're so screwed."

"What does that have to do with anything?" Tollison asked.

"Downtown will be packed with runners and spectators, and traffic will be gridlocked."

Once they'd retrieved the bags, Bissonet checked for their weapons, and the two men crossed the street to the rental car area. Just before they pulled out of the airport parking lot, Bissonet reached over the seat and dug inside his suit coat pocket. He handed Cruz his travel itinerary. "Can you see where we're staying and plug it into the GPS?"

Tollison unfolded and scanned the piece of paper. "Looks like were at the Planters Inn on Market Street."

"Oh, okay," Bissonet said. "No need to plug it in. I know exactly where it is."

They were no more than three miles down I-26 when traffic came to a crawl. "Damn," Bissonet said, pulling slightly over onto the shoulder to see if he could figure out what the holdup was. When he apparently saw nothing, he pulled back onto the highway again.

"Can you google the Cooper River Bridge Race and please tell me it's not this weekend?" Bissonet asked.

Tollison took out his iPhone and typed in the information. "Shit," he said. "You were right."

"Fuck," Bissonet said, smacking the steering wheel with both hands. "It's a miracle we even got hotel rooms."

"Maybe we can get to the gallery, see if our painting has surfaced, and fly out tonight," Tollison said.

Bissonet shrugged. "I'm game if you can find a flight."

Tollison typed "delta.com" on his iPhone and searched for flights. "Not going to work," he said, shaking his head. "The last flight leaves Charleston at six fifty this evening. At this rate, we won't even make it to downtown by then."

"Well!" Bissonet said. "I guess that settles that."

AN HOUR and forty-five minutes later, Beau parallel parked in a spot on Broad Street. Beau led them two blocks down to Church Street and turned right. Another three blocks and they were in front of The Church Street Art Gallery.

Beau put his hands against the window to block out the glare and peered inside. Much like The Royal Renaissance, this gallery also appeared to specialize in Southern art from the Civil War era. There were a number of paintings depicting plantations and cotton fields, as well as a few of Fort Sumter under attack and what appeared to be old Charleston before the war. Before Beau could comment, he heard the door open and saw Cruz's back as he entered the gallery.

"Oh no, he didn't just go in there without me? Shit!" Beau cursed under his breath as he followed Cruz in.

"Is curator Ferry in, please?" Cruz asked the young girl behind the desk.

"May I ask who's inquiring?"

"Yes. I'm Tollison Cruz with Lloyd's of London, and this," he said, gesturing over his shoulder, "is Detective Montgomery Bissonet with the New Orleans Police Department."

"Let me check," the girl said, disappearing through a door located directly behind the desk.

A few minutes later, the young girl reappeared in the doorway with a tall, thin man wearing thick horn-rimmed glasses and a bow tie.

The man removed his glasses and looked at Cruz. "I'm curator Ferry. How may I help you?"

Beau saw Cruz open his mouth to speak, so he stepped between the two men. "Mr. Ferry. I'm Lead Detective Bissonet, and I'm investigating a robbery that took place in New Orleans at The Royal Renaissance Gallery. It's come to my attention that you may have been contacted about acquiring one of the paintings stolen during that heist."

Cruz glared at him again, and Beau flashed a satisfied smile while he waited for Ferry to respond.

Ferry nodded. "I assume you're referring to what the press has dubbed 'The Royal Street Heist'?"

"Exactly," Beau confirmed. "But I'm surprised you heard about this so soon."

"Detective, uh, Bisso…?"

"Bissonet," Beau clarified. "Beau Bissonet."

"Detective," Ferry said. "The art world is a very small one indeed, especially in the South. And those of us who curate similar types of art readily share information with one another."

Cruz took out a notepad and a pen from his inside coat pocket. "So, Mr. Ferry? Have you—"

"I see," Beau said, raising his voice and cutting Cruz off. "So *have* you been contacted by someone trying to divest one of the stolen paintings?"

Cruz lowered his head and looked away, no doubt cursing under his breath.

"As a matter of fact, I have," Ferry said.

Beau cast a sideways glance in Cruz's direction and hoped he conveyed the "keep your damn mouth shut" look. "Can you please tell me about the inquiry?"

"Surely," Ferry said. "I received an anonymous call last evening from someone inquiring about whether our gallery might be interested in a recently discovered and conserved original painting by Louis Mathieu Didier Guillaume of *General Robert E. Lee at the Battle of Chancellorsville*. Of course, by this time I already knew of the robbery, so I quickly declined. I don't know of any dealer who would go anywhere near that painting now. But"—Ferry held up his forefinger—"not before I questioned who was doing the inquiring."

"And…?" Cruz asked before Beau could speak.

"The caller hung up, of course."

Cruz was still taking notes, but he looked up. "What about—"

Beau cut him off again. "Did you happen to check caller ID to see if a phone number appeared?"

This time Cruz cursed loudly enough for Mr. Ferry to look in his direction.

"I apologize for Mr. Cruz," Beau said. "He's having a bit of trouble understanding who's in charge here."

"Oh, I understand clearly who thinks he's in charge," Cruz said. "But the mayor obviously questioned Detective Bissonet's ability to solve this case and asked for my assistance in the matter."

Now it was Beau who was turning his head and cursing under his breath.

"Oh!" Ferry said nervously. "Anyway," he continued, looking at both men, "I checked the caller ID immediately, and the number was blocked. And of course, as soon as he ended the call, I dialed the Charleston Police Department, which I assume is how you found out about the inquiry."

Beau nodded. "I'm sure you won't mind if I contact your local telephone company and try to trace the number that way?"

"Not at all. If it will help, by all means."

Beau shook Mr. Ferry's hand. "Thank you for your time, Mr. Ferry. I'll be in touch if I have any more questions."

Beau turned and walked out of the gallery, not caring if Cruz followed him or not. When Beau turned left on Church Street, he didn't look back. He got to the car, pulled away from the curb, and left Cruz behind.

TOLLISON WAS so mad he was seeing stars. He seriously disliked Bissonet, but they had *worked* relatively well together over the last couple of days with the good cop/bad cop approach, at least in the interrogation room. What had happened to change that?

When he left the gallery, Tollison had seen Bissonet hurrying down the street toward the car. Not in the mood for the confrontation he knew was coming, Tollison had turned in the opposite direction and started looking for a cab. "I know where I'm going," he mumbled. "I don't need that fucker."

He was still grumbling to himself as he climbed into the back of a Green Cab. "What a piece of work," he murmured, then told the driver, "Planters Inn on Market Street, please."

When Tollison stepped into the lobby of the Inn, the first thing he heard was Bissonet's voice. He was berating the front desk clerk for some unknown reason, and it pissed Tollison off even more. He'd worked the front desk of a small hotel when he was in college and knew firsthand that it was hard enough dealing with people all day who were often rude and demanding without having to be yelled at by a piece of shit like Bissonet on top of it.

Tollison stormed up to the front desk and pushed Bissonet aside. "I apologize for the rudeness of my travel companion, ma'am. What seems to be the problem?"

The young girl wiped at her teary eyes. "Mr. Bissonet seems to think we should have two rooms for him, but I only have a reservation for one room. The Inn has been booked solid this weekend for the Cooper River Bridge Race, and I see that the reservation was just made this morning."

Cruz heard Bissonet from across the lobby screaming at someone on his cell phone—the travel department, he assumed. He turned back to the clerk. "Can you call around to see if you can find us another room?"

"I would love to, Mr...."

"Cruz. Tollison Cruz."

"Mr. Cruz," she said. "But I've been on the phone most of the day looking for rooms, and everything in the city is booked solid. The only thing I've been able to find is a single room at the Days Inn in Mt. Pleasant."

"Where is that?"

"About thirty miles from here."

"That won't work," Tollison said. "We have an early flight tomorrow morning. Please at least tell me the room has two beds."

The clerk frowned, and Cruz cursed under his breath. Then she smiled slightly. "But it does have a foldout couch, will that do?"

"It'll have to," Cruz said. "We'll take it. And again, I apologize for my companion."

"I understand the inconvenience, sir, and I'm very sorry. There's just nothing else available."

"It's not your fault," Tollison said as he checked them in and accepted two plastic key cards. When he was finished, he walked across the lobby, flung one of the key cards at Bissonet, and kept walking toward the elevator. "Room three fifteen," he said over his shoulder.

Bissonet apparently took the stairs because when Tollison rounded the corner, he saw Bissonet opening the door. Bissonet stepped inside and Tollison heard the door slam behind him. Tollison took a deep breath and slid his plastic key into the lock. The red light turned green, and when Tollison pushed the door open, Bissonet was waiting for him.

Bissonet kicked the door shut and backed Tollison up against it, pinning him between himself and the door with both hands on either side of Tollison's head. "Listen, fucker! The next time you interfere with my investigation or apologize to anyone on my behalf, you're gonna find yourself flat on your back."

When Bissonet finished his rant, Tollison brought his arms straight up and widened them, dislodging Bissonet's hands from either side of his head, and shoved Bissonet's chest so hard the man went flying across the room. The backs of his legs hit the bed, and he landed flat on his back. Tollison crawled onto the bed and scooted up on his hands and knees, pinning Bissonet's hands over his head and straddling his six-foot frame.

When he was face-to-face with Bissonet, so close he could feel the man's breath against his skin, he spoke. "Now you listen to me, fucker! The next time you cut me off when I'm speaking or even attempt to talk down to me or belittle me in any way, you'll find yourself a lot worse off than just flat on your back. Got it, *bro*?"

Tollison braced himself and waited for Bissonet's retaliation. He quickly prepared himself for all the options: a knee to the groin, maybe a head butt. But when the reprisal came, it hadn't even been a blip on Tollison's radar. Bissonet lifted his head and pressed his lips firmly against Tollison's in a crushing kiss.

WHEN BEAU withdrew, Tollison's only response was dead silence. Their eyes were locked on each other's, and Beau was desperately trying to get a read on Cruz. Beau didn't know what had come over him, but he'd shocked the hell out of himself with this stupid move, and now he was going to pay. His heart raced frantically as he looked into Cruz's eyes, waiting for Cruz to respond. When Cruz didn't immediately pull back, Beau's eyes widened with surprise and he relaxed a little.

Tollison dropped down on top of Beau and rolled off of him, but he didn't make a clean break without Beau feeling Cruz's arousal when their groins met.

Beau knew Cruz had picked up on something between him and Bruce, but he didn't know to what extent. He'd never hidden his sexual preference, but at the same time, he didn't go screaming "I like boys" from the rooftops either, especially in his line of work. He and Bruce had taken a lot of heat when their coworkers had started putting the pieces of the puzzle together, but eventually the ribbing and teasing had slowed as they became old news. They both had a great reputation, and neither had ever let their sex life get in the way of the job. But Cruz? It had taken him just a few days to get under Beau's skin.

Could he be a switch hitter, or maybe even batting for the same team?

Beau and Cruz lay side by side on the bed, neither saying a word. Finally, Cruz cleared his throat. "Uh. Anything you want to tell me, Beau?"

It was the first time Cruz had called him by his first name. He liked the way it sounded flowing off his lips.

Beau hesitated, trying to decide how to answer. "Probably nothing you haven't already figured out," he finally said, the uncertainty in his voice surprising even him.

"I guess you're right," Cruz replied nervously.

"Anything you want to tell *me*?" Beau asked.

Tollison leaned up on one elbow. His dark eyes were guarded and hesitant, but there was more. Could it be lust and desire?

Before Beau could analyze the situation any further, Cruz leaned over and moved his face closer to Beau's. When their lips touched again, Beau had his answer.

Beau shivered and opened his lips hesitantly. He closed his eyes, grabbed a handful of Cruz's shirt, and pulled him closer. Cruz increased the pressure of his lips against Beau's, and Beau groaned softly, no longer able to control himself, finally relaxing into the kiss.

Cruz rolled over on top of Beau and intensified the kiss. The heat was now steadily building between them, and Cruz was the one who growled this time when Beau moved his hand to the back of his head and gripped a handful of hair.

Pulling them even closer together, Beau fought for control as he rolled Cruz over. Cruz's arms tightened around Beau's back, sending a wave of desire through him, and Beau opened his eyes to see Cruz staring up at him. All the anger and hostility were suddenly turning into heat and passion, and Beau had no idea how this was going to play out when it was all over. But for now, he was going along for the ride. Fuck tomorrow. Right now he wanted Tollison Eduardo Braga Cruz and he wanted him desperately.

Beau rarely lost any wrestling match—on the job or during sex— so he was very surprised when Cruz pulled a quick one and Beau was once again on his back. "I knew there was something between you and Jenkins," Cruz said, looking down at him.

Beau bit Cruz's bottom lip. "And I knew you were an asshole. So now we're even."

Cruz hissed with the bite. "Ditto."

Beau huffed derisively. "Are we gonna do this, or are we gonna talk about our personality traits?"

The corners of Cruz's lips turned up slightly, and he nodded. "Oh yeah. We're going to do this all right" was all he said before he groaned and leaned in to steal another kiss.

Cruz's body seemed to fit perfectly against Beau's, and Cruz melted into him. "Clothes," Beau said as he slid a hand through Cruz's hair. "Too many clothes."

Cruz rolled off of him and offered him a hand. Beau accepted and was pulled to his feet. Covering Cruz's lips with his own again, Beau frantically slid Cruz's suit coat off his shoulders and let it fall to the floor. He unknotted the silk tie and slid it through the collar of Cruz's shirt while Cruz unbuttoned his cuffs. Beau grabbed the front of Cruz's shirt and ripped it open, buttons flying in all directions.

"That was a new fucking shirt," Cruz hissed against Beau's lips.

"I'll buy you a new one," Beau retorted.

Beau pulled Cruz's white T-shirt up, breaking the kiss just long enough to get the shirt over Cruz's head, and then their lips met again as Beau fumbled with Cruz's belt buckle. Cruz toed off his shoes just as his pants fell to the floor, and he stepped out of them and went to work on Beau.

Within seconds, they were both stripped down to their underwear, and Cruz was a sight to behold. His muscular, tanned body was even more beautiful than Beau had imagined, and Cruz's erection was stretching the soft cotton fabric of his briefs.

Beau pushed Cruz back onto the bed and looked down at him. He slipped a finger inside Cruz's black dress socks and pealed them off one at a time. "Can't fuck a guy in black knee-high socks," he said before diving on top of Cruz again and claiming another kiss.

Cruz broke the lip-lock and looked Beau in the eyes. "I was the one planning on doing the fucking."

"All in good time," Beau said, demanding another kiss. "How about we take turns?"

"Do you even have condoms and lube?" Cruz asked.

Beau slid off the bed, reached into his duffel, and came out with his leather shaving kit. He dug through it and tossed a condom and a tube of lubricant on the bed, where they landed beside Cruz.

Beau knelt on the bed and hooked his fingers in Cruz's underwear. As he pulled them off, Cruz's erection flopped back against his stomach with a plop. Beau peeled his own underwear down, kicked out of them, and hit the mattress on his hands and knees. He rolled Cruz over and lowered himself onto Cruz's back, his erection fitting nicely in the crack of Cruz's ass. He buried his nose in Cruz's neck and inhaled, breathing in his manly scent before he kissed his way across Cruz's back and shoulders. Beau followed up with light nibbles, leaving little marks as he went, and Cruz whimpered with each bite. The sound drove Beau crazy with desire.

Beau's hands roamed up and down the length of Cruz's body, and Cruz writhed beneath him. With each move Beau was becoming more achingly erect, and he fumbled with the lube and slicked his fingers up before running them slowly down the crease of Cruz's ass. When Beau brushed his fingers against Cruz's opening, the intimate touch made him tense just a little; then he relaxed again. Beau hated the guy, but feeling Cruz squirming and supple under him was the biggest turn-on he'd ever experienced. Stretched out again on top of Cruz, he slid his length back and forth over Cruz's opening. Cruz turned his head, and Beau sought out his lips. Cruz arched his back into Beau's touch, and Beau slid down and did his best to tantalize and relax Cruz's opening, getting him ready for what was to come. He pushed one lubricated finger inside and worked it around as Cruz groaned seductively, tensing beneath him.

"You okay?" Beau whispered.

"Just move," Cruz begged.

Beau took that as a good sign. He buried another finger deep inside Cruz, and Cruz rose up against the intrusion. But when he moaned reassuringly, Beau knew the time had come. He slipped the condom over his painfully hard erection and positioned himself, one hand on either side of Cruz's shoulders, and pushed in.

Cruz gasped and fisted the sheets when Beau breached the muscle protecting his opening, and Beau paused to give him a minute to adjust.

After a moment, Beau began rocking gently, and Cruz tensed, apparently riding out the pain until he was able to relax around Beau and start to move along with him.

Beau lowered himself and pressed his lips against Cruz's shoulder. He rocked again, slowly at first, then going deeper with each movement until he was all the way in. Cruz lifted his hips off the bed and pushed against him, silently begging for more. Beau gave him what he wanted and started to thrust against Cruz's muscular ass. When he reached around, Beau found Cruz's length hard and leaking with his excitement.

"Move," Cruz pleaded as he pushed against Beau's cock and then thrust forward into his hand.

Cruz once again turned his head, obviously in search of Beau's lips. When Beau gave him what he wanted, Cruz gasped out loud. Beau loved having Cruz in this position. He was almost begging, and it was a far cry from their interactions so far. The anger and sarcasm were all gone, and what was left was pure desire. Cruz trembled, and Beau knew he was shaking the man's resolve. It had been a long time since Beau had been with anyone, and this unexpected tryst and the intensity was almost more than he was ready for.

"God, Beau" was all Cruz kept saying. Hearing his name on Cruz's lips as he begged and pleaded for more was sending Beau dangerously close to the edge.

Beau was surrounded by Cruz's heat, and he dug deeper and harder. With each push he was rewarded with a long drawn-out moan. Cruz was now up on all fours, and Beau was pounding into him hard, his hand around Cruz's waist, stroking his erection.

"Harder," Cruz begged in an almost unrecognizable voice.

Beau eased them to the edge of the bed and slid off, planting his feet firmly on the floor. He pulled Cruz against him and rammed into him over and over. Cruz inched forward with each push, but Beau kept pulling him back. Beau groaned passionately from somewhere deep inside him and tried to remember it being like this with anyone else, but he kept coming up empty.

"Cruzzzz," Beau drew out as he felt his body seizing and tensing, so close to letting go. Cruz didn't answer, but he pushed against Beau harder, giving him everything he needed.

"Jesus fuck…!" Beau hissed as he went over the edge, lurching unsteadily as he felt the waves of pleasure and heat coursing through his body. Beau felt Cruz tensing in his hand simultaneously and pumped feverishly as he continued to pound into Cruz's ass. Cruz gave a muffled moan, his face buried in the pillow as he came in Beau's hand, the two of them now working each other as they rode out their orgasms.

Beau released Cruz, and the sight of Cruz's pleasure dripping from his fingers assured him he'd done okay.

Cruz lurched forward and fell to the bed, gasping for air, and Beau collapsed next to him, eyes closed and out of breath. "Fuck," Beau said as he rolled onto his back.

"Yeah," Cruz agreed through breathless attempts at inhaling.

"I knew we should have had separate rooms," Beau murmured.

Cruz huffed. "I guess we don't need that foldout couch after all."

"Prick!" Beau snorted.

"Asshole!" Cruz replied. "I'm hungry."

"Like I care," Beau said.

Cruz rose up on his elbows and looked at Beau. "You mean you're not gonna buy me dinner after that?"

Beau cocked one eye open and looked over at Cruz. The look on his face was priceless. "Fine. I have an expense account anyway. But… that doesn't mean I still don't hate you."

"Likewise," Cruz said.

SIX

CRYMES SAT in his favorite chair and sipped his evening cocktail. Harper was in the kitchen, helping Charmaine prepare dinner while they waited on Jamie to get there.

Now that Charmaine's latest actions were front and center in the news, Harper surely knew how close they'd come to losing everything. But on the bright side, the insurance company had reluctantly paid off the claim once they had confirmed that money hadn't changed hands between Charmaine and Della Penna and Charmaine was not the person responsible for the theft. Because of the payoff, all the debt had been settled.

Except Jamie's gambling debt. Jamie didn't know Crymes knew about any of that, and Crymes wanted to help him, but not until Jamison got the other sort of help he needed and Crymes was sure he wouldn't get back into the same situation all over again. Crymes still hadn't found the right time to tell Harper, and he didn't even know if it was his place to do it at all, but he'd hoped to get a few minutes with Jamie alone tonight to try to figure out what to do.

Charmaine's legal troubles weren't over by far, and although her charges were very serious ones, Jamie was working very hard and Crymes was calling in every favor he could just to try to keep her out of jail. According to Jamie, based on her having no prior record and her age, along with the influences of their friends in high places, there was good chance she might just get off with community service and a slap on the wrist. But for now, she was out on bail, and they were trying to regain some sort of normalcy.

Crymes looked up when he heard the back door open and close. Minutes later Jamie stepped into the living room with a drink in his hand. "Evening, Crymes," Jamie said.

"Jamison," Crymes said with a nod as he gestured to the chair across from him. "Where are the ladies, son?"

"Working on dinner, sir. They said it would be another thirty minutes or so."

"That's good," Crymes said. "That will give us a chance to talk."

"Okay," Jamie said as he raised his eyebrows and inclined his head in interest. "Is this about Charmaine's case?" he asked.

"Not directly," Crymes said. "But look, son. I won't beat around the bush. Detective Bissonet told me about your—" He cleared his throat. "—ah, gambling problems."

The blood drained out of Jamie's face as he nervously looked back and forth between Crymes and the door. "What exactly did he tell you?"

Crymes took a sip of his drink and swallowed. "About your… problem and how much in debt you are to some pretty shady characters."

Jamie's eyes turned flat and emotionless as he listened to Crymes.

"You realize you're still a suspect in all this, right?" Crymes asked.

Jamie looked down into his drink as if the answer to Crymes's question was at the bottom of the glass. "Yes," he finally said.

Crymes leaned forward in his chair. "Jamie, I want to help you, but I'm not going to bail you out only for you to get back into debt again. You need to get help, son. And you need to tell Harper."

"I want to," Jamie said, standing and starting to pace. "But I just don't know how. This all came down like a landslide. One minute, I was betting on a few ponies. Then the next minute, I was borrowing from bookies to cover my losses."

"Son," Crymes said, standing and putting a hand on his shoulder. "Admitting you have a problem is the hardest part."

"No!" Jamie said. "Keeping the secret is the hardest part. Now that it's out, I'll find a way to tell Harper and get the help I need."

"That's good, son. Real good. Let me know after you've told Harper and arranged to get some help, and I'll help you with the debt."

Jamie took Crymes's hand and pumped it a few times. "Thank you so much. I appreciate your support."

CRUZ SLID carefully out of bed and started picking up his discarded clothes. He stole a few glances at Bissonet. The guy was lying on his back, covered to the waist; his blond hair was falling free over his forehead, and he looked as relaxed as Tollison had ever seen him. His chest was very defined, and his arms were huge. What in the hell had they been thinking? Maybe in another place or another time, but not now. They could have just fucked everything up in a really bad way.

After dinner and a few drinks last night, they'd come back to the hotel and started up all over again. Cruz had given it to Beau not once, but twice, and neither had thought about the consequences.

Cruz sat awkwardly on the couch and grimaced at the pain in his ass. He silently cursed Bissonet but thought it was well worth it. Besides, Beau would be feeling the same jolts of pain when he sat, if not worse, and that gave him a little satisfaction. The guy was hot. And the sex was hot. But at what cost?

Cruz glanced over to the bed when he heard Beau rustling. "Morning," he offered lamely as Beau rose up on one elbow and squinted over at him.

Beau rubbed at his sleepy eyes. "What time is it?"

"Five thirty," Cruz answered, looking at his watch. "Our flight leaves at eight?"

Beau nodded.

The silence was awkward. Not knowing what else to say, Cruz stood. "How're you feeling this morning?"

Beau lay back down, stretched, and yawned. "Tired and a little hungover," he said in a sleepy voice. "You?"

Without thinking, Cruz blurted out, "My ass is sore as a motherfucker." He regretted the words as soon as they left his mouth, but it was too late. So he sat back and waited for Bissonet's reaction.

Beau's lips twisted and he offered Cruz a lopsided smile. He wiggled in the bed and his expression changed. "Mine too."

Cruz bit back a smile and decided to just give up on the forced conversation and take a shower. Beau had already told him the sex was going to change nothing between them, so why keep up pretenses?

Cruz frowned when he remembered his suitcase was in the car. "Fuck."

Beau gave him a quizzical look. "What?"

"My bag's in the car."

Beau looked at him thoughtfully and then smiled. "I tell you what. I'll shower and dress first, and while you're in the shower, I'll run down to the car and grab your bag."

Cruz looked at Bissonet with one eyebrow raised. "I thought you still hated me."

"I do."

"Then why are you being so nice to me?"

"I don't know. Call me a sucker for a good bottom."

Cruz shrugged dismissively. "Hell, if that's all it takes."

Beau laughed as he got out of bed and twisted his back and neck, bones popping with each turn. He stood. "Ouch," he whispered grabbing his ass. "My ass really does hurt."

On the way to the airport, their conversation was still strained, but flowed a little better than it had the day before. They discussed the case briefly and collectively decided their next move was to pay a little visit to Dudley Robinette.

After they had exhausted the case, the silence loomed between them again. Not because of any simmering anger, but mostly out of awkwardness.

On the flight back to New Orleans, Cruz brooded over the situation. He had no idea what the fallout was going to be over their recent lack of judgment—well, to be honest it was multiple lacks of judgment—and Cruz felt pretty certain Bissonet was feeling the same hesitancy.

Cruz realized he would love to take another trip on the wild side with Beau Bissonet, but he had to wait and see how this was all going to play out. He went over the different scenarios in his mind.

The way he saw it, one of three things was going to happen. Their romp in the hay would either help them work together better or... it would do just the opposite and add more tension to their already stressful coexistence. The best-case scenario would be that they might actually become friends, solve this case together, and then decide if they wanted to see each other again. And even that was iffy. The sex had been really hot, but so far, he hadn't seen any redeeming qualities in the man who'd fucked him and whom he'd fucked twice.

By the time they got back to New Orleans, retrieved the car, and drove to the station, Cruz was mentally worn out from minding his p's and q's and trying not to say anything to set Bissonet off. He just kept waiting for the guy to turn on him as fast as sushi at a summer picnic. And that was more exhausting than being at each other's throats.

BISSONET UNLOCKED his office door, flipped on the lights, and threw his satchel on the floor as he rounded his desk and plopped down into his chair. Cruz took his normal seat across from him but looked like he was waiting for Bissonet to take the lead. Ever since they'd woken this morning, the guy had almost looked like he was afraid to speak.

Beau rolled his eyes and leaned back in his chair. "Is something wrong, Tollison?"

Cruz snorted and shook his head in amusement. "Tollison?"

"That's your name, isn't it?" Bissonet drawled sarcastically.

"What happened to Cruz?"

Beau checked the door, leaned over his desk, and smiled. "Once I've had my dick up a guy's ass, I like to call him by his first name."

Cruz snorted again, totally surprised by Beau's candor. "Oh" was all he said.

Beau leaned back again. "You never answered my question."

"Honestly," Tollison said. "I like it better when we don't fight, so I'm trying not to say anything that's going to set you off."

Beau grimaced. "Do you really think I'm a ticking time bomb?"

"That's all you've shown me so far."

Beau sighed. "Look. You got dumped in my lap because of circumstances out of our control, and I may have handled it badly, but I am who I am—"

"Welcome back," Bruce interrupted, sticking his head in the door.

Beau forced a smile. "Thanks." *There. That wasn't so hard.*

"Oh! Captain wants to see you immediately," Bruce added.

"I'm on my way," Beau said, standing and sending his desk chair back against the wall.

Tollison stood as well. "Can you stay behind, Mr. Cruz?" Detective Jenkins asked. "I have a couple of things to go over with you regarding the case."

"Sure," Tollison said, sitting back down in his chair.

"Thanks," Jenkins said. "Let me get my files, and I'll be right back."

Bruce followed Beau out of the office, but instead of going after his files, he steered Beau to an empty conference room and closed the door.

Beau gave him a questioning glance. "What's going on, Bruce?"

"I have some news about who was having dinner with Della Penna the night of the robbery, and you're probably not going to like it."

"And…?"

"It was none other than Tollison Cruz."

"What?" Beau asked, not believing his ears. "How do you know it was Cruz?"

"I went to talk to the waiter at Brennan's again to get a better description of the guy, and as she was describing him, all I could see was Cruz's face. I looked up his picture on the Internet and showed it to her, and she ID'd the guy right there."

Beau ran his hand through his hair and started pacing back and forth. "It's Cruz. He's our thief."

"There's more," Bruce said.

"Fuck! How much more?"

Bruce grimaced. "A lot more."

"Okay," Beau conceded. "Let me have it."

"When I looked up Cruz's picture on the Internet, you won't believe what other information I found."

Bruce hesitated.

"Just come out with it, Bruce."

"Okay, but you might want to sit down."

Beau gave Bruce a look he knew Bruce had seen enough times not to ignore. "Bruce!"

"Okay. Okay. Guess what Cruz did for a living before he joined Lloyd's of London?"

"I don't know. A rocket scientist, maybe?"

"Very funny. He was a world-renowned art thief. Well, alleged world-renowned art thief."

Beau shook his head like there was something wrong with his ears. He hadn't just heard what he'd thought he heard, had he? *An art thief?* "What? Get the fuck out" was all he was able to say.

"Yep. Supposedly he was responsible for some pretty high-profile heists, but they could never actually pin anything on him."

"So how did he end up working at the insurance company?"

Bruce smiled weakly. "About five years ago, he went to Lloyd's of London and told them he wanted to make amends for his past crimes. He even told them where they were going wrong with their security."

Beau looked up at the ceiling. "And let me guess. Cruz suggested they hire him, and now they all work together."

"Yep. It looks like his remorse didn't last too long," Bruce said.

"Only now he's added a new crime to his dossier. Murder." Beau shook his head. "It all makes perfect sense now. He's the one who knew how the thief got into the gallery because he was the thief."

"Then he partnered up with us to steer us to Villerie and Della Penna," Bruce added.

The motherfucker played me!

There was a knock on the door, and Captain Trenchard walked in. "Is he really in on this?"

"We're not exactly sure, sir," Beau said. "But the evidence suggests—"

"I want him in custody, Detective," Captain Trenchard said. "Now!"

"Our case is circumstantial at best," Beau explained.

"Then get something concrete," Trenchard demanded. "I will not have my department publicly humiliated."

"Yes, sir," Beau said.

The captain looked back and forth between Bruce and Beau and then walked out of the conference room.

"The thing that gets me," Beau said, "is he doesn't seem to be in too much of a hurry to leave town."

"Then I think we press our one advantage," Bruce said. "He doesn't know we're onto him."

"Exactly," Beau said.

Bruce paced back and forth, feeling like a fool but trying to push those thoughts out of his mind. "So we go after him quietly. How do we do that?" Bruce asked.

"Simple," Beau explained. "The first thing we do is call in every favor we can and get an emergency warrant to search his hotel room. He said he had to go back there this afternoon to write his report to bring his boss up to speed on the case. I'll meet him there, suggest we have an early dinner, and I'll keep him occupied long enough for you and another detective to conduct the search."

"That'll work," Bruce agreed. "But I'd better get on that warrant right away and then get back to Cruz and ask him a few questions before he gets suspicious."

"Go for it," Beau said. "I'll text you when he's out of his hotel room."

Bruce took off and spent about twenty minutes with Cruz while Beau went outside and kicked the building a few times to relieve some stress. *I can't believe I let this guy play me.*

When he was worn out and calm, he headed back to his office, doing his best to play along.

"Everything okay with the captain?" Cruz asked when he returned.

"Yeah," Beau said. "Just wanted to get an update and go over another case with me." Beau sat on the corner of his desk. "I have Jenkins checking on the whereabouts of Robinette, but in the meantime, why don't you head over to your hotel and take care of your business." Not wanting to alert Cruz to any changes, Beau stood and closed his door. He came back and placed a warm, wet kiss on Cruz's lips. "How about I meet you there later, and we can have an early dinner."

Cruz looked surprised at the invitation, but nodded. "Okaaay?" he said, looking at his watch. "It's a little after two now. It'll take me a couple of hours to do my report. So why don't we meet in the bar? Say, fiveish?"

He doesn't want me in his room! Beau thought. "Perfect. I'll see you then. You're at The Royal Sonesta, right?"

Cruz stood and headed for the door. "That's right."

"All righty," Beau said, pressing his lips against Cruz's again. "See you then."

STILL IN his business suit, Beau sat at the far end of the bar with a clear view of the entrance. He had a text message screen open and the word "Go!" typed on the screen. It was almost six o'clock, and Beau was starting to get worried Cruz had gotten wind of what they were planning and had bolted.

Beau relaxed when he saw Cruz step into the doorway and scan the bar. He tapped the Send button, put his phone away, and waved him over. Beau watched Cruz's narrow hips as he walked across the bar, his gait smooth and confident. It was the first time he'd seen the man out of a business suit, and damned if he wasn't one of the hottest things Beau had ever seen.

"You look great," Beau said when Cruz took a seat next to him at the bar. And man, he wasn't lying. The first thing that came to Beau's mind was a GQ model. Cruz was wearing a white shirt, tapered at the waist and accented by a black-and-white paisley print at the cuffs and neckline. His shirttails were casually hanging out, and his lower half was poured into a pair of well-fitting blue jeans. Black loafers finished off the look, and Beau had to keep reminding himself Tollison was a thief and suspected murderer.

"Thanks," Cruz said.

The bartender walked over and stood in front of them, placing a napkin on the bar.

"What can I get you?"

Cruz looked at Beau's half-empty bourbon. "I'll have a Grey Goose martini, straight up and slightly dirty."

"Coming right up," the bartender said.

Cruz then looked into Beau's eyes. "How was the rest of your day?"

Beau had to turn away to avoid getting lost in Cruz's gaze. *Fuck! I didn't think this was going to be so hard.*

He looked down at his bourbon, and the color brought him right back to Cruz's rich dark brown eyes. Beau turned in his seat and faced Cruz, focusing on the man's collar instead of his face. "Oh, you know, just more of the same. Great shirt, by the way," he said, admiring the crisp white fabric, which he could now see had tone-on-tone embossed paisleys covering it.

Cruz flashed that million-dollar smile, and it was a good thing Beau was sitting or his knees might have just crumpled. *What the fuck? Bad-boy syndrome now? I've been able to control myself around this guy, well, mostly, since we met, and now that I know he's a thief and a suspected murder, I can't stop lusting over him.*

Cruz's smooth voice interrupted his thoughts. "Thanks, but look, man. I know you didn't ask me here for all this small talk. I mean, you made it perfectly clear how you feel about me and that we were never going to be friends."

Beau didn't answer right away. He didn't want to lie to Tollison, but he had to keep him busy long enough for Jenkins to search his room. If he pissed Cruz off right now, he would blow the whole thing. "Maybe I was the least bit too hasty in my summation."

Cruz chuckled, tilted his head, and studied Beau. "Is the big bad detective admitting he might just have been wrong about me?"

"There's a first time for everything," Beau said. "You know, I thought I was wrong *once*. But I was *wrong*."

Cruz laughed out loud this time. "Now that sounds more like the Montgomery Beaumont Bissonet I know."

The bartender came over with Cruz's martini and interrupted their banter. Cruz tilted his forward slightly and took a sip. "Nice."

Beau starred at Cruz's Adam's apple as it moved up and then down, and his own mouth was literally watering.

"Just what the doctor ordered," Cruz said as he put the glass down and turned back to Beau. "So where does this leave *us*?"

Beau tried to get that vision out of his mind and chose his words carefully. He needed to keep the conversation going, but again, for some reason, he was having a hard time lying to the man. "I don't know the answer to that" was what came out of his mouth. *There. That was honest,* he thought.

Cruz nodded. "Beau, is this on the record or off?"

"Somewhere in between, I think," Beau said honestly.

"Does that mean I can ask you a personal question?"

Beau merely shrugged. "I guess."

"What's the story between you and Bruce Jenkins?"

Beau figured if he got into that story, he wouldn't have to worry about the night ending too soon. He decided to give him the Reader's Digest version and try to pump Cruz for more information. Give a little, get a lot, he hoped.

"The age-old story, I guess. 'Boy meets boy. Boy falls in love. Boy loses boy.'"

"Is that how it happened in your world?" Cruz asked.

Beau nodded, and took a sip of his drink. "Pretty much."

"I'm sorry," Cruz said, shaking his head. "But seriously. Is that all you're gonna give me?"

Beau felt his shoulders stiffen, and he tried to relax before he spoke. "We met on the force, spent a couple of very happy years together. I got promoted to detective, was trying to juggle an enormous workload and a relationship, and I failed miserably. I helped get Bruce promoted so we could spend more time together."

Beau held up a finger. "Don't get me wrong. He was due, and it was already in the works, I just helped move it along. But unfortunately I was too late."

Cruz raised an eyebrow and tilted his head with interest.

"Too many long nights alone forced Bruce to find what he needed elsewhere. The affair was already over by the time I found out about it, but the damage had been done. I can't love a man I can't trust. It's that simple."

"So you helped him get a promotion, and now you have to work with each other every day?"

"That pretty much sums it up," Beau said.

Cruz paused and took another sip of his drink. "And do I have to ask how that's going for you?"

"Actually it's going better now," Beau said honestly. "Auggie gave me a good talking-to, and it seemed to help."

"What did he say that changed things?"

"He simply pointed out that Bruce wasn't the only one to blame in the situation. If Bruce had been getting what he needed at home, he would have never gone elsewhere."

"Do you believe that's true?" Cruz asked.

Beau thought about the question. "Yeah. I actually do."

"Then why don't you try and patch things up and try again?"

"Like I said," Beau repeated, "I can't be with a man I don't trust. And I can never trust Bruce again." Beau swirled what was left of his bourbon around in the glass. "I know me. And I know that every time I had to travel or work late, I'd be wondering what was going on at home. I could never live like that."

Cruz's expression quickly changed to one of obvious sadness. "I get that completely. It's just sad how one mistake can change things so drastically. To the point that there's never any chance to go back."

Beau's ears perked up by that admission. "You sound like a man speaking from experience."

Before Cruz could respond, the hostess walked up. "Mr. Bissonet, your table is ready, sir."

Perfect fucking timing, Beau thought.

Beau stood and held out his hand, gesturing for Tollison to go ahead as they were led to their table. After they were seated and ordered another round of drinks, Beau broached the subject again. "At the bar, you were about to say something about mistakes and never being able to go back."

Cruz shook his head. "Oh, it was nothing. Have you eaten here before?" he asked, obviously wanting to change the subject.

JENKINS AND Detective Tom Kloor entered Cruz's room with the help of the hotel's head of security. Jenkins whistled. "Man," he added. "This guy gets a suite. All we ever get is a two-bit motel room."

"That's what you get when you work for law enforcement," Kloor replied. "You wanna start in the bedroom, and I'll start out here?"

Jenkins opened a drawer and found a black felt bag. He opened it and was surprised to find a vibrator. "I knew it." He slipped it back in the bag just as Kloor walked into the bedroom. "Find anything?"

Jenkins slammed the drawer shut. "Nothing so far."

"Me either," Kloor said.

"Damn," Jenkins hissed. "There's got to be something here."

"You really want to get this guy, don't you?" Kloor asked.

"It's my job," Jenkins replied.

Kloor frowned. "Yeah, but it seems like it might be about more than that."

Not wanting to disclose what he suspected about Cruz and Beau, he simply said, "Nah. Just keep looking."

THEIR MENUS were lying open on the table in front of them, but neither seemed to be in a hurry to order. Cruz was staring at Beau seductively, and Beau was struggling to maintain his composure. He kept picturing that tight little ass he'd been pounding just about twenty-four hours ago, and damned if, thief or no thief, murderer or no murderer, he didn't want to do it again.

In an attempt to get his libido under control, Beau looked down at his menu. "So what made you decide to become an insurance investigator? It's not really something little boys aspire to be when they grow up."

Cruz seemed to be choosing his words carefully. "Let's just say it was a recent career change."

"Really?" Beau said, looking up and meeting Cruz's eyes. "What did you do before?"

Cruz hesitated, looked around, and then leaned in and whispered, "Actually, I was a thief."

"No fucking way," Beau said, blown away by Cruz's candor.

"That's what the museums referred to me as, but I like to think about myself as an art retriever."

Beau closed his menu and leaned back in his chair. "What's the difference?"

"Well, for starters," Cruz said, "the art I retrieved had already been stolen from other people."

Beau leaned in and gave Cruz a questioning look.

Cruz clarified. "I specialized in returning things back to their rightful owners, starting with a small piece of art stolen from my family during the war."

Beau leaned back again and crossed his arms over his chest. "So you're like a modern day Zorro without the whip and mask."

"Well. Without the whip," Cruz said, his lips twisting in wry amusement.

Suddenly Beau was flushed, and he fanned his face with his hand. "It's getting a bit warm in here."

"I have an idea," Cruz said, leaning back and downing the last of his martini. "I'm suddenly not very hungry. Why don't we skip dinner and go back to my room?"

"What's the rush?" Beau asked. "As I said, the food here is exceptional."

"I'm sure it is." Cruz leaned in close, licked his lips, and spoke in a low, seductive tone. "But what sounds better to you? Exceptional food or an exceptional piece of meat?"

Beau felt the blood rush out of his face and right to his groin. "Ah, the desserts are really good here too."

"Great," Cruz said, dropping a hundred-dollar bill on the table. "After I have you as my first dessert, we can order more from room service."

Cruz got up and started walking out of the restaurant.

Beau stood, reached into his pocket, and took out his phone. He typed "Get out" and hit Send before following Cruz into the lobby.

JENKINS PUT his phone down on the bedside table as he opened the drawer. He removed Cruz's iPad and was scanning his e-mails when Kloor yelled to him from the closet. Jenkins stood and headed his way while still scanning the iPad.

"Look what I found," Kloor said, holding open a suitcase. "The tools of the trade."

"And I found a bunch of e-mails between Cruz and Della Penna, as well as some other dealers. Guess who's trying to sell some Southern art?"

BEAU KEPT checking his phone, but he'd received no reply from Bruce. He and Cruz were walking down the hall to Cruz's room when the text finally came in. "On our way out. Stall."

"Here we are," Cruz said, pointing to the suite at the end of the hall. Beau heard the door open and did the only thing he could think to do. He slammed Cruz against the wall and covered his lips in a crushing kiss.

Jenkins and Kloor came out of the suite and stopped dead in their tracks. Jenkins cleared his throat, and they both turned in his direction.

"Jenkins? What are you doing in my suite?" Cruz said in a surprised tone, looking back and forth between Beau and the two detectives.

"We're here to arrest you for theft. And murder," Jenkins said.

Cruz looked at Beau with an expression that could only be described as hurt.

Beau felt the look in his gut as he put the handcuffs on Cruz.

WHILE CRUZ was being fingerprinted, Bruce filled Beau in on what they'd found in Cruz's suite.

Beau was rubbing his temples. "I don't think he was involved."

"What the fuck, Beau? Now you're telling me the guy's clean?" Jenkins asked.

Beau ran a hand through his blond locks. "Why would he tell me about his former life if he had something to hide?"

"Maybe because you're sleeping with the guy. And... feeding you just enough truth makes swallowing the lies a hell of a lot easier," Jenkins hissed.

Not really surprised that Bruce had picked up on something between them, Beau sighed. "First of all, who I sleep with is no longer any of your concern. But do you really think I'm that gullible I would jeopardize a case over a one-night stand?"

"A one-night stand?" Bruce asked. "What I've been picking up between you two is more than a one-night stand, Beau."

"You know what," Beau said, sounding as frustrated as he felt. "I don't know what's going on between us, but my gut tells me he's not in on this."

Jenkins slammed his fist down on Beau's desk. "And... I think you're thinking with the wrong head."

"I wanna at least hear Cruz's side of the story," Beau said.

"Beau. You're not serious about doing the interrogation?"

"Of course I am."

"You're too close to this, Beau. Can't you see that? Do I have to go to the captain?"

"So help me, Bruce," Beau hissed, "if you take this to the captain, whatever we have"— he gestured between them—"is over. Completely over. No chance of a friendship, no working relationship, nothing, and I'll do everything I can to have one of us transferred out of here."

Bruce looked at him long and hard, and Beau could see the hurt in Bruce's eyes, but Beau had to give Tollison the benefit of the doubt. "I feel like I owe the guy that much, Bruce."

Bruce walked to the door, stopped, and turned. "Fine, Beau. You win. You always win. Under one condition. You can sit in, but I conduct the interrogation. That's it. Take it or leave it."

"Fuck," Beau said, kicking his desk and cringing when the pain in his foot registered in his brain.

BEAU SAT across from Cruz, who wouldn't even look him in the eye.

"I've got to hand it to you, Cruz," Jenkins said, "this whole art con you're doing with the insurance companies—it's extraordinary."

"Cruz, look at me," Beau said.

Cruz finally did. "So we're back to Cruz, huh?"

Beau lowered his head.

Jenkins continued. "Befriending insurance companies, convincing them you want to go on the straight and narrow while you wait for your next score. Makes great sense to me."

Cruz turned to Jenkins. "*What* are you talking about?"

"The only catch was you knew you needed Della Penna for a decoy," Jenkins said. "What you didn't expect was being surprised by Le Moyne also attempting to steal the paintings himself. You were already splitting the proceeds with Della Penna, and you didn't want to split the heist three ways, so you killed Le Moyne. Then you worked your way into our investigation to cover your tracks."

"Come now, Detective Jenkins," Cruz said. "You sound like some mystery writer trying to tie up all the loose ends in a suspense novel."

"I don't need to tie up loose ends. I've got you connected to Della Penna, a well-known art thief."

"Della Penna and I go way back," Cruz said. "I was trying to get information out of him for another case. I didn't know at the time that he had been contacted by Mrs. Villerie to do the heist, not until after I joined the investigation."

"Come on, Cru—" Beau stopped short. "Tollison. If that meeting was so innocent, then why didn't you tell us about it before?"

"Because I'm not particularly proud of the fact that I didn't figure out what Della Penna was up to. If I had, then the paintings might not have been stolen and Le Moyne might still be alive."

Beau thought Cruz sounded convincing. And he was strangely calm, considering he was up against theft and murder charges. *He's either innocent or he's a psychopath.*

"How do you explain the case of tools we found in your hotel room?" Jenkins asked.

"I specialize in recovery," Cruz said. "My boss doesn't care how I get the artwork back. Just that I do."

"So basically you're still a thief." Jenkins said.

"Recovery. Not theft," Cruz corrected.

"Really!" Jenkins said. "And what part of recovery involves trying to sell original oil paintings worth over two million dollars?"

Cruz shifted in his seat. "The thief is surely going to try and sell those paintings soon, and I was trying to flush out any possible takers."

He rested his elbows on the metal table and lowered his chin to his locked fingers. "Listen to me, gentlemen," he said, looking back and forth between the two men. "I did my homework on you guys before I came here. I know you're both smart and methodical investigators with strong instincts that are telling you that I'm innocent. What bothers me is why you're ignoring those instincts. Could I have stepped into a lover's spat?"

Beau cursed under his breath, and Jenkins shook his head. "This is nothing personal," Jenkins said. "And I resent your implications."

"I really don't care what you resent," Cruz said, standing and offering his wrists. "Now either book me and let me call my attorney, or let me the hell out of here so I can continue doing my job."

"Look, Tollison," Beau said. "Your job is recovery, as you call it, and our job is to solve this theft and homicide."

"Then why don't you tell your former lover to put aside his personal agenda and let's get back to solving this case? And… for the record, I was on the phone with my boss when the call came in about the heist."

"Tollison," Beau said calmly, "if you're telling the truth now, why have you been keeping things from me all along?"

"Because, Beau, it's been my experience that the police always hold back information when working with me, which hampers my investigation, so I do the same. And besides, my job is to recover the paintings, not play nice. But you're right," Cruz added. "I've been treating this like a regular case, and clearly it's not. So I promise from here on out, no more secrets."

"That won't be necessary," Jenkins said. "We won't be working together anymore."

Beau turned his head away and cursed under his breath. *This is not his fucking case!*

"Would it make a difference if I told you I have a theory that might lead to an arrest?"

"Yes, it would," Beau said, glaring at Bruce and daring him to challenge his authority.

Bruce rested both hands on his hips. "Seriously, Beau?"

"As a heart attack," Beau said defiantly. "Now, if you want to go to Captain Trenchard, be my guest. I'll be right behind you. I have to see him anyway to bring him up to speed on the investigation."

Bruce stormed out of the interrogation room, slamming the door behind him.

Cruz looked at Beau without any expression. "Am I free to go?"

By the void of any emotion in Cruz's voice, Beau realized that any chance for a decent working relationship with him was probably null and void. Not to mention anything in the bedroom. "I'm really sorry, Tollison. I had to do my job, man."

"Am I *free* to go?" Cruz asked again, his eyes narrowed and full of anger.

"May I remind you that you weren't exactly forthright with what *you* knew?"

Cruz folded his arms over his chest and looked straight ahead. "I was just doing my job, *man*. Now just tell me if I'm free to go or if I need to call my attorney."

"Of course you're free to go," Beau said. "At least let me drive you back to your hotel."

"Why?" Cruz said. "Do *you* need to search my room personally?"

Beau's shoulders slumped. "Come on, Tollison. That's not fair."

"Why didn't you just come out and ask me about all of this shit instead of pretending to hate me. And then… pretending to like me? And then… pretending to want to sleep with me? For God's sake, Beau, is there no length you won't go to, to solve a case?"

"Wait a minute, Tollison," Beau pleaded. "You've got this all wrong."

"Of course I do," Tollison quipped.

"Seriously. In all fairness, I did hate you at first, and then I did like you later, and I had no idea about any of this when I slept with you. I just found out when we got back from Charleston."

Cruz finally looked up and was apparently searching Beau's eyes for something.

The truth, maybe, Beau thought.

Beau sat down across from him and took both of his hands. "I swear to you, man. When we got back and Bruce told me the captain wanted to see me, he pulled me aside and told me what he'd found out about you. By that time, the captain was already involved, so I had to investigate."

"You could have come to me."

Beau ran his fingers through his hair in frustration. Something he'd been doing a lot lately. "Yes, I guess I could have, but the captain gave me an order. And *I* needed proof, one way or the other, before we confronted you. If you really give this some serious consideration, without all the anger, I'm sure you would have come to the same conclusions and done the same thing."

Cruz huffed, and Beau knew he had him.

"I'm sorry it all went down like this, man, but I'm glad it's all over and we can get back to the investigation. Which reminds me," Beau added. "I think you have a theory you wanted to share."

Tollison sighed. "Can we at least get out of the interrogation room so I don't feel like a criminal?"

Beau chuckled and shook his head in amusement. "Sure. Let's go back to my office."

Once back in Beau's office, Cruz looked up when he saw his picture on the crime board along with Crymes Villerie, Charmaine Villerie, Harper Hayes, Jamison Hayes, Anthony Le Moyne, Emanuel Della Penna, and Dudley Robinette. There were Xs through Dudley Robinette and Anthony Le Moyne's pictures, and before Beau took his seat, he drew an X through Cruz's picture.

Tollison smirked and took a seat without saying a word about the gesture. As promised, he filled Beau in on his theory. He had no proof yet, but he detailed the reasoning behind his speculations.

Beau listened intently, and when Cruz was finished, he considered everything he'd just heard. He shook his head and whistled. "I don't know, Tollison, it's pretty convoluted. But it makes very good sense. Now all we have to do is prove it. And I think we should start with Robinette."

"I agree. Do we know where he is?"

"Bruce is trying to track him down. We should have something by the morning."

"'K," Tollison said. "I guess we can't do anything until then."

"Look," Beau said, glancing at his watch. "It's late. Please let me drive you back to your hotel."

"Fine," Cruz said. "But don't even think about coming in."

Beau grabbed his chest like he'd been shot down. "Ouch. Right to the heart."

"That's such bullshit," Tollison said. "You don't have a heart."

"Oh yeah, I forgot," Beau said in agreement and then rolled his eyes. *"Asshole."*

SEVEN

TOLLISON'S BACK was pressed firmly against his hotel suite door and held in place by the weight of Beau's torso. Beau's hands were cupping his face while his tongue searched every inch of Tollison's mouth. The erection grinding at his crotch was making it very difficult to concentrate on getting the keycard into the lock, but by the grace of God, the card finally slipped into the mechanism. Tollison pulled the card out quickly and was rewarded by a little beep. He turned the handle and they both fell into the doorway, landing against the foyer wall while the door slammed solidly behind them.

The ride from the station to the hotel had been quiet for the most part. Beau had tried to make conversation, but Tollison hadn't wanted any part of it. Instead, he'd spent the time trying to decide if he was going to forgive Beau for his indiscretions or not. Of course he'd known deep down Beau had only been doing his job. But that realization hadn't made him any less angry.

And Beau *had* been right when he'd reminded Tollison he'd withheld crucial information. In past cases, Tollison had worked himself into investigations just like this one and had taken all the information he could get. But in the past, it had all been in a day's work. This time it had been different. He'd seen the disappointment on Beau's face, and the fact that Beau had distrusted him hurt way more than he'd expected.

Tollison knew Beau had also hit the nail on the head when he'd said Tollison would have handled the situation very much the same way. He would have. But the fact that Beau knew that about him also pissed him off royally.

By the time they pulled into the hotel, the Jekyll and Hyde routine had played itself out, and Tollison had decided not to cut his nose off to spite his face. Hurt, trust, or betrayal, Tollison would take every opportunity on offer to get Beau under him again, and that was the bottom line.

Beau had brought the car to a stop and looked at Tollison like he was waiting for some sign. Tollison, without saying a word, simply reached over and turned the ignition off. Apparently that was all Beau needed. He flashed a smile, jumped out of the car, and gave the keys to the valet. They made a beeline for the elevators, disappointed when there were several other people waiting. They nervously rode up to Tollison's floor, and when the elevator doors opened and they were again alone, they made out all the way to Tollison's suite.

Beau growled, slipped out of his suit coat, and dropped it to the floor. He moved his hands down to the front of Tollison's shirt like he was going to rip it off again.

"No!" Tollison moaned into Beau's mouth, putting his hands on Beau's chest and pushing against him.

Beau broke the kiss and stepped back with a confused expression on his face.

"Two-hundred-dollar shirt!" Tollison quipped. "No ripping."

Beau's lips formed a knowing smile. "Got it! This will be more fun anyway."

He covered Tollison's lips with his own and, by feeling his way down, slowly released every button, spreading the shirt open to expose Tollison's chest. Beau broke the kiss and lifted Tollison's left hand to his mouth. Tollison's cock jumped when his fingers slipped into Beau's warm, wet mouth, and Beau nibbled on them one at a time while he unfastened the button on his cuff. Tollison's cock was jumping repeatedly by the time Beau finished with his other cuff.

Beau slowly lowered the shirt over Tollison's shoulders and tossed it onto the foyer table. Tollison gasped when Beau covered one of his nipples with his mouth. He sucked it in and ran it gently between his teeth. By this time, Tollison was frantically running his hands through Beau's hair, gripping the back of his neck and pulling him forward.

Tollison threw his head back as Beau devoured one nipple and then the other, the light biting and licking tantalizing him. He was so caught up in the moment he didn't feel Beau working on his belt and jeans until they were around his ankles. Beau hooked his fingers in Tollison's underwear and rested them there while he kissed his way across Tollison's chest, eventually dropping down to his knees and taking Tollison's underwear down with him.

Beau took Tollison's erection into his mouth all the way up to the hilt, and Tollison went weak in the knees. He put his hands on Beau's shoulders to steady himself as Beau began to move slowly up and down his length. When Tollison regained control of his legs, he moved one hand to the back of Beau's head and guided him as he rode the waves of pleasure from the soft heat surrounding him. Beau shoved his index finger into his mouth alongside Tollison's cock and slicked it up before moving it to Tollison's opening. When he breached the tight muscle, Tollison hissed and almost lost his knees again. Beau instinctively zoomed in on the right spot and kept brushing his finger against it, coursing more waves of pleasure through every inch of Tollison's being.

The combination of Beau's finger continually grazing his prostate and Beau's warm lips surrounding him, moving in unison with his finger, was sending him into heightened-sense euphoria. Tollison tensed up and grabbed a handful of Beau's hair and held on tightly as his impending orgasm began to flood his core. Tollison threw his head back as he screamed Beau's name. "Beauuu! I'm—"

Beau increased his speed and intensity and, unable to hold back any longer, Tollison came deep into the back of Beau's throat. Beau took everything Tollison could give. He brought his other hand up and slid it along Tollison's length, squeezing every drop of thick, white release from him.

Tollison's knees finally gave way, and he closed his eyes as he slid down the wall, attempting to catch his breath and stopping when his ass hit his calves. He winced when Beau's finger eased out of him, but quickly recovered when Beau covered his lips in a crushing kiss.

Tollison tasted a hint of his release on Beau's tongue and reveled in it, still feeling the aftershocks of his orgasm.

"Jesus, Beau," Tollison murmured, still barely able to breathe.

"That's what's called taking the edge off," Beau said. "I've got lots more planned for you."

Beau moved to the side as Tollison dropped down onto his ass and stretched his jean and underwear clad ankles out in front of him.

Beau slipped off Tollison's loafers and socks, grabbed the hem of Tollison's jeans, pulled them off along with his underwear, and tossed them aside. Tollison felt Beau's gaze as he sat on the chilly marble foyer floor, naked and exposed.

"This isn't fair," Tollison muttered.

Beau ran his eyes up and down Tollison's body again and offered a sinister grin. "Seems pretty fair from my point of view."

Tollison got to his feet and offered both his hands to Beau, who pulled him up and led him to the bedroom. On the way, Beau removed his shoulder holster and tossed it onto the chair next to the bed.

Tollison wasted no time getting Beau naked, except for his socks. He had plans for those. He reached down and yanked the coverlet off the bed, put his hand in the middle of Beau's chest, and pushed, sending him down onto the bed. Tollison disappeared into the bathroom and returned with condoms and lube. The first thing he did when he returned was pull Beau's socks off.

"Can't fuck a guy in black socks," Tollison said as he threw the foil packet and lube bottle onto the bed next to Beau, remembering Beau's comment to him during their first encounter.

Beau gave Tollison a lopsided grin as if to say, "Touché."

Tollison climbed on top of him and covered his lips in a forceful kiss.

"This is just how it all began," Beau said, looking up at Tollison and smiling.

After the episode in the foyer, Tollison was planning on Beau fucking him into the mattress tonight, but he was already hard again and suddenly decided he needed to top Beau instead. Maybe he needed a show of dominance after the day they'd had. Whatever the reason, at the moment he didn't really care. He was going to fuck Beau and fuck him hard.

"Yeah, almost!" Tollison said through a menacing smile. "Except this time I'm the one doing the fucking."

Beau's crystal blue eyes widened in surprise as Tollison leaned in and kissed him, taking his already hard length in hand and pumping feverishly. Tollison slid down Beau's long body until he was eye to eye with his cock. The tip was moist, revealing Beau's excitement, and Tollison surrounded it and slid all the way down, causing Beau to suck in a breath and arch his back into the action.

Tollison slid his mouth up and down several times and then focused on the underside of the head, teasing and making Beau's cock jump and jerk with every lick. Tollison released Beau from his mouth, flipped open the top of the lube bottle, and squeezed some into his palm. He covered Beau's cock generously and pumped a few times before lifting Beau's legs and resting them on his shoulders. He squeezed more lube and circled Beau's opening with this thumb, causing another gasp to escape his lips.

Probing lightly at first, Tollison worked one finger and then another inside Beau until Beau had relaxed around them. He positioned himself and eased into him with one fluid motion, Beau's warmth instantly surrounding him. Beau hissed, grabbed a handful of sheets, and again came up off of the bed. Tollison held his position, allowing Beau time to adjust, but within seconds Beau's hands were on Tollison's thighs guiding him in and out.

"Move! Please!" Beau begged.

Beau's head was thrown back and thrashing from side to side. The expression on his handsome face was one that could only be taken for pure pleasure. Tollison was mesmerized and couldn't look away. He thought this might be one of the most beautiful and sensual things he'd ever seen.

Tollison grabbed Beau's cock and pumped in time with his own thrusts. With each stroke, Beau made a whimpering sound that sent chills of excitement down Tollison's spine. Tollison released Beau's cock and took his legs by his heels, lifted them higher, and spread them farther apart, giving himself deeper access. He was rewarded with a guttural growl that sent jolts of desire throughout his body. Beau took himself in hand and stroked feverishly, one hand still guiding Tollison in and out. He moaned in between whimpers, and Tollison felt the first sign of Beau's imminent release as Beau tensed around him.

"Now," Beau pleaded. "Harder! Oh God...."

The first wave of Beau's release hit his chest as Tollison fucked him harder and deeper. The next spasm covered Beau's torso, with the final spurts dripping over his hand and fingers.

Tollison continued to slam into Beau until he felt his balls tighten with his approaching orgasm. Beau was now looking up at him, eyes wide as Tollison pounded his ass as hard as he could.

"Oh my God...," Tollison screamed as his first load filled the tip of the condom deep inside of Beau. Spasm after spasm rushed through Tollison's body until he was no longer able to support his own weight.

He collapsed on top of Beau, who wrapped his arms around him and held him tightly.

Tollison's heart and pulse were racing out of control, and he fought to regain some sort of composure. Beau didn't seem to be any better off, and their hearts pounded against each other's chests.

Beau tensed and moaned when Tollison slipped out of him. Tollison slid off the bed, removed the condom, and went into the bathroom, returning minutes later with a warm, wet cloth. They cleaned the remains of their releases from the bed; then Tollison tossed the wet cloth into the bathroom.

Tollison lay on his back with Beau resting his head on Tollison's chest. They lay there in silence for a long time before either one spoke. Beau was the first to break the silence. "What's with us?" he asked. "That was fucking incredible."

"It was," Tollison agreed. "Do you mind if we not try to analyze it right now and just bask in the afterglow for a little while?"

Beau chuckled. "Sorry. Bad habit."

Tollison tightened his grip on Beau and closed his eyes.

WHEN TOLLISON rolled over and reached for Beau, he found nothing but cold sheets. He opened his eyes in disbelief and stared at the empty spot on the bed. He glanced at the clock. Five forty-five. He reached over to the bedside table and turned on the lamp when he heard a slight squeak. Tollison saw Beau tiptoeing out of the bathroom, partially dressed, tie hanging loosely around his neck, carrying his shoes and his suit coat. Beau froze and looked up.

"Sorry, I was trying not to wake you," he whispered.

"Were you just gonna sneak out without saying good-bye?"

Beau gestured with his head to the bed, his brow almost up to his hairline.

Tollison looked down and saw a folded piece of paper lying on the pillow. He unfolded it and read, "Had a great time. See you when you get to the office. How about dinner at my place tonight?" Signed with a simple "B."

A slight grin appeared on Tollison's face. "At least get over here and kiss me good-bye before you leave. And sure!"

"Sure what?" Beau said as he walked over to the bed, placed his knee on the mattress, and leaned in.

"Dinner at your place," Tollison muttered as he grabbed a handful of Beau's shirt and pulled him down onto the bed, his coat flying in one direction and his shoes in another. In a surprise move, Beau ended up on his back with Tollison straddling him and looking down at him, feeling very satisfied. "That'll teach you to try and sneak out without telling me good-bye."

"I left a note," Beau said in his defense.

"Yeah, and if I hadn't awakened, you would have missed out on this." Tollison leaned down and brought his lips very close to Beau's before he stopped and backed off the bed. "Don't move."

A minute later he came back and resumed his position. "Had to brush my teeth."

"No fair!" Beau protested. "I didn't have a toothbrush."

"Shut up," Tollison said as he crushed his lips against Beau's in a long, steamy, wet kiss. He could feel Beau instantly hardening under him, and he smiled against Beau's lips. "Okay! Now you can go."

Beau lifted his hands in the air and looked up at Tollison. "Seriously?"

Tollison slowly unbuckled Beau's belt, unhooked and unzipped his pants, never taking his eyes off the man. He yanked his underwear down, cupping them under Beau's balls, and fisted him and squeezed. "Fine. But I'm only doing this so the next time you try to sneak out without a good-bye, you'll know what you're missing."

BEAU STOOD in the doorway to his office. Tollison was already sitting in his usual spot, sipping his coffee with a satisfied grin on his face.

"Morning," Beau said, looking around to make sure there was no one else in earshot. "Again," he added with a wink.

Tollison lifted up his coffee mug. "Morning, hotshot."

Beau stood tall, feeling a little flattered. "Hotshot, huh?"

"I think it's fitting, don't you?"

Beau noodled on that for a second. "Well, I've been called a lot worse."

"Don't I know it," Tollison said. "And mostly by me."

"Among others," Beau added, taking his seat at his desk.

"Speak of the devil," Tollison said as Bruce stepped into the doorway.

Bruce gestured angrily at Tollison. "Why is he still here?"

"Now, now, ladies," Beau said, looking back and forth between the two of them. "Let's keep it professional. We have a job to do. And speaking of… any luck on finding Robinette?"

"Yeah," Bruce confirmed, tearing a piece of paper off his notepad and handing it to Beau. "He has a small office on Magazine Street. Here's the address. And we're still looking into Jamison Hayes. In my opinion, something's not adding up where he's concerned."

Tollison looked at Beau and winked.

"What about surveillance footage around the gallery?" Beau asked.

"We found a variety of security cameras at personal residences and nearby businesses surrounding the gallery, with enough footage to paint a pretty thorough picture. We're reviewing it all now and should have something in a day or two."

"Thanks," Beau said. "Let me know if you come up with anything else. Oh! Any word from Auggie?"

Bruce nodded. "I talked to him this morning. He's still flat on his back, but he says he's a little better."

"Good. I'll call him later." Beau looked at Tollison. "You up to paying Mr. Robinette a visit?"

"Just say the word and I'll follow you to the ends of the earth," Tollison teased.

Beau rolled his eyes. He could tell Bruce was getting more pissed by the second and knew he needed to get these two apart. "Let's get out of here, then."

BEAU PULLED in front of a parking meter in the thirty-nine-hundred block of Magazine Street. He saw Tollison slapping his thighs, apparently checking for loose change. He looked at Beau. "I don't have any change."

"Don't need it," Beau said as he put his Official Police Business card on the dashboard.

Tollison raised an eyebrow.

Beau smiled wryly. "One of the perks of the job."

The two men strolled down Magazine Street, passing one antique shop after another. They stopped in front of a small storefront in the forty-one-hundred block with a sign in the window that said Estate Liquidators.

Beau looked up and thought the place was very cool. It looked like something right out of downtown Mayberry, and he half expected to see Aunt Bea, Andy, Barney, and Goober inside.

Beau opened the door to the sound of a tiny bell ringing and allowed Tollison to walk in ahead of him. Much to his surprise, an elderly lady who indeed reminded him of Aunt Bea stood up and smiled warmly. "May I help you, gentlemen?"

Beau flashed his badge. "I'm Detective Bissonet with the NOPD, and this is Mr. Cruz. We'd like to have a few words with Mr. Robinette, please."

"Oh my," the receptionist said, raising her hand to her heart. "I hope he's not in any trouble?"

"I'm not at liberty to say, ma'am. Will you please tell him we're here?"

"Unfortunately he's not in at the moment."

Beau looked at Tollison. "And where might we find him?"

"He's managing an estate liquidation on Louisiana Avenue today."

"What's that address?" Tollison asked, taking a notepad out of his inside coat pocket.

"Why, I'm not sure I'm allowed to give out that information," the receptionist said.

"Look, Ms…?" Tollison paused.

"Ball," the lady said. "Iona Ball."

Iona Ball? Seriously? "What a lovely name," Tollison said, glancing at Beau and trying to keep a straight face. "Did Mr. Robinette advertise the estate liquidation?"

"Thank you. I got it when I married my late husband, Earl Ball. And yes. It hit the *Times-Picayune* in last Sunday's paper."

Tollison nodded and smiled sincerely. "Was the address in the advertisement?"

"As a matter of fact it was," Ms. Ball said, apparently starting to get a clue.

"So if it was in—"

Ms. Ball held up her hand. "I see where you're going with this, Mr. Cruz. The address is—" Ms. Ball flipped through a notebook. "—thirteen twenty-four Louisiana Avenue."

"Thank you," Tollison said.

"And his cell phone?" Beau asked.

Ms. Ball frowned. She opened her mouth and from the look on her face, it was to object, but then she closed it again, apparently deciding she wasn't going to win. She jotted down the number and handed it to Beau.

"Thank you, ma'am. You have a great day."

Tollison nodded in her direction, and they both left the way they came.

"Is THAT name for real?" Tollison joked. "Iona Ball? I wonder what her maiden name was. Unless it was worse than Ball, I think I would have kept *it* instead."

"There are all sorts of possibilities with that one," Beau teased. "Iona Dick. Iona Twat. Iona anything. The possibilities are endless. Sounds like a drag queen's name."

Tollison laughed out loud. "You're right."

"Here we are," Beau said, putting the car in park.

Tollison looked out of the window and whistled. "This is some estate."

"Looks like our Mr. Robinette does pretty well for himself. I wonder what percentage of the proceeds he gets to keep."

The front door of the house was open, and people were coming and going. Beau stepped inside and waited for his eyes to adjust to the dimly lit room.

Tollison was right behind him as they slowly made their way through the house. When they got to the kitchen doorway, Beau stopped dead in his tracks. He was shocked to see Della Penna leaning on the counter, arguing quietly with a short dumpy man with his back to the door.

Beau stepped away quickly and put his arm out to stop Tollison, gesturing to the kitchen and smiling. "Look what we have here," Beau whispered.

Tollison peeked into the kitchen and stepped back. "Della Penna."

"And Dudley Robinette, I presume," Beau added, "arguing."

Beau listened intently. The two men were speaking softly, but heatedly, and he couldn't quite make out anything they were saying. "Can *you* hear what they're arguing about?"

Tollison shook his head from side to side. "No. Talking too low."

Beau figured the element of surprise was his only option at this point, so he gestured for Tollison to follow him.

"Good morning, gentlemen," Beau said as he stepped through the doorway with Tollison right behind him. Because of the way Della Penna was facing, he was the first to lock eyes with Beau. The two men held each other's gaze.

Della Penna's expression turned "hand in the cookie jar," but he quickly regained his composure and smiled boldly. "Detective Bissonet. Investigator Cruz. We meet again. You still strike me as such an odd pair."

"We've heard that before," Beau said, winking at Tollison.

By this time, the other man had also turned around. The words "Detective Bissonet" obviously piqued his interest, and producing a nervous smile, he said, "How may I help you, gentlemen?"

"Mr. Robinette, I presume?" Beau said.

"Yes, I'm Dudley Robinette."

After introductions, Beau said, "What a surprise to find you here, Mr. Della Penna. I didn't realize you two gentlemen knew each other. And quite the heated conversation."

"The New Orleans art community is a very small one," Della Penna responded, skipping over the "heated conversation" comment. "We all run into one another eventually."

"And how did you happen to be here today?" Beau asked.

"I saw the advertisement for an estate sale and thought I might check it out."

Beau flashed his best fake smile. "How odd. It was my understanding you stole art, not purchased it."

Della Penna pursed his lips and his eyes narrowed. "That was a long time ago, Detective."

"That's what you keep reminding us anyway."

"Am I being detained?" Della Penna asked.

"Not at the moment," Beau replied.

"Then if you'll excuse me, gentlemen, I'll be on my way."

"I'm sure I don't have to repeat your instructions not to leave the state."

Della Penna waved his hand over his head as he left the room but didn't respond.

Robinette fidgeted with some papers on the counter and then looked up. "Again, Detective Bissonet, how may I help you?"

"I have a few questions about the artwork you sold Crymes Villerie of The Royal Renaissance art gallery."

Robinette's eyes turned upward and he rested his forefinger on his chin. "Crymes Villerie? Doesn't ring a bell."

"Come now, Mr. Robinette. How often do you sell original paintings from the Civil War era?" Tollison said.

"And you are, again?" Robinette asked, his gaze one of obvious annoyance.

"Tollison Cruz, insurance investigator for Lloyd's of London."

"Mr. Cruz. With all due respect, in my line of work, I sell hundreds of paintings every year. In fact, almost all of my estate sales have some type of art to be liquidated. How long ago was this supposed sale?"

"A little over six months ago," Beau said.

"And they were sold by me?"

"Yes, Mr. Robinette," Beau said in an impatient tone. "Maybe I can help jog your memory."

Robinette tilted his head and offered a small semblance of interest.

"The two paintings in question are *The Little Soldier* and *General Robert E. Lee at the Battle of Chancellorsville*. They were both from the Le Moyne estate on St. Charles Avenue, and you sold them to Mr. Crymes Villerie. And... as soon as they were restored—or conserved, as you people in the business like to say—they were stolen from The Royal Renaissance Gallery after a gallery event a few nights after the opening. Does any of this ring a bell?"

"Vaguely," Mr. Robinette said. "But again, I sell so many paintings; it's just hard to keep track of them all. I think I recall seeing something about this on the news."

Tollison slipped his phone out of his pocket and pulled up pictures of the paintings and Crymes Villerie he'd downloaded from the gallery's website. He slid his finger along the bottom of the phone and showed the three images to Robinette. "Maybe this will help you remember."

Robinette looked at the images and shook his head. "I'm sorry, but these pictures are just not ringing a bell."

Beau looked at Tollison. "Okay, then. Tell me about your relationship with Mr. Della Penna."

"Relationship? I hardly know the man. Although—" Robinette looked over his shoulder and around the room. "—I do know of his reputation as an art thief. If someone stole some valuable art, I certainly wouldn't rule him out."

"Thanks for the heads-up," Beau said, "but you two seemed to be in a heated conversation when we arrived."

"Oh that," Robinette said, waving his hand through the air nervously. "Just art stuff."

"Oh goodie," Tollison said, clapping his hands together quickly. "I love art stuff. Care to share?"

Robinette snorted in a derogatory manner. "Hardly. Now, gentlemen, if you'll excuse me. I have an estate sale to manage."

The man turned anxiously on his heels and walked out of the kitchen.

"He's lying," Beau and Tollison said simultaneously.

"Big time," Beau added. "I think I'll have Bruce do a little background search on our Mr. Dudley Robinette and see what it turns up."

"Good idea."

ONCE BACK in the car, Beau got on the phone, focused on filling Bruce in on their conversation with Robinette and simultaneously maneuvering through the heavy traffic on the streets of uptown New Orleans. Tollison studied him closely, and damned if he wasn't really starting to like the guy. He was great in bed and certainly easy to look at. His sometimes gray, sometimes blue eyes and the way they changed color and intensity with his moods were downright mesmerizing. But the guy could be so damn arrogant and condescending. Beau could make Tollison's blood boil in a split second and then minutes later look up at him through his sandy-colored hair, focus those intense eyes, flash a million-dollar smile, and all was forgiven. The man could play him like a fiddle, and Tollison knew it. That pissed him off more than anything.

Tollison knew the arrogance and condescension were things that served Beau well in his career and aided his interrogation style, but when it came to the two of them, the attitude needed to stay in the interrogation room. Tollison knew he would never tolerate such behavior in a boyfriend. *What? You did not just say boyfriend*, Tollison thought, shaking his head. *Or did you?*

"Care to share?" Beau asked, apparently paying attention now that he was off the phone.

Tollison thought quickly. "Oh, just thinking about Robinette," he temporized, not quite ready to talk about what was going on between them.

Beau tilted his head and gave Tollison an incredulous look. He eventually nodded, evidently giving Tollison the benefit of the doubt. "Yeah. That guy knows way more than he's letting on, and we just need to figure out what. And the way he threw Della Penna under the bus. Amazing."

"I'll bet there's a history between those two," Tollison said. "I can just feel it."

"I agree. And if there is, Bruce will flush it out. And speaking of Bruce," Beau added, "you know you two are gonna have to find a way to get along. At least until this investigation is over."

At least until this investigation is over, Tollison thought. *I guess I am the only one who was thinking beyond sex. Stupid me.*

Tollison vaguely heard the word "station," but was startled out of his thoughts when he heard his name. "What?"

"I said, how about some lunch before we go back to the station?" Beau repeated. "Are you okay, man?"

"Yeah I'm fine. And a little lunch sounds great. Thanks."

TOLLISON LOOKED up when Beau parked in front of a restaurant on Poydras Street and stuck his Official Police Business card on the dashboard again. The sign in front of the building said Mother's Restaurant.

"Best of New Orleans right here," Beau said, putting the car in park.

Tollison showed as much enthusiasm as he could muster. "Sounds good."

They'd driven to the restaurant mostly in silence, Tollison looking straight ahead as Beau gave him questioning glances every now and then. He didn't know why, but that one little statement—"At least until this investigation is over"—was bothering him a lot. He reminded himself he'd just met the guy. And had instantly hated him. But in less than a week, Beau had managed to get under his skin, and Tollison wasn't the least bit happy about it.

The restaurant was a mad house with the busy lunch crowd, and when they were finally seated, Beau ordered an oyster po'boy and sweet tea, and Tollison tried his hand at jambalaya and sweet tea as well.

After the waitress brought the tea, Beau linked his fingers and rested his elbows on the table. "So you wanna tell me what's on your mind?"

Tollison said the only thing he could think of that made any sense without revealing his true thoughts. "What if Della Penna and Robinette were somehow involved in this thing together?"

"I'm listening."

"So let's just say Robinette knew the paintings were originals and kept it from the owner. Then he called Villerie, knowing he would buy the paintings, have them conserved, and then try to resell them. Once that part was done, he hired Della Penna to steal them."

Beau looked like he was mulling over the question. "But why wouldn't Robinette just buy the paintings himself?"

"There could be a clause in his contract that forbids him from buying any of the merchandise. Or… if Robinette knew the paintings were worth two mil and bought them from the estate for two hundred and fifty thousand, word might get out, and his reputation and business would be ruined."

"Could be," Beau said with a nod.

"Or," Tollison added, "maybe it's as simple as he just didn't have the two hundred and fifty thousand dollars and needed someone to fund his project."

"That's also a very good possibility," Beau said. "But remember, Della Penna has an airtight alibi."

"Yeah." Tollison admitted. "I'm still working through that part."

The food came, and Tollison was happy for the distraction. Beau attacked his food the same way he attacked everything else, with a vengeance, while Tollison merely picked at his. He'd been thinking too much about him and Beau, and he needed to stop. This thing between them *was* what it *was*, and when the case was over, it would all come to an end. And besides, it was starting to affect his job, and he needed to focus on solving this case.

The good thing was when Beau had picked up on his mood change, he'd been forced to come up with some reason for being so preoccupied, and Della Penna and Robinette was the first thing that had popped into his mind. He hadn't thought much about them consciously, but the link between them must have been working in the back of his mind. Now that he'd voiced his speculation, the connection made perfect sense. He and Beau still had a theory to prove, and this new connection between Della Penna and Robinette might prove to be very instrumental in making his case.

"You're doing it again," Beau said with a shred of lettuce hanging out of his mouth.

Tollison tapped his finger against his mouth to let Beau know food was dangling. "Doing what?" he asked.

Beau put his po'boy down and passed his napkin across his face. "Thinking again."

"It's my job," Tollison said. "I'm trying to work through this in my head."

"Can't you take a few minutes off to eat? You barely touched your jambalaya. How is it, by the way?"

"It's really good. You want to try some?"

Beau reached his fork across the table and took a large bite of Tollison's food. "This *is* good."

"Here," Tollison said, pushing the plate across the table. "I'm done. Have at it."

Beau sighed. "No thanks. Let's talk this through some more."

Tollison shook his head. The last thing he wanted to do was talk. "No thanks. Not just yet. I've got a few things to iron out in my head. But by the time we get back to the station, I should be ready to bring you up to speed."

"Suit yourself," Beau said, filling his fork with another bite of jambalaya and lifting it to his mouth. He froze, fork to mouth, when his cell phone rang. "Damn. So close."

He pulled the phone out of his pocket and looked at the screen. "It's Bruce," he mumbled.

Beau slid his finger across the bottom of the phone. "Montgomery. … Yeah," Beau said, nodding his head.

Tollison watched Beau's eyes widen and his expression change several times.

"No fucking way," he said. "Okay. We're on our way." Beau ended the call and looked directly at Tollison. "Robinette is dead."

Tollison laid both hands flat on the table. "What?"

"Someone just found him, and you won't believe how."

WHEN THEY got back to the Louisiana Avenue estate, Beau was surprised at how quickly the place had been overrun with squad cars, crime scene investigators, and news media trucks.

"Fucking press," Beau said, flashing his badge at the officer on guard and stepping under the yellow crime scene tape. He held the tape up and motioned for Tollison to follow. "These guys are unbelievable. They must sit around all day and do nothing but monitor police broadcasts."

Beau looked up and saw Bruce standing on the front porch.

"Where is he?" Beau asked, smiling when the he saw Bruce give Tollison the evil eye.

"Follow me," Bruce said, stepping through the front door.

When they got to a room at the back of the house that appeared to be a study or office of some sort, they found Robinette sitting in a leather chair behind a large mahogany desk, eyes staring blankly ahead. Beau couldn't help but smile when he saw the large gold-framed painting around his neck.

"Won't know for sure until the autopsy, but based on this"— Bruce pointed to a thin red mark encircling Robinette's neck—"it appears he was strangled to death."

"By a painting?" Tollison asked.

Beau chuckled, but Bruce ignored the comment and kept talking.

"We believe the painting was placed there after he was unconscious or already dead."

Beau looked at the painting more closely. It was of an older gentleman, sitting behind the same or a very similar desk. The odd thing was that Robinette's head was sticking through the canvas exactly where the gentleman's head would have been.

Beau looked at Tollison. "You thinking what I'm thinking?"

"Della Penna?" Tollison replied.

"Precisely," Beau said. "Bruce?"

Bruce reached for his cell phone. "I'm on it. Oh, and by the way, I forgot to mention this, but we have video of Della Penna on Royal Street the night of the theft about seven forty-five in the evening one block from the gallery."

"You mean he was at the fund-raiser?" Tollison asked.

"Apparently so," Beau said, turning to Tollison. "What time did you meet him for dinner at Brennan's?"

"Around nine o'clock."

Beau did the math in his head. "With a fifteen-minute walk from the gallery to Brennan's, assuming he did walk, that would give him at least forty-five minutes or more to case the gallery and still get to the restaurant by nine o'clock."

Beau looked at Tollison. "How long does it take to case a joint?"

"Depends," Tollison said. "But that gallery? No more than thirty minutes."

"Any helpful surveillance footage from later in the evening?"

"Not yet, but we're still reviewing."

"Perfect," Beau said. "Oh, and Bruce. Bring Villerie in to see if he can identity Della Penna as being at the gallery."

BEAU, TOLLISON, and Bruce, along with Crymes Villerie, stood in front of a two-way mirror watching Della Penna sitting at a table in the interrogation room.

"Not only was he at the gallery," Villerie said, "he was also at the estate on St. Charles Avenue the day I bought the paintings. He introduced himself and even commented on another painting I was considering."

"Eureka," Beau said. "I think we are looking at our thief, gentlemen."

"But where are the paintings?" Tollison asked. "I mean... I agree Robinette and Della Penna were somehow involved, but unless my theory is off base, I don't think Della Penna is the thief."

"Maybe your theory *is* wrong," Bruce said matter-of-factly.

Beau interrupted. "Let me spend a little time with Della Penna alone and see if I can break him."

"TWICE IN one day, Mr. Della Penna. If I were you, that would make me pretty nervous," Beau said, now sitting comfortably across from their number one suspect again.

"Really. Why? I have nothing to be nervous about."

"Oh, come now," Beau said. "You're a well-known convicted art thief—"

Della Penna cut him off, holding up a finger. "Former art thief. And... I did my time."

Beau continued, "And you had some sort a relationship with Dudley Robinette, with whom you were having a very heated discussion earlier today, and who just happens to be dead."

Della Penna's eyes widened. "Dead?" He turned his head away and cursed under his breath. "I had nothing to do with that."

"Have you ever been to The Royal Renaissance art gallery?"

"I can't say for certain that I have," Della Penna said. "I go to lots of openings. I may have been there at one time or another."

"Let's try this another way. Have you ever met Crymes Villerie, the owner of the gallery?"

"Not to my knowledge."

"That's very interesting," Beau explained. "Because we have you on surveillance video just one block away from the gallery, heading in that direction. And... Crymes Villerie has identified you as not only being in the gallery the night of the theft, but says he also met you at a St. Charles Avenue estate the day he purchased the paintings you later stole."

"As I said, I go to lots of openings, and I meet lots of people," Della Penna admitted very calmly. "It's quite possible I did both. But... I didn't steal any paintings or kill anyone."

Beau slapped the table, stood, and started pacing. "So am I to assume you just happened to be having a very heated discussion with the man who's now dead who sold the now-stolen paintings to the gallery owner. The same gallery owner you met the day he was buying the paintings, and the same paintings you observed at the gallery a little over six months later?"

"Assume what you like, but I have an alibi for the entire evening, Detective. By the way, you never asked who I had dinner with that night."

Beau smiled. "That's because I already know with whom you dined."

"And did he tell you he got nothing more out of me than you're going to?"

"I don't need Mr. Cruz to tell me anything. I'm a big boy, and I'm conducting my own investigation."

"Then why do you keep trying to pin this on me?"

"Because all the evidence keeps pointing back to you. And the evidence never lies."

"In this case, your evidence is wrong. Are you sure you've exhausted all your suspects? Maybe your thief is right under your nose."

"I can see this is going nowhere," Beau said. "If you'll excuse me."

BEAU JOINED Tollison and Bruce again. "I feel like he's trying to tell us something. But what?"

"I think he knows something," Tollison said. "But he can't tell us without admitting he was there." Tollison looked back between Beau and Della Penna. "Let me talk to him."

"You're kidding, right?" Bruce said. "He's a suspect and you're not even a cop. Beau, this is crazy."

"No. I'm a thief," Tollison said. "Just like him. He'll talk to me."

"Do it," Beau said, raising his hand to stop Bruce before he protested.

"SO! BAD cop struck out so good cop gets a turn," Della Penna said. "Except you're not even a cop. Who are you really, Investigator Cruz?"

"It depends on who you ask," Tollison said, taking a seat. "I have a lot of names in my past. Names that you may or may not recognize, depending on how well traveled you are. In Zurich, I'm known as Luca Birrer. In Spain, Police Nationals know me as Cruz Del Olmo, and in Britain, Scotland Yard knows me as Kiwi. But you probably know me as Kane Pousso."

Della Penna sat upright in his chair. "San Francisco Museum of Fine Art, 2006? Are you saying that was you?"

"Yep," Tollison said.

"How did you get by the sound sensors?" Della Penna asked.

"I had the Chinese build me a wave cancellation box," Tollison said.

"I'll be damned."

Tollison leaned back in his chair and smiled.

"But now you're here, working with the cops," Della Penna said. "So that means you must have been caught."

"Nope. I got smart," Tollison said, leaning forward again. "I realized that one day this was all going to catch up with me, and someone was going to get hurt and I didn't want it to be me."

"I didn't kill Robinette or Le Moyne," Della Penna said.

"But you were at the gallery the night Le Moyne was killed and the paintings were stolen, and we overheard you arguing with Robinette."

Della Penna stared at Tollison for a long time before he spoke. He sighed. "I wasn't hired to steal the paintings. My contact told me that I was being paid to test their security system and identify their vulnerabilities. That's it. And for my trouble, I got a hundred grand in advance. When you heard us arguing, Robinette had just asked me to unload the paintings for him. We were arguing because I told him to go and fuck himself. I wouldn't do business with that man if my life depended on it. He's the reason I spent five years in prison for the New Orleans Museum of Art heist. He hired me to do it and then testified against me. I served the time, and he got off without as much as a slap on the wrist."

"Where *are* the paintings now?" Tollison asked.

"Don't know. I've never actually seen them."

"Shit!" Tollison said under his breath. "Who hired you, then?"

"If you truly are who you say you are, you know that everything is done through a third party. Much safer that way."

"Yeah, until someone sets you up," Tollison said.

"That's why I was so surprised when Robinette called me personally. He must have really been desperate."

"In the beginning, Robinette needed you to tell him how to go about stealing the paintings, and then later, he needed you to unload them."

Della Penna rolled his eyes. "Apparently. But I don't really know if I was working for Robinette. Why would he start off by using a third party and then blow his cover and call me directly?"

"Maybe it's like you said," Tollison agreed. "He was desperate."

"Maybe," Della Penna said. "But there *is* one person who acted very strange while I was at the gallery. Watched me like a hawk the entire time I was there."

"And who is that?" Tollison asked.

Cruz listened as Della Penna explained what he'd observed the night of the fund-raiser.

By the time Della Penna had finished, Cruz couldn't hide the smile on his face. He kept glancing back at the two-way mirror, hoping Beau was on the other side, listening to the commentary. This new information only strengthened his theory, and he wanted Bruce to hear it as well.

"Very interesting," Tollison said as he stood. "Okay. Just stay put."

"Not like I have any choice at the moment."

"I'll see what I can do."

WHEN HE closed the door to the interrogation room, Beau was waiting for him. "You get all that?"

"I got it. But—"

"Come on, man, he's got no reason to lie," Tollison pleaded.

Beau ran his fingers through his hair as he paced. "He's a thief. He has plenty of reasons to lie."

"Not about this. He knows you've got nothing on him except a shitload of circumstantial evidence. And he also knows he just has to wait and you'll have to release him. He's been down this road before. He knows the ropes."

"Fine. Bruce! Let him go. But make sure he doesn't leave the state."

BACK IN his office, Beau took his seat. He propped his elbows on the desk and held his head in his hands. "You think Robinette is behind all this?" he asked.

Tollison walked around the desk, rested his hands on Beau's shoulders, and massaged the tense muscles for a few minutes while he thought out loud. "If Della Penna is telling the truth, and I believe him, I think he's involved in some way."

Beau rolled his head as Tollison massaged his shoulders. "That feels really good. But I feel like we're missing something."

"Okay, so playing devil's advocate, if Robinette did the heist himself, I'd bet my life that he was Le Moyne's killer, but you know what I think," Tollison said.

Beau shook his head. "Yeah, but that would leave us no leads on Robinette's killer."

"Or motive," Tollison added. "On the other hand, if Robinette hired someone to do the heist, that person probably killed Le Moyne and then turned on Robinette for some reason and did him in as well. All we need to do is find out who that person is, and maybe that will also lead us to the artwork."

Tollison gave Beau's shoulders one last squeeze before he walked around the desk and took his normal seat.

"Thanks. That felt great."

"I'm glad, but look, man. Now that Della Pena is out of the picture, does my theory sound any more likely?"

"Were you buttering me up with an agenda?" Beau asked with a light smile.

"Maybe. Did it work?"

"Sadly, yes," Beau said in amusement. "But thinking something and proving it are two different things. And so far… we haven't been able to prove anything."

Beau and Tollison both turned when they heard a tap on the door. Bruce stood in the doorway with a slight smile on his face. "Got something," he said. "Check your e-mail."

Beau motioned for Tollison to come behind the desk and join him. He opened the latest e-mail from Bruce and clicked on the attached video.

The video was very dark, but he could clearly make out a figure in a hoodie walking out of the alley behind the gallery, head down and hands tucked in pockets. Beau looked at the timestamp on the bottom of the video. Three thirty! "It's the right time, but that's not Robinette."

"Yes!" Tollison whispered.

Beau looked up over his shoulder. "Are you thinking what I'm thinking?"

Tollison nodded.

"But if this is our guy, then where in the hell are the paintings?"

"What if the paintings never left the gallery?" Tollison asked.

Beau considered Tollison's question. "It would surely account for why they haven't surfaced yet."

"All the other footage *was* clean," Bruce added.

"What about Robinette?" Beau asked, grabbing his coat and his keys. "Did anything show up in his background check?"

"Nothing so far but his connection to Della Penna," Bruce said. "And Della Penna was telling the truth, by the way. Robinette did testify against him and was largely responsible for putting him away."

"Okay, let's go, gentlemen," Beau said, rounding his desk. "We have a gallery to search."

EIGHT

"MR. VILLERIE. I hope you don't mind, but we need to look around a bit more," Bruce explained as Beau and Tollison walked around the gallery searching for possible places to stash the stolen artwork.

Crymes raised his hands. "By all means. Anything to help the investigation."

"Is Mrs. Hayes here?" Tollison asked over his shoulder.

"Unfortunately not," Crymes said. "She took my wife to a spa in Shreveport for a couple of days for a little rest. She's still struggling with—well, you know—and she needed a little time away."

"We understand," Bruce said, nodding his head. "We'll make it as quick as we can and be out of your hair."

"Thank you. I'll leave you to your investigation, then. I'll be in my office if you need anything," Crymes said, turning and disappearing up the stairs.

"OKAY, LET'S talk this through," Beau said, pacing back and forth. "Thief number one, who we think is Le Moyne, and thief number two, who we think is Robinette or someone Robinette hired, enter through either the first-floor courtyard door or the third-floor french doors leading to the rooftop deck. At some point, one of them surprises the other, and Le Moyne takes a bullet to the head."

Tollison jumped in. "And thief number two possibly runs out of time, stashes the paintings somewhere in the building for later retrieval, and escapes though one of the aforementioned entrances," Tollison added.

"Now, if we can just find a couple of paintings to back this up, we've got it made," Bruce said.

Beau wandered through the gallery, checking every closet or area that might be capable of housing the largest of the unframed paintings, which was approximately three feet by three feet. Short of stashing the paintings in the walls, which would have been impossible not to detect, the only area he found on the first floor was a small kitchenette, which he assumed was used for catering openings and special events. Unfortunately, none of the cabinetry or storage areas were large enough to accommodate either of the paintings.

"Let's check out the upper floors," he said, taking the stairs two at a time.

When he got to the top of the stairs, Crymes was standing in the doorway to his office.

"We're gonna search the second and third floors," Beau said. "Has anyone stayed in the guest apartment since the night of the theft and murder?"

"Absolutely not," Crymes said, looking at Bruce. "Detective Jenkins told us it was still a crime scene, so I locked it up tight."

"Can you unlock it for us, please?" Tollison asked.

"Absolutely," Crymes said, disappearing into his office and returning with a set of keys. He unlocked the door and pushed it open. "Help yourselves, gentlemen. May I ask what you're looking *for*?"

"The paintings," Beau said nonchalantly while walking past the man.

Crymes froze with a shocked expression on his face. "That's preposterous. Why would the thief leave the paintings here?"

Beau didn't stop. "Guys, fill Mr. Villerie in on what we know so far," he said over his shoulder. Beau tried to tune out the chatter between Bruce, Tollison, and Crymes as he observed his surroundings.

From what he remembered, the apartment was exactly as it had been the night of the murder and theft. The small foyer opened to a large sitting room with twelve-foot ceilings surrounded by very heavy crown molding and full-length windows.

Beau stepped to the left into a tiny kitchenette with a small sink, apartment-sized refrigerator and dishwasher, microwave oven, and coffeemaker. He could barely turn around in the tight space and immediately ruled it out as a potential hiding place.

Stepping back into the sitting room, he then stuck his head into a powder room under the stairs. With nothing there but a toilet and sink, he ruled out that tiny space as well.

He hadn't paid much attention to the decor when he was here last, but glancing around now, he realized Villerie must put up some very important customers here. The sitting room was extremely well appointed; the word that came to mind to describe it was simply "handsome." The place was full of antiques, or at least they appeared to be antiques to Beau. They could have all been reproductions, as far as he could tell, but they were good-looking either way.

Tollison came up behind him and whistled. "I didn't pay much attention the last time we were here, but this place is pretty nice, huh?"

"I'll say," Beau agreed, looking into Tollison's eyes. "I could easily live here."

Tollison smiled. "Yeah. Villerie's customers must be predominantly male. This place is pretty masculine."

"'Handsome' was the word that first came to my mind, but you're right, 'masculine' is a better fit."

Beau stepped across the room and inspected the wall-to-wall bookcases. They were built in, and nothing could get behind them and none of the lower cabinets were big enough. He glanced across the room and stopped when he saw Tollison's ass. It was up in the air as he bent down and looked under the couch. He took a second to admire the view and pictured what he hoped he'd be doing to that ass later that night.

Once Tollison was back up on his feet and the show was over, Beau opened a short door under the lower part of the stairs. He got to his knees and flipped a light switch he felt to the left of the door. As he peeked in, he saw it was a storage closet and housed a vacuum cleaner and a bucket of cleaning supplies. The paintings might have fit through the door, but the closet wasn't deep enough to get the paintings in all the way.

As Beau stood, he furrowed his brows in frustration. Between him and Tollison, they'd covered the entire room and found nothing. Beau made a gesture to the stairs, and Tollison started to climb with

Beau behind him, Tollison's ass once again in Beau's face. Tollison looked over his shoulder, and his lips twisted into a slight smile. *I know he's doing this to torture me,* Beau thought, readjusting his crotch.

Tollison stopped short at the top of the stairs and Beau, still staring at Tollison's ass, ran right into the back of him.

Beau stayed put, rested his hands on Tollison's hips, and wiggled his erection against the man's backside. "Oh no, big boy," Tollison whispered over his shoulder. "I'm gonna be buried so deep in your ass tonight, you're gonna feel it in your throat."

Beau sighed, amused, and kissed the back of Tollison's neck. "Don't threaten me with a good time," he whispered, thrusting his hips forward again.

"Are you two going to fuck each other right here?" Bruce said in a huff as he passed them at the top of the stairs. "How about a little professionalism, huh?"

Beau cleared his throat. "Ah, yeah. We were just, ah—"

"I know what you were 'just, ah' doing," Bruce mocked, storming through the doorway just ahead.

When a chuckle escaped Tollison's lips, Beau slapped him on the ass, and Tollison lunged forward theatrically. "And stop distracting me, Investigator Cruz," Beau added.

"Yes, sir," Tollison said, heading down a short hall.

Beau shook his head and smiled as he opened a door to his right. He found a laundry room just big enough for a stacking washer and dryer, and a broom and dustpan hanging on the wall. He closed the door and opened the adjacent door. There he found the heating and air-conditioning unit, with nothing more than a few filters leaning against the wall.

When he closed the door, Tollison was on the other side. "Anything?" he asked.

"Not a thing. You?"

"Just a linen closet, but nothing else."

"Let's try the bedroom, then," Beau said.

"Are you sure you can control yourself around me in a bedroom?"

"Pretty sure," Beau replied. "On second thought, as long as Bruce is in there, I guarantee you're safe."

Beau stepped into the bedroom, and Bruce was nowhere to be found. "Bruce?"

"I'm searching the bathroom," Bruce yelled.

Beau and Tollison looked at each other. "Jesus," Beau said. "Would you look at this place?"

The bedroom was the size of the sitting room downstairs, but it had lower ceilings, with two dormer windows facing the front of the building overlooking Royal Street and the french doors facing the back. To the right, draperies hung the entire length of the wall, forming a backdrop for the king-size bed, which was upholstered and dressed in the same fabric. Across the room from the bed stood a dresser, and a flat-panel television hung on the wall above it. In the corner, facing out, was a writing desk and chair, and opposite that was a fainting couch in front of one of the dormer windows.

Beau felt his way all along the draperied wall, reaching as far up to the ceiling as he could and then back down to the floor, anticipating finding two paintings hidden behind the heavily gathered fabric, but much to his surprise, he found nothing.

Tollison was once more on his hands and knees with his ass in the air, looking under the bed. Beau was determined not to let himself get distracted again, so he crossed the room and opened a door. He ran his hand up the wall just inside and flipped a switch. Light flickered and the room was instantly filled with the familiar humming of fluorescents. *Of course. A walk-in closet.* The walls were lined with drawers, shelves, and hanging space but virtually empty of any personal belongings, which made it very easy to search.

Beau was about to turn off the light and move on when he spotted what looked like a door-sized cutout in the drywall behind one of the hanging spaces. He slid his fingers into the cracks to try to pull whatever it was away from the wall, but he had no luck. In a fit of frustration, he slapped his hand against the cutout area, and lo and behold, the door popped open.

"I'll be damned," he said.

Behind the door was a six-foot-high safe with a six-inch-diameter dial and a lock on the handle.

"Look what you found," Tollison said, stepping up behind him. "Nice work."

"Thanks," Beau said, bowing at the waist. "Hey, Bruce! Get Villerie, would ya?"

Bruce popped his head in the closet. "What?"

"Get Villerie," Beau repeated. "And tell him to bring the combination and key to his safe."

VILLERIE SPUN the dial to the right. Then left. Then right again. He slid the key into the lock and turned the handle. Beau heard a click, and Villerie pulled the large door open. Standing on end were about two-dozen paintings.

"Looks like we hit the mother lode," Tollison said.

"Not so fast, gentlemen," Villerie said. "This is simply our inventory."

"Inventory?" Beau asked.

"Yes," Villerie explained. "We rotate our inventory continuously to keep everything fresh. If something doesn't sell quickly, we replace it with another painting and store it here. Then behind the scenes, we try to sell it by contacting specific collectors and offering it to them in a private showing. That way our gallery is ever changing and doesn't get old and tired."

"I see," Beau said. "But if you don't mind, we'd like to see each of these paintings. If for nothing more than to satisfy our own curiosity."

Villerie nodded. "By all means. But please be careful, Detective. These paintings are worth a lot of money."

"I tell you what," Beau offered. "You can handle them all. Just pull them out one by one and let us verify that none of these are the paintings in question."

Villerie pulled out each painting and laid them against the closet wall. When the safe was empty, Beau walked inside and inspected all three walls. "No secret compartments. Nothing," he mumbled.

When Villerie started replacing the paintings, Beau sighed. "Back to square one, guys. Thanks, Mr. Villerie. Bruce, would you give him a hand?"

Beau walked back into the bedroom, stood in the center of the room. "If I were a thief, where would I hide a painting?" He looked around the room again. Suddenly, he froze and smacked himself in the forehead. He ran to the bed and pulled the covering and sheets off. "Give me a hand, Tollison."

Beau and Tollison flipped the mattress off of the bed and it landed on the floor with a thud. Beau totally expected to see the paintings lodged between the mattress and the foundation and cursed under his breath when they weren't there. With one hand on his hip, he rubbed his forehead. "What are we missing, Cruz?"

"Wait!" Tollison said, pointing to the underside of the mattress. "Look."

Beau looked at the mattress and could barely make out the outline of something almost square. Tollison dropped to the floor next to the mattress and inspected the piping. "This has been cut and restitched," he said.

Beau fished for his pocketknife and slowly cut along the piping as Villerie and Bruce walked in.

"Stop!" Villerie yelled, running over to the bed. "What are you doing?"

"I'm ripping this case wide open," Beau said.

He cut a piece of the sheet, used it as a glove, and reached in, putting his hand on something solid. He then slid the knife inside the mattress and slit the covering from the inside out so as not to damage the contents.

"You're ruining it," Villerie screamed. "For what purpose?"

When Beau ripped the remaining mattress covering apart, the eyes of Robert E. Lee were gazing back up at them. "Fucking A. For that purpose," he said as he withdrew the painting from the partially hollowed-out mattress. And just as he'd suspected, the smaller painting was nestled inside the back of the larger one.

"What the hell?" Villerie said. "The paintings were here all along?"

"That way, the thief didn't need to worry about smuggling them out and could walk down the street unnoticed," Tollison said.

Beau held up a hand. "We know that whoever stole the paintings was the same person who killed Le Moyne and more than likely Dudley Robinette. And… they had a lot of time to unmake the bed, rip the mattress open and partially remove the stuffing, slide the two paintings inside, sew it up again, remake the bed, and dispose of the mattress stuffing. How much time do you think that would take?" he asked Tollison.

"At least an hour," Tollison replied.

Beau nodded. "At least. And… how could the robber/murderer do all this between the time the alarm sounded and the police arrived?"

Villerie's expression suddenly changed. "You think this was an inside job," he said.

Beau nodded. "Bruce?"

"Wait!" Villerie said. "It wasn't me."

Beau smiled. "You mean it wasn't *just* you? Tell me. How did Le Moyne, Della Penna, and Robinette fit into all this?"

"I have no idea," Villerie said. "I just met Robinette and Della Penna for the first time at the estate sale, and I only met Le Moyne the night he stumbled into the gallery. I swear it."

"Look," Tollison said. "It's no secret you were in financial distress and about to lose everything you owned, so you had the paintings stolen and stashed in your very own business with no one else's knowledge. Very clever, I might add. Then you collected the insurance money and paid off your debt. Much later, when everything died down and the time was right, you could resell the paintings on the black market or to one of the many people you mentioned in that database of yours who specialize in Civil War art. All very nice and neat. You get a double payoff for the same artwork."

"No!" Villerie said. "That's not right. I'm not even going to be here. I signed the business over to   " Villerie stopped short. "No, it can't be…."

"Over to whom?" Beau asked.

"My daughter."

Bruce looked at Beau, who looked at Tollison, who simply smiled.

"No! Not Harper." Villerie said. "It couldn't have been Harper."

"Bruce, call a cruiser and—" Beau said.

"I got it," Bruce interrupted. "Mr. Villerie, you're under arrest for possession of stolen property," he said as he read the man his Miranda rights.

"And," Beau said, "in the very near future, I hope to be able to add conspiracy to murder and theft to that charge."

"I had nothing to do with any of this," Villerie pleaded.

"Bruce, find out which spa the ladies are visiting, contact Shreveport PD, and have Mrs. Hayes picked up, booked, and transported back to New Orleans. Tollison and I are out of here."

Beau saw a flash of distress on Bruce's face, and he regretted the words, but Bruce seemed to recover pretty quickly. "Will do."

"I'll interrogate Mrs. Hayes in the morning," Beau added.

Tollison tore the piece of sheet in two and picked up both paintings. "These are now property of Lloyd's of London. I'll contact my boss first thing in the morning."

"We'll need to take them downtown and book them into evidence and check for prints, but as soon as all that's done, we can release them to you on behalf of the insurance company."

Beau took one of the paintings from Tollison, careful to make sure he used the sheet, and together, they carried them out to the SUV. He was feeling something he couldn't quite put his finger on. He was uneasy and unusually melancholy, especially after getting so close to solving a case. Normally that gave him a high like no other. Then it hit him. Now that Tollison had recovered his paintings, he'd probably be heading back to Atlanta. Was what they'd embarked upon over before it really got started?

"I guess you were right all along," Beau said as they drove downtown. "Good job."

Tollison smiled. "It was just a hunch, but thanks."

"A hunch that hopefully will pay off tomorrow morning."

Tollison didn't respond.

Beau cleared his throat. "I guess since you recovered the paintings, you'll be heading back to Atlanta soon, huh?"

"Probably. It'll take me a day or so to wrap up all the loose ends, but yeah, soon."

Before Beau could respond, he pulled into the station parking lot. They took the paintings upstairs to the evidence room and had them recorded and stored.

When they got back to Beau's office, Beau jotted down his address and handed it to Tollison. "I need to bring the captain up to speed on the case, but why don't you go back to your hotel, shower, and grab some things and stay the night with me?"

Tollison smiled. "Sounds good. What can I bring?"

Beau looked at the door to make sure the coast was clear and he took a handful of Tollison's crotch. "Just this," he said, kissing him hastily and letting go.

"He goes where I go," Tollison drawled, licking his lips.

"Then I think we're all set. I'll see the both of you in, say… an hour and a half?"

Tollison looked at his watch. "That's doable."

TOLLISON STROLLED out of the precinct with mixed emotions. He was excited about the evening ahead of him, but he also knew this might very well be his and Beau's last night together, and that was the part that kept nagging at him.

When he reached his car, he popped the locks but didn't get in right away. He leaned against the driver's side door and folded his arms over his chest. He was ass deep in emotions he didn't want to deal with when a squad car pulled up alongside of him. A uniformed police officer got out and opened the back door. He reached in and placed his hand on the head of a handcuffed Villcric to make sure the guy didn't hit his head as he slid out of the backseat.

Moments later the passenger's side door opened, and Bruce popped out of the car, putting away his cell phone. When their eyes met, Tollison saw a look in the other man's eyes that he didn't recognize. It had been pretty easy to identify the loathing and scathing glances Bruce had given him all the way through this investigation, but now there was an unrecognizable softness to his gaze.

Bruce looked at the officer. "Take him in, Tom, and I'll be right behind you."

The officer led Villerie toward the building.

"Hey," Bruce said, stopping in front of Tollison. "You all right? You looked pretty deep in thought."

Surprised by the sentiment, Tollison smiled weakly. "Yeah, I'm okay."

"I thought you and Beau would be celebrating about now," Bruce said.

Tollison thought about the best way to respond, knowing the guy still had feelings for Beau. He didn't want to be cruel, but in the end, he decided on the truth. "He's briefing Captain Trenchard, and we're hooking up later."

Bruce's expression changed, and Tollison recognized the pain on his face. It was pretty clear Bruce still had it bad for Beau, and Tollison waited for the onslaught.

Instead, Bruce sighed, stood next to Tollison, and leaned against the car, staring off into the distance. He appeared to want to say something but was hesitating.

"Go ahead," Tollison said. "Let me have it."

Bruce turned and looked into his eyes. "Yeah. About that, I'm sorry."

Tollison's mouth dropped open, and he used his finger to close it. "That was the last thing I was expecting to hear."

"I figured as much," Bruce said wryly.

"But thanks for saying it."

Bruce nodded and then hesitated.

"You've got something else on your mind?" Tollison asked.

"It's really none of my business."

"Go for it," Tollison said, giving the guy an opening and preparing for whatever was heading his way.

Bruce cleared his throat. "Ah… this thing with Beau. Is it… you know… serious?"

Tollison chuckled. "I've known the guy for less than a week, and we didn't exactly get off to a good start, but I know I like him. A lot."

"The thing is," Bruce said, "he's a great guy, and I still love him."

"Look, Bruce—" Tollison began, but Bruce held up a hand to silence him.

"Please, let me finish."

Tollison nodded.

"But," Bruce continued, "I know it's over for us. Beau is a man who thrives on fidelity and trust, and I broke that trust. He's the type of guy who can never go back."

"It takes two to tango," Tollison said. "From what he tells me, you weren't the only one at fault."

"Yeah, but I'm the one who cheated. Who turned to someone else," Bruce admitted. "And I'll regret that for the rest of my life."

"Listen, man," Tollison said, suddenly feeling sorry for the guy. "We all make mistakes and do stupid shit over the course of our lives. It's not the mistakes that define us; it's what we do about the fallout that distinguishes us from others. Don't beat yourself up. You've admitted your mistakes and hopefully learned from them, and it's time to let it go and move forward."

"Thank you," Bruce said. "Maybe it *is* time I let myself off the hook. Let both of us off the hook, really."

"I think you might be right."

"I want him to be happy, you know. You're the first person he's shown any interest in since our demise, and he looks happy for a change. Hell, he's even treating me like a human being again."

"I think he realizes he was being pretty hard on you."

"I guess so," Bruce agreed. "But in the beginning, I thought it was because he was starting to forgive me and maybe wanting to try again. But now I realize it was because he met you and he was finally able to let go of me and all those bitter feelings and start to move on."

"I'm sorry, man," Tollison said. "I know what it's like to love someone who doesn't feel the same way."

"Sucks, huh?"

"Yeah."

"Are you going back to Atlanta soon?"

"As soon as Beau releases the paintings, I'll be on my way."

"Atlanta's not that far away, you know," Bruce said. "Maybe you guys can still see each other."

"I have no idea what Beau is thinking, but I'd like that. It's just…."

"Long-distance relationships never work?"

"Exactly."

The two men stood in silence for a few more minutes. Bruce straightened and offered his hand. "I love Beau enough to want him to be happy, and if you make him happy, I'm all for it."

Tollison accepted the outstretched hand. "Thank you, Bruce."

Bruce wiped a tear from his cheek, turned on his heel, and walked away without looking back.

TOLLISON ENTERED his hotel suite, threw his keys on the foyer table, and went straight to the minibar. After popping the top on a Stella, he slipped out of his suit coat, kicked off his shoes, and opened the doors leading to the balcony overlooking Bourbon Street. The warm night was alive with tourists, drinking and taking in the sights as they moved up and down the street. The aroma of New Orleans cuisine filled his nostrils, and the sounds of jazz wafted up to his suite.

He watched the people without much thought as they maneuvered the streets of the French Quarter. His mind was strictly on Beau. He remembered the things Bruce had said to him and wondered if he *did* make Beau happy. It was much too soon to tell if anything would come of their fling, but he knew there was some sort of a connection between them. At least on his part.

What bothered him most was the fact that he would probably never know if there was a possibility of anything lasting between them. Bruce had been right. Long-distance relationships rarely worked, and now that Beau seemed to be forgiving Bruce and ready to move on, he didn't seem like the type to stay on the market too long. From all Tollison knew, he was a good man—smart, witty, good-looking, and built like an Adonis—and someone would scoop him up in a heartbeat.

Besides, Beau had never indicated he wanted anything more than what they had now, so why was he torturing himself? *You've got one more night. Maybe two. So why don't you just enjoy this time and make the best of it?*

Tollison stepped off the balcony and closed the door behind him. He downed the last of his beer and walked through the bedroom and into the bathroom, where he turned on the shower and stripped. He stepped into the glass enclosure and sighed when the steam encompassed him and the hot water began to soothe his tense and aching muscles. He planted his hands on either side of the showerhead and leaned against the wall, head hanging forward, as the water beat on his shoulders and back, washing his stress away.

In his protective cocoon of steam and hot water, Tollison found his mind drifting back to Beau. He pictured the man on his back, those silvery-gray eyes looking up and boring into his soul. His dick instantly filled, and he became rock hard with desire. He sat on the bench at the opposite end of the shower and filled his right hand with shower gel. He leaned back, his legs falling open, and ran his soapy hand over his erection, squeezing and fondling, enjoying the sensation of his callused hand against his soft skin. He let his left hand roam freely over his chest, pinching and rubbing his nipples.

In his mind, Beau's legs were over his shoulders, and Beau was moaning and whimpering as Tollison drove harder and harder into him. With each stroke of his hand, he imagined moving in and out of Beau. His release was quickly building, and within minutes, Tollison was the one moaning as he threw his head back and shot his load onto the shower floor. Out of breath and sated, Tollison remained in that position, regaining his composure, until he was able to stand again and finish showering.

He dressed in jeans and a polo shirt, threw a few things in a bag, grabbed a suit and a clean shirt for Mrs. Hayes's interrogation tomorrow morning, and headed out the door.

He plugged Beau's address into his GPS and let the system guide him through the French Quarter, across Canal Street, and eventually into the uptown area. Twenty minutes later he put his car in park in front of a mint green Acadian-style cottage with Charleston green trim, a large front porch with two rocking chairs, three floor-to-ceiling windows, and a front door with a stained-glass transom above it. Tollison had no idea what he'd been expecting, but he liked what he saw. The style suited Beau's personality to a T. It was masculine and tasteful but still had a certain playfulness to it.

Stepping onto the porch with his bag over his shoulder and holding on to his suit hanger, Tollison raised his free hand to knock. But before his knuckles hit the wood, the door flew open, and there stood a barefoot Beau, looking like a million bucks. "Hey there," he said, smiling broadly. "Let me help." He took the suit out of Tollison's hand.

Tollison's feet were frozen in place as he stared at Beau, unwilling to look away. *He looks incredible.*

Faintly, Tollison heard John Legend singing from somewhere in the background, but he tuned everything out except the man in front of him. For the first time since they'd met, Beau appeared to be relaxed and carefree. Tollison was literally speechless. Beau's hair was wet and slicked back, and he was wearing a powder blue T-shirt and khaki shorts.

Beau laughed, apparently noticing Tollison's stare. "You okay?"

Tollison nodded as he pushed his way inside, slamming the door behind them. He dropped his bag to the floor and jammed Beau against the back of the door. He buried his face in Beau's neck and inhaled the clean, fresh scent of a recent shower combined with his own spicy aroma. He licked his way up Beau's neck to his chin and eventually covered Beau's lips in a crushing kiss.

When Tollison pulled back and smiled, Beau smiled back. "I could certainly get used to hellos like this," Beau said.

"And I could most definitely get used to giving them. You look delicious, by the way."

"Likewise," Beau said. "And welcome to my humble abode."

"I really like it," Tollison said honestly. "At least what I've seen so far."

"Let me show you the rest, then," Beau said, laying Tollison's suit on the couch.

When Tollison turned around, the place was considerably more contemporary than he'd expected, but with some traditional touches. The room was largely monochromatic, with bursts of color here and there. And the furniture was quite sleek, with ultraclean lines. Again, Tollison had no idea what he'd expected, but he was pleasantly surprised by Beau's knack for decorating.

Next was the dining room, and it was more a mix of contemporary and traditional. A long, narrow, glass-topped dining table with a chrome scissor base sat in the middle of the room, surrounded by eight black leather-and-chrome chairs. On the opposite wall was a mahogany sideboard. A traditional oriental rug tied it all together. Tollison didn't miss the romantic setting for two at one end of the table, complete with china, crystal, and silver candelabrum.

The dining room opened into a large den and kitchen area with a powder room off to one side. The kitchen was lined in cherrywood cabinets, black granite countertops and backsplash, and stainless steel appliances. But when Tollison looked at the den area, it was all Beau. This is what he now realized he'd expected to see.

The room simply looked lived-in and comfortable, and Tollison could tell this was where Beau spent most of his time. The entire right side of the room was an exposed-brick wall with a large flat-screen television hanging above an old fireplace. An L-shaped brown leather sectional with brass nailheads sat in the middle of the room, with a sofa table and a couple of end tables bordering it. The room was warm and inviting, with overstuffed pillows and throws everywhere. Tollison loved it.

"Upstairs are two bedrooms and two bathrooms, which I'm sure you'll see later," Beau said with a wry smile.

"I sure do hope so."

Beau opened the fridge. "How about a beer or a glass of wine? Oh, and I have Grey Goose and olives if you'd prefer a martini?"

"What are you having?"

"Beer for now, and then I'll switch to wine for dinner."

"I'll have the same, then."

"Is Blue Moon all right?"

"Sure," Tollison said. He drew in a breath. "Something smells incredible."

"I hope you like rack of lamb."

"I'm impressed," Tollison said. "And yes. One of my favorites."

"Don't be too impressed. I didn't have time to start from scratch, so I picked up a rack from the gourmet deli on Magazine Street. Along with rosemary potatoes and asparagus. I'm just warming it all up. But… I did make the salad."

Tollison laughed. "I'd say you're a very resourceful man."

"And I'd have to agree with you. Goes with the job, I guess."

Tollison sat at the breakfast counter, sipping his beer and watching Beau move about his kitchen with ease, stirring this and checking that. He liked seeing the man so at home in his own environment. They chatted about anything and everything except the case, and by the time they sat down to dinner, Tollison couldn't remember the last time he'd had such a nice evening.

Beau plated the food, poured the wine, and lit the candelabrum. Over dinner, Tollison told him about his interaction with Bruce.

While Tollison recounted the conversation, he watched for any signs of emotions that might lead him to believe Beau wasn't quite over his ex, but in the end, he saw nothing he could identify as pain, hurt, or jealousy.

Beau put his fork down and looked at Tollison. "So he gave us his blessing? Like I couldn't move on unless I got that from him?"

"I didn't get the impression it was like that at all," Tollison said. "He still loves you, Beau. He knows he messed up, and he knows he'll never have another chance with you, but he still wants you to be happy."

"That's so fucking thoughtful of him."

"Come on, Beau, cut him some slack. Can you imagine how hard that must have been for him? How hard it is to watch us together, knowing what we're doing outside of the case? I'm not sure I could have done that if the situations were reversed."

"Now you're starting to sound like Auggie."

"Well, maybe you should listen to both of us."

"I really have been trying to foster a better working relationship, but that's all he's gonna get right now," Beau said. "Maybe in time we can be friends, but I'm still so pissed off at the guy it's hard to look at him without flattening him."

"That's pretty obvious," Tollison said. "But what bothers me is why. Do you think you could possibly still be in love with him?"

Beau exhaled. "Of course I'm not in love with him. I mean, I'll always love him, but I'm not *in* love with him anymore. Besides, what kind of man would I be if I got involved with you while I was still in love with him?"

Tollison's ears perked up. "Are we involved?"

"I'd like to be," Beau said. "I know it's only been a week or so, but I feel like there's something there. And personally, I'd like to explore it and see where it goes."

Tollison reached over and took Beau's hand in his. "I agree, but when I leave here, there's gonna be five hundred miles between us. And in my experience, long-distance relationships never work out."

Beau squeezed Tollison's hand. "It's an eight-hour car ride or an hour-and-a-half flight. I think two adult men can handle either of those for a while."

"But I travel so much," Tollison said. "When would we get to see each other?"

"We'd find a way if we really wanted to. Look, I've got several months' vacation stowed away, and I can use as much as I want, when I want."

"And when that's all gone?" Tollison asked.

"If we're still happy to be together, we take the next step. I mean… the way I see it, there are endless possibilities."

"Like?" Tollison asked.

"Like, I could join you in Atlanta, or you could see if your company would allow you to work from New Orleans. If things progress and we really want this, we'll find a way to make it happen."

Tollison was suddenly overcome with emotion and fighting back tears. Beau believed everything he was saying, and the conviction behind his words went right to Tollison's heart.

As if on cue, John Legend starting singing "All of Me," and Tollison stood and offered his hand to Beau. "Dance with me."

Beau accepted his hand and stood. For a moment they struggled over who was going to lead, but Tollison took control, and Beau eventually gave in. With Tollison's left hand in Beau's right and his arm wrapped around Beau tightly, they swayed to the music, cheek against cheek. Beau felt so good in his arms. How could he have even considered not seeing where this was headed?

Tollison dropped his head and nibbled at Beau's neck as he tightened his hold at the small of Beau's back. He turned one way and then the other, moving easily with the music, and much to his surprise, Beau was keeping up with him effortlessly.

When the song ended, Tollison lifted Beau's chin and pressed his lips against Beau's, kissing him deeply. "That was nice. You're a pretty good dancer."

"Thanks. I love to dance," Beau replied. "And for the record, that was nothing. You should really see me bust a nut."

Tollison chuckled. "I'll remember that."

"Hey," Beau said. "Why don't we get these dishes in the dishwasher so we can relax and enjoy the rest of our evening."

"Absolutely," Tollison said, picking up his plate and silverware.

Beau blew out the candles, picked up his own place setting, and lead Tollison into the kitchen.

"Drop these right here, and I'll take care of everything," Beau instructed. "You get the wine, and I'll meet you on the couch."

Minutes later Beau came over to the couch and sat on the coffee table. He lifted Tollison's left leg and slipped off his shoe, giving his foot a quick rub, and then did the same to the right. He spun Tollison's legs around until he was stretched out lengthwise on the couch. Beau climbed on top of him and slid in between Tollison and the back of the couch. He rested on one elbow and rubbed Tollison's chest with the other. "This is nice," he said.

"I can't believe I have to leave tomorrow," Tollison whispered.

"Not if I don't release that artwork," Beau said wryly.

"Good point. How long do you think you can keep it without causing an uproar?" Tollison asked.

"At least until we put this case to bed, and we still haven't done that."

"I almost hope Hayes is innocent so we have to start all over again."

"I know what you mean," Beau said, placing a gentle kiss on Tollison's cheek. "But I think we got her red-handed."

"I'm not so sure about that. Of course, you know I've always thought her husband had a hand in all of this."

"I don't know. And maybe you're right. Time will tell."

"Look at us," Tollison said. "We sure have come a long way in a week. When we first met, you couldn't stand to look at me, never mind collaborate on the case."

"Yeah, I was quite an ass. But you got one thing wrong." Tollison raised a brow, and Beau continued. "I could certainly stand to look at you, and boy, did I. I had to continuously remind myself that I didn't like you."

Tollison chuckled. "I know. I saw you lusting after me when you thought I wasn't looking."

"Is that so?" Beau said, smacking Tollison on the chest.

"Yep. But I sure as hell liked it. And for the record, I thought you were hotter than shit."

"Yeah?" Beau asked.

"Absolutely."

"Then what do you say we take this party upstairs?"

"Lead the way," Tollison said, bringing Beau's hand to his lips and kissing it gently.

When they got to the base of the stairs, Beau took two steps before Tollison spun him around, raised Beau's arms over his head, and pinned them against the wall. Tollison lifted Beau's T-shirt over his head and tossed it to the floor. He buried his lips in the crease in Beau's neck and nibbled gently while pinching each of Beau's nipples. Beau sucked in a breath and lowered his arms, gripping Tollison's head between his hands. He brought Tollison's face closer until they were nose to nose. His eyes were a deep gray and as intense as Tollison had ever seen them. Beau smiled seductively and bit Tollison's bottom lip, pulling back and sliding his teeth against the tender skin. Tollison felt a jolt that sent twitches right to his cock. He was growing harder by the second; Beau's actions were driving him closer to a full-on erection.

In a surprise move, Beau spun him around and repeated what Tollison had done to him. Tollison saw his shirt fly through the air and felt Beau's lips press against his left nipple. Beau bit softly and licked and then bit again, driving Tollison crazy. He cupped the back of Beau's neck, pressing his face against his chest, encouraging Beau to continue. Beau kissed his way across Tollison's chest and attacked the other nipple with the same dedication. Tollison's socked foot slipped on the hardwood stairs, and he felt himself falling, but Beau caught him under the armpits and brought him back up. Beau dropped to his knees and lifted each of Tollison's feet, pulled his socks off, and tossed them over the railing.

They kissed their way up the stairs, and by the time they reached the second floor, Beau was already unbuckling Tollison's belt and unbuttoning the fly of his jeans. Beau yanked the jeans down to Tollison's knees and nuzzled his face in the cotton boxer briefs. Tollison felt Beau nibbling at his erection through the thin underwear and Beau's hot breath against his skin.

"Off," Beau mumbled as he tugged at Tollison's jeans. Tollison lifted each foot, and Beau ripped the jeans off and flung them over his shoulder. Beau rose to his feet again, lifted Tollison off the ground, and carried him to the bedroom. Tollison felt the bed against the back of his legs as Beau set him down. In one swift move, Tollison's underwear was around his ankles and he was flat on his back on the bed, feet still on the floor. Beau bent down and tugged the underwear off, dropped his own shorts and boxers to the floor and stepped out of them.

Tollison watched as Beau knelt at the end of the bed and ran his tongue under his balls and licked his way to the tip of his cock, circling and teasing the sensitive underside. Tollison gasped when Beau's warm, wet mouth swallowed his erection in one gulp and took him to the back of his throat. Beau held him there and swallowed, taking him in a little deeper.

"Holy Jesus," Tollison hissed, gripping the bedcovers and closing his eyes.

As Beau slid up and down his length, Tollison imagined Beau straddling him, riding his cock in slow, even strides. As if reading his mind, Beau released him and reached over to the bedside table, retrieving a condom and lube. He tore the foil packet with his teeth and put the condom in his mouth. Beau once again eased down onto Tollison's erection and unrolled the condom all the way to the base, using his tongue and teeth. With the condom securely in place, Beau released Tollison again and stood over him. Tollison thought he might just blow from simply watching Beau prepare himself.

Beau tossed the bottle of lube next to Tollison, climbed onto the bed, and flashed a wicked but intense smile. When he straddled Tollison, Tollison's heart started racing with anticipation. Tollison reached to his side for the lube, opened the bottle, coated his hand, and grabbed Beau's erection, working it slowly.

Tollison shivered with eagerness as Beau positioned his cock at his opening and started moving up and down in slow, short motions as he adjusted to the impalement. Tollison continued to work Beau's cock as Beau slid lower and lower until his ass was resting flat against Tollison's hips, enveloping Tollison in his warmth.

Beau held his position momentarily before he started moving again. He leaned back and rested his hands on Tollison's thighs, rose up and slid back down, riding Tollison's excitement. Tollison felt Beau relaxing around him with each motion, and he worked Beau's cock in unison.

Tollison watched Beau closely and thought this was probably the most sensual thing he'd ever seen. Beau's head was thrown back, his eyes were closed, and he was moaning with pleasure as his body relaxed around Tollison. Tollison began thrusting his hips upward each time Beau was on the downstroke, and Beau moaned even louder, tightly squeezing and then releasing Tollison's thighs.

Tollison couldn't take his eyes off Beau, who must have sensed the intensity of Tollison's gaze, as he opened his eyes and met Tollison's stare. He smiled smugly and leaned forward, covering Tollison's lips in a heated kiss as he continued to ride the waves of pleasure apparently coursing through him.

"I want you on your back," Tollison whispered, rising up on his elbows to meet Beau's warm lips. "Please."

Beau slid off Tollison, moved farther up the bed, and lay on his back, gazing up at Tollison. Tollison knelt between Beau's legs, lifted them over his shoulders, and positioned himself at Beau's core. He pushed in slowly, and Beau once again threw his head back and held on to Tollison's thighs, guiding him forward until he was all the way in.

Tollison held his position, giving Beau time to adjust until Beau pleaded with him. "Move, Tollison. Please."

Tollison pulled out almost completely and then slid back in.

"Yes," Beau hissed as his head rolled from side to side and he stretched his arms out, fisting the sheets.

Tollison found his rhythm and picked up speed and intensity, once again taking Beau's cock into his hand and moving in unison with his thrusts. With each stroke over the head of Beau's cock, Tollison felt Beau tighten and release around him.

Beau's muscles tensed visibly, and he quickly pushed Tollison's hand away from his cock. "Not yet," he pleaded. "I want to last as long as you can."

Tollison moved slowly, gliding in and out, each time trying to brush against that sensitive bump that drove him crazy when he was in Beau's position. He was apparently succeeding because Beau's moans became louder and more intense with every stroke, and he was now moving his hips up and down as they moved as one.

Tollison allowed Beau's legs to fall on either side of him as he bent down and crushed his lips against Beau's. Beau immediately rose up and wrapped his arms around Tollison's back as Tollison pumped in and out of him frantically. Beau's cock was pressed tightly between them, and Tollison could feel it jumping and twitching as Tollison plowed him.

"Oh my God," Beau mouthed against Tollison's lips. "I'm going to come."

Tollison picked up speed. "I'm right there with you."

Tollison felt his balls tighten and draw up as his release built. Goose bumps covered Tollison's body, and he felt everything inside of him tense as he emptied his load deep inside of Beau.

Beau held on tighter and moaned into Tollison's mouth as he came, Tollison feeling the warm, wet liquid spilling between them. Tollison continued to thrust in and out as fast as he could, hopefully giving Beau time to ride out his orgasm until the bitter end.

When Beau released him, Tollison slowed his movements and eventually collapsed on top of Beau, so out of breath he couldn't make a coherent sound. Beau looked to be in the same shape, if his heaving chest was anything to go by. Tollison felt Beau flinch when he slipped out of him, and Tollison rose up on his hands, slid down to Beau's abdomen, and licked every bit of Beau's release from his stomach until he was once again clean. He then took Beau into his mouth and milked every last drop from him.

Exhausted and sated, Tollison rolled over onto his back and pulled Beau close to him. Beau removed the condom from Tollison's semierect cock and hopped out of bed. He returned a couple of minutes later with a warm cloth and wiped Tollison clean. He tossed the cloth into the bathroom doorway and once again snuggled against Tollison.

"That was really hot," Beau said. "You felt really good inside of me."

"You should have felt it from my perspective," Tollison teased.

"Tollison," Beau whispered. "I really—" He stopped midsentence.

"You *really* what?" Tollison asked, lifting his head up and casting a look at Beau.

Beau looked hesitant.

"Out with it, Bissonet."

"Like you," Beau said softly. "I really like you."

"What a coincidence," Tollison said. "I really like you too."

"No, seriously," Beau explained. "You don't understand. This is the first time since Bruce that I've wanted to go beyond the sex with anyone."

Tollison turned onto his side and propped his head up with his elbow. "For the last couple of days, I've been stressing about leaving New Orleans without knowing where this was headed. You really hadn't, up until tonight, given me any indication of what you were thinking, and, well, let's face it, we're grown men, not teenagers. I mean… we've only known each other for a week, and… you know how the first couple of days went."

"I thought that was all behind us?" Beau asked.

"It was—I mean it is, but you—"

Beau interrupted. "I… I was just being an asshole."

"You're right," Tollison agreed. "You were being an asshole, and to be truthful, I see the way you treat Bruce, and I never want to be on the receiving end of that assholeness."

Beau rolled over and looked up at the ceiling, smiling wickedly. "It's pretty simple, Tollison. If we go farther, and eventually hit a rough spot, just don't cheat on me, and you never will."

"I'm not the cheating kind," Tollison clarified. "If I don't want to be with you anymore, I'll just tell you. No cheating. No drama. No fighting. It's that simple."

"Then, the way I see it, we have no issues."

"I guess not," Tollison agreed.

They lay quietly for the longest time, Beau rubbing Tollison's head and playing with his thick black hair.

"Have you even been in a long-term relationship?" Beau asked softly.

"I have," Tollison replied.

"Do you mind me asking what happened?"

"My line of work," Tollison said with a matter-of-fact tone in his voice.

"He had something against insurance investigators?"

Tollison chuckled. "Before that."

"Ohhhh," Beau said, suddenly realizing what Tollison meant. "So he had something against art thieves."

"Exactly."

"I'm very glad we met much later, 'cause I kinda do too."

"I get that, Beau, but there was a method to my madness back then. I felt like I had to right a bunch of wrongs."

"What kind of wrongs?"

"I traveled the world and was paid handsomely to recover art that had been previously stolen to put it back in the hands of its rightful owners."

"Who hired you?"

"Sometimes the rightful owners of the art, sometimes a particular country's government. It all just depended on the circumstances."

"Did you enjoy the work?"

"I enjoyed the rush," Tollison admitted. "And... there was a certain satisfaction to helping put the art back where it belonged."

"How long?" Beau asked.

"How long what?"

"How long was your relationship?"

Tollison held up his open hand. "A little under five years. That's how long it took him to finally figure out what I did for a living. And when he did, he was gone."

"Do you still keep in contact with him?"

"No," Tollison replied. "To the best of my knowledge, he's still in Geneva, where we were living at the time. I did leave him a voice mail when I went to work for Lloyd's of London, but he never returned my call. I guess that said it all."

"I'm sorry," Beau said. "But his loss is my gain."

Tollison laughed out loud. "You're a strange bird, Montgomery Beaumont Bissonet."

"Not really," Beau replied. "I'm just a normal guy who goes after what he wants."

Tollison snuggled down against Beau, wrapped an arm around him, and whispered in his ear, "I'm glad you did."

NINE

BEAU AND Tollison walked into the station and went straight to Bruce's office. "How's our Mrs. Hayes this morning?" Beau asked.

"Not very happy," Bruce said. "Apparently she's been one pampered little girl. By the time she arrived back to New Orleans, it was four o'clock in the morning, and she demanded to see her attorney and wanted breakfast to boot. Her husband slash attorney tried to raise every judge her father knew in the city, but since the mess with Mrs. Villerie and the fact that Mr. Villerie was being held as well, none of them wanted to get involved."

Beau looked at Tollison and smiled. "I guess it's time we do our magic, then."

"After you, Houdini," Tollison said, sweeping his hand toward the door.

When they walked into the interrogation room, Mrs. Hayes looked up at them and glared.

"Good morning, Mrs. Hayes," Beau said with a condescending smile. He gestured to Tollison. "You remember Investigator Cruz?"

Harper flashed an equally condescending smile. "I demand to be released."

"Mrs. Hayes, you're not in any position to demand anything. We're in the process of booking you on murder and conspiracy charges unless you have some really compelling evidence otherwise."

"I didn't kill anyone and I didn't steal those paintings from my father," Harper said.

"Come now," Beau said. "We know you wouldn't have been stealing from your father. He told us he just signed the gallery over to you."

Harper's face lost all expression for a second; then she composed herself. "And what business is that of yours?" she asked. "I see no reason why I should have to justify my family inheritance to you."

"Because this particular family inheritance just happens to have stolen artwork in it."

Harper sat up straight. "You found the paintings?"

"Yes," Tollison said. "Right where you put them."

"Where I put them?" Harper repeated. "I told you I didn't steal the paintings."

"You know," Beau said, tilting his head to the side. "If I were you, I'd be trying to decide how you're going to justify killing Le Moyne and Robinette. Unless this was some self-defense or horrible accident, this could make a thirty-year difference in your prison sentence."

"I did not kill either of those men," Harper said.

Beau stood and started his usual pacing. "Mrs. Hayes, we've obtained a warrant for your financials and we *will* find evidence of the hundred grand you paid Della Penna to point out your deficiencies in security."

"I'm sorry," Harper said. "Now you've lost me."

Tollison tried a little dishonesty. "Della Penna confessed that you paid him to scope out the gallery."

"Well, he lied," Harper said. "But even if I had, what's wrong with making sure the gallery is secure?"

"For starters," Tollison said, "most people don't hire a convicted art thief to do it."

"I think that would have been the perfect choice," Harper said. "If I had done it."

"In addition," Tollison said. "The paintings are now being checked for fingerprints, and I'd bet my life yours are gonna be all over them."

"They belonged to the gallery," Harper said. "Of course my prints are going to be on them, along with my father's."

Before Beau could answer, there was a tap on the door and it opened slowly. Bruce stuck his head inside. "Sorry to interrupt, but I need to see you both."

Beau gave Bruce the "this better be good" expression, and Bruce nodded. "Excuse us for one moment."

He and Tollison stepped out of the room. "Whataya got?" Beau asked.

"We just got the fingerprint results back."

"And…?" Beau asked.

"We found prints matching Robinette, Crymes Villerie, Harper Hayes, and one other set of prints mixed with blood that matched Le Moyne's." Bruce explained.

Beau raised his brows nearly up to his hairline.

"Let me guess," Tollison said. "Jamison Hayes."

"Bingo!"

"I knew it," Tollison said. "I just knew something wasn't right with that guy."

"This case just keeps getting more interesting by the minute," Beau said. "Bring him in. But in the meantime, we'll go figure out what else Mrs. Hayes knows."

Back in the interrogation room, Beau apologized for the interruption again and looked at Tollison. "Now, where were we?"

"You were explaining the fingerprint situation," Tollison said.

"Oh, right. Tell me something, Mrs. Hayes. Did your husband handle the paintings at any time?"

"I don't think so," Harper said. "He couldn't have. I unpacked them when they arrived from the conservancy, and Crymes picked out the backdrop and hung them himself just before the opening."

"If your husband didn't have an opportunity to touch the paintings before they were hung, why do you suppose his fingerprints, mixed with Mr. Le Moyne's blood, were found all over them?"

Harper started to tremble, and the blood drained out of her face. "Jamie's prints are on the paintings?"

"Mixed with Mr. Le Moyne's blood," Beau repeated.

Harper looked away. "Oh my God, Jamie," she said as she started to weep.

"Mrs. Hayes," Beau said softly, handing Harper a tissue. "You can make it easier on yourself and him if you tell us everything you know."

WHEN BEAU and Tollison entered the next interrogation room, Jamison Hayes was sitting in a chair with his head in his hands.

"Mr. Hayes," Beau said. "I'm sorry to tell you, but the gig is up. As you already know, we're holding your wife and your father-in-law, and unless you tell us everything you know, they're both going to be arrested."

Jamison looked up. "Detective, I'm an attorney. I know you can't hold them very long without charging them. And you have no evidence against them to do that."

"That's where you're wrong, Mr. Hayes," Beau said. "We now have all the evidence we need."

Jamison gave him a questioning glance.

"That's right," Beau said. "With Investigator Cruz's help, we recovered the paintings where they were hidden in the gallery. Unfortunately for your family, both your wife's and your father-in-law's fingerprints are all over both of them. Furthermore, we know you and your wife had a lot more to gain because Mr. Villerie had just signed the gallery over to you. In addition, your wife confessed to hiring Della Penna to case the gallery for her. All in all, I think we have as much evidence as we need to arrest them both."

"No!" Jamison yelled slamming his fist down on the table. "Harper didn't hire him."

"She says she did," Beau argued.

"Well she didn't, okay? She's covering for me. I hired him. There. Are you happy now?"

"Very!" Beau said.

Jamison rubbed his face and dropped his head in his hands again. Beau took the opportunity to give Tollison a gratified smile before he continued.

"Mr. Hayes. Either you tell us exactly what happened, or your wife is going to take the fall."

When Jamison looked up his eyes were wet with tears. "She knew nothing about any of this. I swear. No one was supposed to get hurt. This is all Dudley's fault. If he hadn't called me to borrow money, none—"

"Wait?" Beau interrupted. "Dudley Robinette contacted you?"

"Yes. He was my first cousin," Jamison explained. "He had these two paintings he wanted me to buy for him. He explained that the owner of the estate was an elderly woman, and her late husband had been an art connoisseur. She had no clue as to the value of any of the artwork, and Dudley knew the two paintings in question were originals.

He wanted me to buy them from the estate for him, and when he resold them, we would split the profit. I saw his plan as a way out. A way to pay off my gambling debts."

"The only problem is," Beau said, "you didn't have the money."

"Exactly," Jamison said. "So the next best thing was to get Crymes involved. I knew these paintings were right up his alley, and if he saw them, he would definitely find the money to buy and restore them."

Tollison nodded. "So Dudley made that anonymous call inviting Crymes to preview the estate."

"Yes."

"But wait," Beau asked, "if Dudley was out of the transaction except for the commission on the estate sale, how were the two of you going to profit?"

"Dudley was going to get Della Penna to steal the artwork once it was restored," Jamison said.

"But Della Penna refused?" Beau asked.

"Not at first," Jamison said. "Initially, he agreed. But my dingbat of a mother-in-law must have called him shortly thereafter, and he backed out. She was going to pay him to do the heist, and he was going to get to keep the paintings."

"And all the profits," Tollison added.

Jamison held up a finger. "Remember, Della Penna didn't trust Dudley to begin with. Dudley was the one who testified against him after the New Orleans Museum of Art heist."

"And that's when your plan started to deteriorate."

"By that time, Harper had already found out Crymes was in serious financial trouble and was about to lose everything, including the gallery."

"Her inheritance," Tollison added.

Jamison nodded. "I figured if I stole the paintings, hid them in the gallery, Crymes would get the insurance money. He could catch up on everything and maybe have enough left over to loan me the money I needed to settle my gambling debts as well. My 'associates,'" Jamison said, using his fingers to make air quotes, "were starting to threaten Harper and to expose me to my law firm. I couldn't let any of that happen… to any of us. I saw it as the only way out at the time."

"I'm curious about something," Tollison asked, "what were you planning on doing with the paintings?"

"When things died down and the trail got cold, Dudley was supposed to sell them."

"And why didn't he?" Beau asked.

"He got cold feet after you questioned him. He was afraid at some point you were going to make the connection between us."

"And that's why you killed him?" Tollison asked.

"He was going to turn me in," Jamison said, lowering his head.

"Why all the drama, though?" Beau asked. "The painting over his head was very theatrical."

"Everyone in the art world knew Della Penna and Dudley hated each other, and Dudley called me and told me you overheard them arguing. So I thought I could make it look like Della Penna did it. Everyone would believe that."

Beau looked at Tollison and shook his head.

"Tell me everything you can remember about the night you stole the paintings and killed Le Moyne," Beau said.

Jamison stood and started pacing. "I waited for Harper to go to bed, and then I slipped out of the house. I entered the gallery through the front door and disarmed the security alarm. I removed the paintings from the wall, took them out of the frames, and carried both of them upstairs."

Beau interrupted. "Is that where you ran into Le Moyne?"

Jamison stopped pacing and looked Beau right in the eyes. "Yes. He showed up out of the blue. After his drunken rant at the opening, I guess he decided to take back what he thought was his. We both froze when we saw each other. He must have heard me downstairs because he was coming out of Crymes's office and he was pointing Crymes's gun at me. We struggled, and I was able to wrestle the gun out of his hand."

"Le Moyne was a big guy," Beau said.

"He *was* a big guy, but I was quicker. Le Moyne reached for the gun again, and what else was I supposed to do? I pulled the trigger."

Beau flattened his hands on the table. "Just like that? You killed a man."

"I had no choice," Jamison replied. "It was him or me. But I swear, killing him was never part of the plan."

"Go on," Beau said.

"I dragged him into the bathroom and closed the door behind me. I carried the paintings into the apartment bedroom and unmade the bed. I ripped the mattress open at the piping, removed enough stuffing to slide the paintings in, sewed everything back up, and remade the bed."

Beau looked at Hayes. "That explains why we have your fingerprints mixed with Le Moyne's blood on both paintings."

Hayes winced.

Beau continued. "And then you went back downstairs, rearmed the security system, and then set it off."

"Yes. But not before I disassembled the security sensor on the courtyard door to make it look like it had been the escape route."

"How did you rearm the system if the door sensors were disassembled?" Tollison asked.

"I just made sure the sensors were still aligned before I reset the alarm and then purposely set off the motion detectors. I ran up the stairs and exited through the third-floor rooftop deck and down the fire escape."

"Where is the murder weapon now?" Tollison asked.

"At the bottom of the Mississippi River."

"Jamison Hayes," Beau said, "you are under arrest for insurance fraud and the murders of Dudley Robinette and Anthony Le Moyne."

TOLLISON WALKED out of the interrogation room as Beau finished reading Jamison his Miranda rights. He made his way back to Beau's office and realized he was a serious mixed bag of emotions. He took his usual seat and contemplated his situation. On the one hand, he should be ecstatic about solving the case. With the missing art recovered, he would make a shitload of money, not to mention a little more status with the company. But on the personal front, he was feeling pretty dismal. Beau would be forced to release the recovered artwork, and he'd have no reason to stay in New Orleans.

"Shit, Tollison! You're not a schoolgirl with a silly crush," he murmured. "Snap out of it, man."

"Snap out of what?" Beau asked, putting his hands on Tollison's shoulders from behind, squeezing and massaging.

"Ah, nothing," Tollison said. "Just talking to myself."

"Well," Beau said, "Mr. Hayes is on his way to being booked, and we released Mr. Villerie and Mrs. Hayes. This was some case, huh?"

"Pretty intricate," Tollison agreed. "But I had a hunch all along Jamison had something to do with it. I just couldn't prove it."

"Not until we got those bloody prints," Beau added.

Beau kissed the top of Tollison's head, squeezed Tollison's shoulder's one last time before he took a seat behind his desk. "Now the fun part," he said.

"The paperwork," they both said succinctly.

"Speaking of. I need to call my boss and bring him up to speed and then get down to business myself. By the way," Tollison added hesitantly, "he's gonna want to know when the paintings will be released."

Beau looked like he was considering his answer very carefully. "Well, I certainly can't release the evidence until my paperwork is completed and the case is completely closed. That'll take me at least a day and a half, and since today's Friday, it'll be Monday afternoon at the earliest, maybe even Tuesday."

Tollison smiled. "That long, huh?"

"I'm afraid so," Beau said, matching Tollison's smile.

"Okay, then. I'll tell him."

Beau's eyes were expressive and hopeful. "And while you're at it, why don't you check out of that hotel and spend the weekend with me?"

Tollison considered the proposal. "I think I'd like that," he said, keeping his voice gentle.

Beau winked and smiled. "Good. I'll see you back here as soon as you're all done. And try to make it quick. It's Friday afternoon, and I want to get the weekend started."

Tollison gave him a mock salute. "Yes, sir, Detective."

Beau's face lit up in amusement. "Asshole," he finally said, shaking his head. "Now get out of here so I can at least attempt to concentrate on getting some work done."

TOLLISON WENT back to his hotel suite and was sitting cross-legged in the middle of the bed, in his sock feet, with his laptop in front of him. He speed dialed his boss, held the phone against his ear with his shoulder as he tapped away on the keyboard while bringing him up to speed on the case. Needless to say, his boss was quite pleased with the outcome, and as expected, asked him to stay in New Orleans until the paintings were released and he could oversee their packing and shipment back to Atlanta.

Of course, Tollison made it sound like he was taking one for the team by staying on until the first part of next week, but inside he was ecstatic to have another few days with Beau.

"How did things work out with that crackpot detective?" his boss asked. "I know he wasn't happy that you were involved with the case."

"Let's just say we made our peace," Tollison replied with a chuckle.

"Good to hear. Nice job down there. I'll expect your report ASAP."

"Thanks. I'm working on it as we speak and will send it over as soon as it's complete. See you next week."

"Next week? Why is it taking so long for the good detective to release our property?"

"From what I can tell," Tollison said, playing stupid, "Detective Bissonet wants to close the case completely before he hands it over to us."

His boss just grunted "We'll see about that" and ended the call.

Tollison tossed his phone onto the bed in front of him.

Three and a half hours later, he autosigned his report detailing the investigation and hit the send button. "There," he mumbled. "That should keep the boss busy all weekend."

He closed his laptop and laid it on the bed next to him, stretching and stifling a yawn. He debated on whether he could curl up and take a quick nap, but then he looked at his watch. "Shit! Where did the afternoon go?"

BEAU SIGHED. "Another one bites the dust," he said as he closed the folder on his desk. He didn't suspect there would be much more to this case since he'd gotten a full confession out of Hayes. Of course, there would be a trial and a sentencing, and unless Hayes withdrew his confession, it would be a slam dunk. He looked up when he heard a familiar clearing of the throat.

"Hey, Bruce. What's up?" Beau said, turning in his seat to slide the folder into the filing cabinet behind his desk.

"Um… nothing, really. I'm about to head out for the weekend and wanted to make sure you didn't need anything from me for the case report."

"Thank you. But no, I'll finish it on Monday and e-mail it to the captain." Beau leaned back in his chair and linked his hands behind his head. "Do you have a minute?"

Bruce looked at his watch. "Sure. Whataya need?"

"Come in and close the door. Would ya?"

When Bruce took a seat, Beau leaned forward and rested his arms on his desk.

"Tollison told me about the conversation the two of you had about me, and I just wanted to say thanks."

Bruce dipped his head. "I meant everything that I said, Beau. All I want is for you to be happy, and if Cruz makes you happy, I'm all for it."

Beau leaned back again. "It's way too soon to determine if either one of us makes the other happy long-term, but I do like the guy."

"The long-distance thing is gonna suck, though," Bruce said.

"Yeah. That's the toughest part, but I've accrued a lot of vacation and personal time, and I'm gonna use it. Maybe—" Beau stopped. "Never mind."

"*Maybe* what?" Bruce asked. "Come on, Beau. Isn't it time we're honest with each other?"

Beau nodded. "I was just going to say that maybe if I had used that time when we were together, we wouldn't be where we are now. That's all."

Bruce's bottom lip started to tremble and a single tear slid down his cheek. He wiped it away quickly, but his expression changed to one of relief. "Thank you for saying that," he murmured, looking down at the floor, his hands fidgeting in his lap. "You know I've reconciled everything in my head over and over, and it always came down to me. I'm the reason we're at this point in our lives, and I finally figured out that you shouldn't have to suffer any more for my indiscretions."

Beau got up and walked around the desk and leaned on the edge right in front of Bruce. He lifted Bruce's face up by the chin. "We're where we are today because of things we both did, not just you. And… it's time I stop blaming it all on you. There's more than enough blame to go around."

Beau stood, offered Bruce a hand, and urged him to his feet. When he stood, Beau wrapped his arms around him and held him tightly.

"We're both at fault."

Bruce returned the embrace, buried his face in Beau's neck, and began to openly sob. Beau could feel the burden easing in Bruce's hold, and he was thankful he could give him that. As Bruce cried on his shoulder, Beau wondered what could have changed in a little over a week. The only thing that came to mind was Tollison. Tollison had changed everything. In the short time they'd known each other, Beau had finally started to let go of all the feelings of anger and betrayal. He realized he'd held onto those feelings for so long, they'd consumed him and kept him from moving on with his life. He'd been miserable and in turn made Bruce's life just as miserable.

"It's time to move on, Bruce," Beau said. "For both of us. I have no idea where this thing with Tollison is going, but I'm willing to find out, which is a big step for me. And I think it's time you do the same."

Bruce pulled away and wiped at his eyes with his shirtsleeve. "I know. Believe it or not, I have a blind date tomorrow night. You know, it's funny," Bruce continued. "This guy is a friend of a friend, and he's been calling me for the last few months asking me out, and I've been turning him down. But he called right after my conversation with Cruz, and for some reason, I said yes. Maybe letting you go was what I needed to do to move on as well."

"I'm glad, Bruce. It's time."

Bruce took a step back and smoothed the front of his shirt. He wiped at his eyes again, ran his fingers through his hair, and looked at Beau.

"You look fine," Beau said. "No one will know you've been crying."

"Thanks."

Bruce slapped Beau on the arm. "You better get a move on. I'm sure Cruz is waiting for you."

"Yeah, I do need to get out of here."

Bruce turned and headed for the door. He put his hand on the doorknob and looked back over his shoulder. "Be happy, Beau."

"You too, Bruce. And good luck tomorrow."

Bruce offered a weak smile as he opened the door and disappeared into the hallway.

Beau walked around his desk and dialed Tollison's number.

"I KNOW I'm late. I just finished my report and I'm packing now," Tollison said in a hurried tone, without even saying hello.

Beau laughed heartily. "Relax. I almost finished my paperwork as well. Hey look, instead of coming downtown, why don't you just meet me at my place?"

"That sounds good," Tollison said. "I'll be out of here in less than thirty minutes."

"I'll see you in about an hour, then," Beau said. "And Tollison?"

"Yeah?"

"I'm really looking forward to this weekend. Drive safely, would ya?"

"Me too," Tollison said. "And you do the same."

TEN

BEAU WAS ten minutes from home when his cell phone rang. He looked at the number flashing on his dashboard and recognized it as Bruce's number. "This can't be good."

He answered the hands-free call. "I thought you were going home."

"So did I," Bruce replied with a huff. "Hey look, I wanted to let you know I just got a call that Jamison Hayes retracted his confession and changed his plea to 'not guilty.'"

"Fuck! I was afraid of that," Beau yelled, the sound echoing around inside of his SUV.

"I know. I know," Bruce said. "His own law firm is now going to represent him, and he's requested a bail hearing on the grounds that he was coerced into an admission of guilt."

"That's fucking bullshit," Beau said. "We may have used a little white lie or two, but he confessed all on his own and, might I add, he went into great detail while doing it."

"You're preaching to the choir, man, but I just wanted to keep you in the loop."

Beau pulled into his driveway and put his SUV in park. "I appreciate it. Will you let me know if he makes bail?"

"Sure, but I'm certain he will. His family has friends in very high places."

"Yeah," Beau said through a sigh. "If this goes to trial, it's going to be a fucking circus."

Bruce laughed. "I think you're right. We better strap ourselves into the clown car for a very bumpy ride."

"Oh no!" Beau exclaimed. "No clown car for me. I'm riding a white stallion into the ring for once. This was a very high-profile case, and I made a special point to dot all my i's and cross all my t's. We have the entire confession on video, and we have you and Tollison as witnesses."

"My guess is he's going to draw this out and his attorneys are going to try and get a plea to shorten his sentence."

Beau switched the call from Bluetooth to his cell and got out of the car, slamming the door behind him. "Probably," he agreed. "But once the district attorney sees the video of Hayes's confession, I don't think he'll go for that."

"Time will tell," Bruce said. "I'll call you as soon as I hear about bail."

"Thanks."

"And Beau?"

"Yeah?"

"Thanks again for, well… this afternoon, and for letting me off the hook. I feel like a weight has been lifted off of my shoulders and I can finally start to move forward."

Beau listened to Bruce's words, and they did sound lighter in a strange way. And that made him happy. "I think it did us both some good. Have a good weekend."

"You too."

Beau walked up the steps to the porch, hit his speed dial for Auggie, and sat in one of his rocking chairs. He'd kept Auggie up to speed on the case all along in hopes that he would be back sooner rather than later and wanted to give him the latest.

When Auggie answered, Beau could tell he was still hurting. His voice sounded strained, but Auggie said he *was* doing somewhat better and hoped to be back at work on Monday. Beau filled him in on Hayes's confession and retraction, what had transpired between him and Bruce earlier, and what was happening between him and Tollison.

"Man, I missed a lot in a week," Auggie said. "But… I'm glad you and Bruce finally talked, and maybe now you can both move on."

Beau cut the conversation short when Tollison pulled into his driveway. "Hey, man. Good talking to you, but I gotta go. Tollison just pulled up. Feel better, and I hope to see you on Monday."

"Have a great weekend," Auggie said, laughing raucously as Beau disconnected the call.

Beau walked down the front porch steps and met Tollison at the trunk of his car, where he was sorting through his luggage.

"Hey there," Beau said, stealing a kiss and looking down into the trunk. "You sure do have a lot of luggage."

"Hey, I didn't know how long I was going to be here," Tollison teased, pushing Beau's hair out of his eyes. "I won't be needing a suit, will I?"

"Since I don't plan on letting you out of the bedroom all weekend, I don't think you'll need any of this."

"Okay, then," Tollison said, attempting to close the trunk without retrieving a single piece of luggage.

Beau caught the trunk just before it closed. "On second thought, I might want to take you out to a nice dinner, so pick one," he said, looking down at two large roller boards.

Tollison handed a bag to Beau and reached for a carry-on. "Can't forget this one. It has the condoms and lube."

Beau flashed a smile. "By all means." He slipped his arm around Tollison's waist and walked him to the front door. As Beau pushed the front door open, he stopped. "Oh! I got a call from Bruce, and Jamison Hayes retracted his confession."

"What?"

"Apparently his own law firm is going to represent him, and they say he was coerced into confessing."

"That's a load of crap."

"Exactly what I said," Beau stated, closing the front door behind them. "And he's trying to get a bail hearing set up immediately."

"Can he do that?"

"His family is pretty connected," Beau explained. "If a judge believes he was coerced and takes pity on him, he could be out by tonight."

"The way I see it," Tollison said, "he probably wants to get out so he can kill himself and avoid spending the rest of his life in prison."

Beau dropped Tollison's bag, shoved him up against the back of the door, ran his hands over his chest, and looked him directly in the eye. "He might not have to," he murmured, placing a gentle kiss on Tollison's neck. "The death penalty for first-degree murder is alive and well in Louisiana," he added, licking his way up to Tollison earlobe, biting gently. "He can argue that Le Moyne was self-defense. But the way he left Robinette was definitely premeditated. Now! Enough about this case," Beau whispered, plunging his fingers into Tollison's hair and covering his mouth with a hot and hungry kiss.

When they came up for air, they were both flushed and struggling to breathe. "The hellos just keep getting better and better around here," Tollison huffed out, still holding on to his shoulder bag.

Beau readjusted his aching cock and gave Tollison one last peck before he picked up Tollison's suitcase and headed for the den. He looked over his shoulder. "I have set the bar pretty high, haven't I?"

Tollison laughed. "Yes, you have. But it's really gonna be fun to watch you try to continually top yourself."

"Top myself, huh?" Beau teased. "Boy! There have been times when I wish I could have done that."

"Not what I meant," Tollison said, dropping his bag next to the suitcase and taking a seat on the leather couch.

"I know, but a guy can dream, right?" Beau said. "How about a beer?"

"Absolutely."

Beau plopped down next to Tollison and handed him his beer. "God! I feel like I've been working for the last two weeks straight."

Tollison slid down to the end of the couch and put his beer on the end table. He patted the space next to him on the couch. "Put your feet up here."

Beau immediately liked where this was going. He swung his legs around and stretched out with his feet in Tollison's lap.

Tollison untied Beau's shoelaces and slipped both of his shoes off, dropping them to the floor one by one. He took Beau's left foot into his hands and massaged the soles with his thumbs, paying special attention to the balls and arches.

"God, that feels good," Beau said, laying his head back and closing his eyes. "Please don't ever stop," he pleaded.

Tollison continued with Beau's left foot and then the right, Beau thinking he might actually start purring like a kitten. When Tollison stopped, Beau opened one eye and peeked at him. He was smiling broadly and taking a sip of his beer.

Beau eased over on the couch and knelt in front of Tollison. "That was really nice."

He loosened the tie from around Tollison's neck and tossed it to the floor, unbuttoned Tollison's dress shirt and cuffs, and pulled the shirttails out of his pants. Tollison leaned forward, and Beau slid the shirt over his shoulders and tossed it to the floor as well. Now there was only a thin white T-shirt separating Beau from what he wanted. He urged Tollison's arms up and pulled the shirt over Tollison's head. He sighed when his hands came in contact with Tollison's warm, tanned skin.

"God, you're beautiful," Beau whispered. *I wonder what in the hell does he see in me?*

As if on cue, Tollison leaned up and pressed his lips against Beau's in a hungry kiss filled with desire.

Don't care! Beau thought. *I'm just going with it.*

Beau broke the kiss, desperate to get out of his own clothes. He removed his own shirt and T-shirt, and before he finished, Tollison's hands were immediately roaming over his chest. Beau hissed and threw his head back when Tollison pinched both of his nipples and squeezed. He then rubbed each one softly, soothing the sting. Tollison leaned forward again and kissed his way down Beau's chest and stomach, teasing Beau's bellybutton and nibbling at the skin just above his belt.

Beau pushed Tollison onto his back and dove on top of him, fingers roaming over his warm skin and digging in possessively.

Tollison cupped the back of Beau's neck and drew him in close enough to steal another kiss before Beau pulled away and started working his way up and down Tollison's chest. He bit Tollison's left nipple, then licked it softly as he moved on to the other, repeating the process.

As he thrust his erection against Tollison's, Beau again covered Tollison's lips with his own. Beau took in a harsh breath when Tollison slid his hand down Beau's pants and grabbed a handful of his hard cock and squeezed, running his thumb over the opening, causing a spasm of pleasure to course through Beau's body. Tollison sat up and quickly unbuckled Beau's belt and unfastened his pants, yanking them and his underwear down his thick thighs and stopping at his knees.

Beau got to his feet, standing on the couch and looking down at Tollison. He moaned loudly when Tollison rose to his knees and took him into his mouth. Beau cupped the back of Tollison's head and guided him gently, watching his cock slide in and out of Tollison's warm mouth over and over again. Tollison released his cock and sucked on his balls, sending tingles up his spine and waves of pleasure coursing through his body.

Beau dropped back down to his knees and pushed Tollison onto his back again. He could feel Tollison's erection through his pants and couldn't wait to get his lips around what was just beneath the navy blue fabric. He released Tollison's pants, pulling them down and off, along with his underwear and socks, and dove back on top of Tollison, taking him into his mouth. Beau swallowed him to the back of his throat and pulled back up slowly and deliberately, then swallowed him again. Tollison was moaning and gyrating, his head thrown back and his eyes closed.

Beau licked his finger and dropped it between Tollison's legs, rubbing and teasing his opening. "Jesus, Beau," Tollison hissed. "Just do it."

As Beau fisted Tollison's cock and moved his mouth over the head, he plunged a finger inside, drawing a loud groan from his lover. He hooked his finger and searched for that little bump that would send Tollison into a tailspin. When he found it, Tollison tensed, buried his head in Beau's neck and ran his fingernails down Beau's back.

Beau slowly moved his finger back and forth as Tollison wiggled and rode the sensations Beau knew he was feeling.

"Where are those condoms and lube?" Beau asked, slipping his finger out, so desperately needing to replace it with his cock.

Tollison opened his eyes and pointed to his bag on the floor. Beau unzipped the bag and found what he needed, ripped the foil packet open with his teeth, and rolled the condom onto his erection. Tollison rolled over onto his stomach as Beau coated himself and prepared Tollison for what was to come, one finger at a time, until Tollison was relaxed and ready for him.

He positioned himself at Tollison's opening and pushed in gently, giving Tollison time to adjust. "Go," Tollison hissed when he was ready for Beau to start moving.

Beau pulled almost all the way out and pushed back in, drawing a long, guttural moan out of Tollison. He lifted Tollison's hips and plowed into him over and over again, each time coercing the same response.

After a while, Beau pulled out and lay on his back, and Tollison followed his lead, straddling him, one leg on the floor and one on the couch. He rode Beau like a bucking bronco, never breaking eye contact.

Beau loved the way Tollison felt rocking back and forth on top of him as he took Tollison's erection in hand and stroked in time with their movements. Tollison finally gave in and threw his head back. He closed his eyes, whimpering like a baby.

In one fluid movement, without breaking contact, Beau lifted Tollison's six-foot-one-inch frame up like he weighed twenty pounds and tossed him onto his back and mounted him. Tollison grabbed his feet and held them back, giving Beau everything he wanted and more. Beau stood on the couch and rested his hands on Tollison's chest, slamming into him repeatedly. Tollison's hands gripped the back of Beau's thighs, urging him deeper with each thrust.

Beau wrapped his hands around Tollison's ankles and pushed the man's legs back over his head, gaining even more access as he plowed into him. In turn, Tollison grabbed his calves and opened his legs wider, taking every one of Beau's plunges like a champion.

The sight of his own cock disappearing inside of Tollison and Tollison happily accepting him was sending him over the edge.

Beau felt the build of his impending release. His entire body seized, and his muscles cramped as he dug his fingers into Tollison's ankles. "Oh my God, Tollison, I'm so close."

Tollison took himself in hand and stroked as Beau continued to plummet into him. He threw his head back and called Beau's name as he shot his load all over his chest and abdomen.

The sound of his name escaping Tollison's lips tipped the balance and he came deep inside of his lover. He pumped and ground into Tollison continually, riding the waves of pleasure until he simply collapsed from exhaustion.

Both men were out of breath. Beau started gasping and laughing at the same time, desperately trying to breathe. Tollison started laughing as well until they were both snorting hysterically.

"Jesus, Beau," Tollison said when he could finally speak. "I won't be able to walk for a week."

"I'm really sorry," Beau said, thinking he'd gone a little too far.

Tollison placed a finger on his lips. "Don't apologize. I loved every minute of it. I love a sports sex workout every once in a while, and this was just what the doctor ordered."

Beau felt relief wash through him, and he kissed Tollison lazily, with no sign of the desperation he'd felt just minutes ago.

"You're amazing," Beau said when the kiss ended.

"Ditto," Tollison whispered, stealing another kiss.

Beau got to his feet and offered Tollison a hand. "How about a shower, some dinner, and maybe some of that dancing we talked about?"

"Sounds like fun."

"I don't know about you, but I'm in the mood for a big juicy burger," Beau admitted. "And if you're up for it, I know just the place."

"I can totally go for some red meat," Tollison agreed.

AT 1:55 the next morning, they crawled into bed, exhausted. Beau nuzzled up close and rested his head on Tollison's chest, and Tollison stroked his hair gently as he replayed their incredible night in his head.

After their episode on the couch earlier, they'd gone up to take a shower, and one thing had led to another, and they finished round two shriveled and flushed. They'd dressed casually, and Tollison rode shotgun on the way to the restaurant as Beau explained he was taking him to Port of Call on Esplanade Avenue, one of his all-time favorite burger spots in New Orleans.

After driving around for thirty minutes trying to find a place to park on the busy avenue, they waded through the crowd of people on the sidewalk and got to the front door of the restaurant. Beau had pushed his way through and stepped aside to allow Tollison to walk ahead of him. Tollison had slowly cut a path to the bar, maneuvering through the other patrons, and he remembered loving the feel of Beau's hand at the small of his back, guiding him along possessively. *I could really get used to that.*

The wait to get a table had ended up being over an hour, but they'd spent the time at the bar laughing and simply enjoying each other's company.

They were eventually seated at a little table for two way back in the corner and were both thrilled with the privacy it afforded. Beau had held Tollison's hand across the table and gazed into his eyes, smiling occasionally, obviously very relaxed. In fact, Tollison had never seen the man as relaxed as he'd been this evening, and he had to admit, Beau wore it well. His face had been totally stress free, and he'd looked as if he didn't have a care in the world. When the little bit of light in the restaurant had reached Beau's eyes, they'd sparkled like crystals, and it had taken Tollison's breath away. Even Beau's sandy hair seemed darker and more distinguished in their dimly lit corner of the restaurant.

Tollison had asked question after question, trying to learn as much as possible about Beau in the little time he had and was having a great time getting to know what made the other man tick. Beau answered each question patiently, and when the food came, it almost seemed like an intrusion. Until… Tollison bit down into his burger. Then it was suddenly no longer an intrusion, but a heavenly experience. Tollison's mouth almost started to water as he thought about his dinner. It had been quite possibly one of the best burgers Tollison had ever tasted, and he could clearly see why Beau loved that place so much.

In turn, Beau had grilled him about his childhood, his family, past boyfriends, his favorite color, his favorite food, what type of house he lived in, what kind of car he drove, and anything else that came to his obviously brilliant and chaotic mind. Tollison had thoroughly enjoyed the inquisition and the interest Beau was taking in his life.

After leaving the restaurant, Beau had led him down Esplanade Avenue to Bourbon Street and to the Bourbon Pub and Parade dance club in the heart of the French Quarter. Halfway there, Beau had draped an arm over Tollison's shoulder and kept him close all the way, warming Tollison to his core. He remembered the feeling of Beau taking his hand and holding him close, once they were inside the club, as they made their way to the dance floor through the crowds of buff and half-dressed men. That's where Beau had totally surprised him with his dance moves. The man was a natural, moving fluidly with an ease Tollison hadn't expected from a semi-uptight detective with the NOPD. They'd danced the night away until they were both exhausted and soaked with sweat down to their underwear.

Tollison was as content as he'd been in a very long time. He tightened his hold on Beau, who was now breathing evenly and snoring lightly, and closed his eyes, giving in to the sheer exhaustion of a perfect evening. Just as he was dozing off, Beau's cell phone started chirping.

"Fuck," Beau mumbled as he reached over and plucked the phone from the bedside table.

He laid his head back on Tollison's chest and looked at the caller ID. *Bruce.*

"This better be good," Beau answered, using the speakerphone.

"Sorry to wake you, but you asked me to keep you in the loop," Bruce said. "I just got the call. Hayes made bail."

"What?" Beau turned his head into Tollison's chest and cursed. "How much?"

"A mil," Bruce said.

"How in the hell?"

"It appears that Villerie and Hayes Sr. are very well connected. They applied some pressure and finally got a judge to leave a dinner party and set up an emergency bail hearing."

"Are you shitting me? Who's the judge?"

"Guess?" Bruce asked.

"Noooo. Michelson?"

"Yep."

"I swear, that judge is the head of the 'Good Ole Boy' network. Can this city get any more corrupt?"

"I just thought you should know."

Beau sighed. "Thanks for the call. Keep me posted, will ya?"

"Will do. Good night."

"This city fucking amazes me," Beau hissed, tossing his phone back to the bedside table. "Villerie and Hayes must have done some serious favors for Michelson for him to call an emergency bail hearing on a Friday night. Especially since he wouldn't go near Villerie when he was arrested."

"Maybe the judge wanted to distance himself from Villerie until he found out whether Villerie was guilty or not."

"You're probably right," Beau said, bringing his knee up and resting it on Tollison's cock. He moved his leg up and down as he nuzzled his face in Tollison's neck, kissing him gently. Tollison's cock immediately sprung to action, and he raised his hips to heighten the contact.

"What this?" Beau asked, slipping his hand down and fisting Tollison's growing erection.

"Just a little something that popped up," Tollison teased.

"Nothing at all little about this thing," Beau said, giving it a squeeze. "It'll be a while before I'm able to go back to sleep, so I'm gonna take advantage of the time."

"Good idea."

BEFORE TOLLISON could blink his eyes, it was already Sunday evening. The two days had flown by. Beau had been the ultimate host. On Saturday they had taken a horse-and-buggy ride through the French Quarter, shopped along the River Walk, and even sat at the roulette table at Harrah's for a few hours. On Sunday morning they'd risen early and taken the trolley car down St. Charles Avenue for breakfast at another of Beau's favorite spots and then spent the afternoon tossing a Frisbee around and napping lazily on a blanket at Audubon Park.

On the way home from the park, they'd made a stop at Rouses seafood market and the wine store. Tollison was making his mother's Portuguese fisherman's stew for dinner, and he wanted a certain bottle of wine to accompany the meal. While the stew simmered, they sprawled on the couch, watching a Braves game, Tollison's bare feet propped up on the ottoman and Beau lying with his head in Tollison's lap.

Beau's phone chirped again.

"I'm not answering it!" Beau yelled.

"Sure you are," Tollison said, glancing at the caller ID and handing the phone to Beau. "It's Bruce again."

"Shit," Beau said, sitting up and hitting the speaker. "More good news?"

"You're not going to like this," Bruce warned.

"Let me have it."

"They just found Hayes in his garage. Dead."

Beau looked at Tollison and mouthed, "Fuck! You were right."

"What's the address?"

"I'll text it to you as soon as I hang up."

"We're on our way," Beau said and ended the call. He blinked at Tollison. "How did you know that?"

Tollison stood and walked into the kitchen to turn off the stew. "He was a well-to-do kid. Probably had everything handed to him on a silver platter. If that were you, could you disgrace your family by being on death row? Or even worse, imagine being behind bars for the rest of your life? Now his family can claim his innocence and concoct some story that he just couldn't stand the thought of going to jail for a crime he didn't commit."

"Good point," Beau said, joining Tollison and slipping his arms around his waist. "I'm sorry. This isn't exactly the way I wanted to spend this evening."

"If I'm gonna date a detective, I guess I better get used to it."

"I like the way that sounds," Beau said, stealing a kiss. "Will dinner keep?" he asked, referring to the pot of stew.

"For a couple of hours, at least."

"Good. Then let's go so we can get back."

BEAU AND Tollison arrived at the crime scene to a wailing Harper Hayes sitting on the patio with her face in her hands and her parents and in-laws attempting to console her.

They walked right past her unseen and stepped under the yellow crime scene tape to enter the garage. Bruce was talking to a uniformed officer, and Hayes was hanging from one of the open rafters, a red jumper cable around his neck and a ladder lying on its side under his feet.

Bruce walked over. "Hey, guys. Sorry to bring you out on a Sunday evening."

"Not your fault. What have we got so far?"

"For starters, the coroner's on his way. But from what Hayes and Villerie tell me, they were all together at church this morning, and Hayes seemed fine."

Beau cocked an eyebrow.

"Probably for appearance. Society family and all," Tollison said. "You know. To show a united front."

Bruce continued, "After church, they went to Brennan's for brunch, and according to everyone, Hayes was still in good spirits. After brunch, Harper and Jamison came directly home. Harper said she went to the gallery for about an hour or so, and when she returned and the automatic garage door opened, she found Hayes hanging just like he is now."

"Was there a suicide note?" Beau asked.

"Yep," Bruce said, handing him a handwritten note on Hayes' personal stationary, sealed in a ziplock bag.

> *To My Family,*
>
> *Thank you for believing in me. Although the evidence against me is overwhelming, I just can't bear the thought of spending the rest of my life in prison for a crime I did not commit. Harper, I'm so sorry for disgracing you and our families by taking the easy way out, but if I were to be convicted, I surely would have been put to death eventually; I simply saved the judicial system the trouble. I think this is better for everyone involved. I love you all.*
>
> *Jamie*

"You were right again," Beau said, handing the bag to Tollison.

Tollison read the note and shook his head. "The last thing he could do was try to save his family's reputation."

Tollison handed the note back to Beau.

"Bruce, have the handwriting analyzed to make sure Jamison wrote that note. The last thing we need is another murder on our hands."

"I already put in a request in for samples from his law firm."

"I guess I need to give my condolences," Beau said. "God! I hate this part."

Beau and Tollison walked to the patio area where the Hayeses and the Villeries were still trying to console Harper. "Mrs. Hayes," Beau said. "I'm very sorry for your loss."

Harper looked up and glared at Beau. Even through her tears, the anger and hatred were very obvious. "This is all your fault," she screamed, standing and lunging at Beau. Her father caught her just before her fists landed on Beau's chest and pulled her back. "If you would have just left him alone," she cried. "He had a disease."

"I'm sorry, ma'am," Beau said.

Villerie offered him a sympathetic look and drew his daughter close to him. "If you'll excuse us," Villerie said, leading Harper into the house.

Beau and Tollison walked back to his SUV. When he was out of earshot, he looked at Tollison. "Get her! Hayes stole from his father-in-law and killed two men in the process. And… it's all my fault."

Tollison chuckled and the quickly apologized. "Sorry, I didn't mean to laugh. It's just when you put it that way, it sounds so preposterous."

"It is preposterous," Beau agreed. "But it used to really get to me."

"And now?"

"Not so much," Beau admitted.

Tollison stopped and faced Beau. He put his hands on Beau's shoulders. "Not so much? Beau, what's even more preposterous than Harper blaming you is you listening to her."

"Logically, I know, but I feel sorry for the woman. The man she married was a killer and a thief, but she apparently loved him. And now he's dead."

"I feel sorry for her too, but I'm not blaming myself for her husband's actions."

"I'm not really blaming myself either," Beau said. "It's just sometimes this job really gets to me."

"Let's go home, and I'll draw you a hot bath while I finish dinner. That'll help you relax."

"That sounds nice. But only if you'll join me."

"If I do that, there'll *be* no dinner, and you know it."

Beau rubbed his stomach and offered a sloppy grin. "I've been meaning to lose some weight anyway."

Tollison laughed. "Just get in the car, will ya?"

Beau hesitated. "Let's look on the bright side. With this latest development, you'll probably have to stay on awhile longer until we get this handwriting thing ironed out."

"Good point."

LATER THAT night when they slipped into bed, they simply held each other, every part of their bodies touching in some way. Beau had gotten his hot bath, a blowjob, great wine, and the best Portuguese seafood stew he'd ever eaten. But now his restless thoughts threatened to derail him. Beau knew what was simmering just under the surface, but it seemed like neither one of them wanted to bring it up. *Tollison's leaving in a couple of days* kept running through his head. Beau knew it and Tollison knew it, and they had no idea when they'd see each other again.

Beau tried to ignore the obvious. He pretended that one of the best things that had ever come into his life wasn't leaving him just as quickly.

"Montgomery Beaumont Bissonet, I can hear you thinking."

"Tollison Eduardo Braga Cruz. Not only are you a handsome man, a perfect lover, and a great investigator, you're also a mind reader."

Tollison howled with laughter. "First of all, how in the hell did you remember my full name? I think I only mentioned it once. And secondly, you wear your heart on your sleeve. You're so easy to read."

"*First of all,*" Beau repeated, "I paid attention, and secondly, fuck you!"

Tollison howled again. "No one ever remembers my name except my parents."

"And me," Beau said again, resting his head on Tollison's chest with his leg thrown across Tollison's midsection. The fingers of Tollison's right hand were linked with Beau's left, and Tollison was drawing little circles on Beau's back with the forefinger of his other hand.

"Can we talk about the elephant in the room?" Tollison asked.

"If you're not referring to my extra-large endowment, then the answer is no," Beau teased.

"Come on, Beau," Tollison pleaded, keeping his voice low. "We can't ignore the fact that we've only got a couple more days together before I leave. We have to talk about it."

Beau exhaled. "I don't want to talk about it."

"Okay. Let me try another approach."

"I'm listening," Beau said.

"Why don't we plan our next rendezvous?"

"Okaaay," Beau said. "I'm liking this approach much better."

"I got an e-mail earlier today from my boss telling me that as soon as I wrapped up this case, I was needed in Prague."

"How long will you be there?" Beau asked.

"I don't know," Tollison replied. "Much the same as my trip here. It all depends on how quickly I can recover whatever has been stolen."

"I changed my mind. I'm no longer liking this approach," Beau whined.

Tollison ran his fingers through Beau's hair. "I tell you what. As soon as I get back from Prague, I'll take a couple of weeks off, and you can come to Atlanta and we can head up to the North Georgia mountains for a little getaway. How does that sound?"

"Good," Beau said, dipping his head into Tollison's touch. "That sounds fun. Now I just need to get through however long you're overseas."

"Hey," Tollison said, lifting Beau's face so he could look into his eyes. "It'll be just as tough for me."

"Really," Beau questioned.

"Yes. Really. I've become quite attached to you, Mr. Bissonet."

"Likewise," Beau said.

"So it's settled," Tollison said, kissing the top of Beau's head. "As soon as I'm back from Prague, we're off to the mountains for two whole weeks."

Beau didn't reply, but he nodded.

Tollison lifted Beau's head again until they were face-to-face. He placed a gentle kiss on Beau's lips, then deepened the kiss until Beau was moaning and his hand was lazily rubbing Tollison's chest.

They made love. Slow and easy, each exploring every part of the other's body. They dozed off wrapped tightly in each other's arms and then woke and made love again. Beau desperately wanted to memorize every inch of Tollison's long, tight, muscular body, and the feeling seemed to be mutual. The frantic lovemaking sessions Beau had offered and experienced up until now were replaced with languid worshiping.

WHEN THE sun peeked over the horizon, Tollison was standing naked at the window, holding the drapery back and gazing at the new dawn. Last night he'd been strong for Beau, but it was breaking him to leave this man he'd known for such a short time, but who had somehow worked his way into Tollison's heart.

Tollison was angry that he had no control over his life. He had to go where the work took him. Or did he? He had more than enough money, and he'd always promised himself that when he stopped enjoying the work, he would give it up.

Had he stopped enjoying the work? He'd been too busy up until now, going from one case to the next, to stop and figure it out. He wasn't happy now, but he knew that had a lot to do with leaving Beau. How would he feel if Beau had continued to be an asshole? He'd probably be running for the airport the minute he had the stolen artwork. But Beau wasn't an asshole. He was an incredible man, and Tollison would have a hard time leaving him. He knew he enjoyed the work. It was the traveling that took its toll. Year after year, he barely slept a full month in his own bed, and he was tired of that for sure. But was he ready to give it all up?

Feeling eyes on him, Tollison looked over his shoulder to see Beau leaning on his elbow, resting his head in his hand. "You're gorgeous," he said, holding up the sheet and blanket, inviting Tollison back into bed.

Tollison did his best to muster a weak smile and walked over to the bed and slipped in.

"You're chilled," Beau said, covering Tollison with his body and kissing him gently. "Good morning, handsome."

Tollison smiled. "Morning."

"You okay?"

"Yeah. Just feeling a bit dismal."

"I know. Me too, but we can manage this," Beau reassured him. "I know we can."

Tollison grinned impishly. "Maybe I don't want to manage it."

Beau's expression changed to one of concern.

"No!" Tollison said when he realized what Beau was thinking. "I didn't mean it *that* way. I meant I'm tired of the lifestyle that accompanies my job. I hate the traveling. But I like you. A lot. I want to see where this is going, but I also want to give it a fair shake, and I'm not sure I can do that if I'm gallivanting around the world chasing thieves."

"What are you saying?" Beau asked, sounding encouraged.

Tollison got out of bed again and started pacing the room. He ran his fingers through his hair. "I don't know what I'm saying. Maybe I'm over this job, or maybe I just need a change. No. I like my job, but hell! I want a normal life. A life I can share with someone... someone like you." His voice was sincere and hopeful.

Beau climbed out of bed, dragging the blanket with him. He took Tollison in his arms and wrapped the blanket around them both. He pulled the drapery back. "Look!" he said, pointing to the impending sunrise. "Today is a new day, and let's say it's just for us. Don't make any rash decisions about your job. Get through Prague, and then we'll go on our vacation. If we're still as happy as we are now, we'll figure out a plan together. Deal? We still have tonight. Right?"

Tollison sighed and tightened his hold on Beau. It wasn't perfect, but it was a plan. One with promise and hope, and he could live with that. Together they watched the dawning of the new day. "We do have tonight, and thank you."

ELEVEN

WHEN BEAU and Tollison walked into the station, Captain Trenchard was waiting for them, and he didn't look too happy. "In my office, Bissonet."

Beau looked at Tollison, squared his shoulders, and followed the captain into his office, closing the door behind him. Before Beau could take a seat, the captain turned and looked him in the eye. "You know what I got hit with first thing this morning?"

"I have no idea, sir."

"I got a call from a bigwig at Lloyd's of London."

Beau cocked his head. "And?"

"They want their recovered artwork, as well as their investigator, back. Apparently they have another job for him overseas, and they want him to leave ASAP."

Beau's heart sank, but he managed to mask his feelings. "Sir! I was waiting until we closed the case," he said with no hesitancy in his voice.

"With Hayes now dead, I think you can consider the case officially closed."

"But, sir," Beau said, his frown growing deeper. "We haven't matched the suicide note with any handwriting samples yet. I want to confirm that Hayes wrote that note and we don't have another murder on our hands."

"The way I see it, the stolen art has been recovered, and that part of the case has been resolved. If we have another murder on our hands, it has nothing to do with the paintings or Lloyd's of London. They want their shit, Bissonet."

Beau opened his mouth to protest, but Trenchard held up his hands. "Release it."

"Yes, sir," Beau mumbled through gritted teeth.

Trenchard took his seat. "That's all, Detective."

Beau opened the door and walked out, not bothering to close it behind him.

When he got to his office, Tollison was leaning on the corner of his desk, arms crossed over his chest, with a concerned look on his face. "Is everything okay?"

"He told me I had to turn the recovered artwork over to you immediately so they could send you overseas. Apparently someone at Lloyd's of London is getting impatient."

Tollison looked down at the floor, then back up through his eyelashes. "I was afraid of that."

Beau raised both eyebrows.

"My boss wasn't too happy that you were holding on to it. I tried to explain that you wanted to close the case first."

"Shit!" Beau cursed.

"I mean, it's not like we didn't know this was coming," Tollison said with dread in his voice. "But I thought we had at least one more day."

"I know," Beau said. His voice was laced with disappointment. "I'm sorry. I thought I could buy us some more time. You know, just until we were able to match Hayes's suicide note to his handwriting samples and put this thing to bed. Or put something to bed, at least one more time."

Tollison smiled affectionately. "That would have been nice. But I guess I need to start making some arrangements to get me and those paintings back to Atlanta."

"Can I stow away in your luggage?" Beau asked, walking around his desk and plopping down in his chair.

"I wish you could," Tollison said, hanging his head.

He eventually sighed, pushed himself off of Beau's desk, and stood. "Do you mind if I use one of the conference rooms so I can get started with the arrangements?"

"No. Stay here," Beau said, standing. "I have a staff meeting in five minutes, and it will last at least an hour."

"You sure?" Tollison asked.

"Absolutely."

Beau glanced up at the door out of habit and then stole a quick kiss. "I'll see you in a little while," he said as he turned to leave.

Tollison squeezed Beau's shoulder, and he stopped momentarily. He looked back and tried to smile, then kept going. Tollison trailed a hand down Beau's arm as he walked out of the office, their fingers brushing ever so lightly before the contact was gone.

BEAU RETURNED to his office a little over an hour later. Tollison was on the telephone, looking frustrated and dejected. It was obvious he was talking with one of the airlines, trying to book a flight. "That's not going to work," he said into the phone. "When's the next earliest flight?"

"Damn," Tollison cursed, looking at his watch. "It's gonna be tight, but I think I can make that one. The tricky part will be turning in my rental car."

Beau waved his hand.

"Hold on," Tollison said, putting his hand over the receiver and looking at Beau.

"Let me do that," Beau said. "The rental car return is right there at the airport. I'll follow you to the airport, walk you to your gate, drop off your car, and I'll walk back and get mine. No biggie."

"That sounds like a lot of work for you," Tollison said sympathetically.

"Not at all. I was planning on going to the airport with you anyway."

Tollison smiled. "You sure?"

"Yes! I'm sure. Book the flight."

Tollison confirmed the flight, hung up the phone, and looked at Beau. "I tried to get a much later flight so we could at least have dinner, but everything is booked."

"What time were you able to get?"

"Two fifty-five."

Beau frowned. "What about the paintings?"

"I have a company meeting me here at noon that specializes in transporting valuable cargo."

Beau looked at his watch. "That's two hours," he mumbled, looking disappointed.

"I'm sorry, but that's the soonest they could get here."

"No!" Beau said apologetically. "I was just hoping we could sneak away for a little while before you left."

"Now I'm really sorry," Tollison said, gazing into Beau's eyes.

When there was a tap on the door, they both looked up in unison. "Sorry," Bruce said. "Am I interrupting?"

"No. It's fine," Beau said. "Tollison is just making his arrangements to fly out this afternoon."

Beau watched Bruce's reaction and saw nothing but sympathy for them.

"Wow! I thought you were holding on to the art until the case was closed."

"So did I," Beau said. "But the captain received a call from someone at Lloyd's of London who is very impatient. They want their property immediately."

"I hate to be the bearer of bad news," Bruce said. "But the handwriting results are back and it's a 100 percent match. Hayes wrote that note."

"It's so fucking amazing to me how efficient our people can be sometimes," Beau said thorough a smirk. "When you really need something quickly, it's excuse after excuse. When I was hoping for a little time…. Well, here we are."

Bruce looked down at the floor like he didn't know what to say.

"Well," Beau said, looking between them. "I guess the case is officially closed."

Tollison's frown grew deeper. "I guess I would have been leaving today either way."

"Sorry, guys," Bruce said. "Tollison, for what's it's worth, I think you were an asset to the team. I know I didn't show it at first, but eventually I came to my senses."

"You know what they say," Tollison replied. "Better late than never."

Bruce offered his hand and Tollison accepted it sincerely.

"By the way," Beau asked, "how was your date?"

Bruce looked at Beau and smiled shyly. "It was really good. Thanks for asking."

Beau nodded. "I'm glad."

Bruce looked back at Tollison. "Safe travels, and I hope to see you again very soon."

"Same here."

After Bruce left, Tollison looked at Beau. "You two seem to be getting along better."

Beau nodded. "It only took a stiff kick in the pants from Auggie and me finally getting interested in someone else to help me let go of the anger. But I think we're starting to make our peace."

"Whatever it took, I'm happy for you both."

BEFORE THE transport truck arrived, Tollison ran to Beau's house to gather his things and got back just in time to meet the truck and hand over the goods.

He ran back upstairs to meet Beau and found him in his chair with his back to the door and his feet up on the console behind his desk.

Tollison cleared his throat. "You okay?"

Beau spun around. "I'm good," he said in a defeated tone. "Everything okay with you?"

"Besides the obvious, yeah. Paintings are on their way back to Atlanta, so I guess it's time to go."

Beau got up, walked around his desk, and closed his office door. He took Tollison in his arms and kissed him deeply. When the kiss ended, they were both breathless, and Beau's lips were numb and tingly. "*Now* we can go," he said.

THE RIDE to the airport seemed to pass in seconds. Tollison had this stupid urge to glance at his rearview mirror every couple of minutes to make sure Beau was still following him. He knew in his head he was back there, but his heart kept making him verify it. He pulled into the parking garage, and Beau parked right next to him. Before Tollison could get out of the car, Beau was seated beside him, leaning over and covering Tollison's lips with his own once again. To Tollison, the kiss felt hesitant and desperate all at the same time, and he didn't want it to end. He gripped the back of Beau's neck and pulled him in even closer, the strong attraction starting to boil.

Tollison thought he was acting like a silly schoolgirl after only a couple of weeks with Beau, but damn, the man felt so good in his arms, and more importantly, it felt real. But God help him, he didn't want to leave. He wanted to stay right here and see where this thing would go.

Tollison's heart was racing, and all sorts of crazy things were running through his mind. He could quit his job right now and stay. But he reminded himself that Beau hadn't asked him to do that. In fact, it was just the opposite. Beau suggested he go to Prague and think things through before he made any rash decisions.

Deep down he knew Beau was right. In his travels he'd had affairs before, but they were just that. Affairs. This didn't feel like an affair, at least to him. It had never been this hard to leave before.

Tollison knew he needed to check his bags and get through security, or he'd miss his flight. *That's an idea. I could just miss my flight.*

He slid his hands to Beau's shoulders and pushed gently, reluctantly breaking the kiss. "I'd love to stay right here, but if I'm gonna make my plane, we need to get a move on."

"You're right," Beau said. "I'm so close to begging you to stay right now, but I know I have no right."

"Please don't," Tollison begged. "Because if you do, I'll throw caution to the wind, forego all my responsibilities, and stay wrapped up in your arms for as long as you'll have me."

"In that case," Beau said. "Will you—"

Tollison put his finger over Beau's lips. "Don't."

Beau smiled. "Can't blame a guy for trying."

THEY WALKED to the terminal hand in hand, neither caring nor even paying attention to any heads, if they were turning. After Tollison checked his bags, they walked to the security gate. Tollison turned to say good-bye again, but Beau was already flashing his badge. "Official business," he said. "I'm escorting this gentleman to his plane."

They both cleared security, and Tollison stopped. "How did you get through with your gun?"

Beau winked at him. "I didn't. I left it in the car."

"Smart man."

By the time they got to Tollison's departure gate, the plane was already boarding.

Beau led him to a secluded corner, shoved him up against the wall, and again pressed their lips together in a crushing kiss. "That's to remember me by," Beau said when he pulled away.

"I don't think I'll need anything to remember you by, but that was nice just the same."

Beau walked him to the Jetway and kissed him again on the cheek. "Call me when you land."

"I will," Tollison promised as he gave his phone to the gate agent for her to scan his electronic boarding pass.

Tollison walked to the Jetway, then stopped and looked back over his shoulder, locking eyes with Beau one more time. He smiled and winked, biting his bottom lip as he turned and hurried down the long tunnel to his awaiting plane.

TOLLISON CALLED Beau when he landed and again when he got home. For over two hours, while Tollison unpacked and repacked, they talked. Tollison gave Beau all the details of his task in Prague, which was to recover a piece of valuable crystal stolen from a private home during a recent charity event.

When it got to be pretty late, Tollison reluctantly said his good-byes, with a promise to talk or Skype every day while he was away. Beau offered to help as a sounding board if Tollison got stumped on the case, and Tollison gladly accepted his offer.

TWELVE

TOLLISON HAD been in Prague now for just over two very long and excruciating months. The case had been a difficult one because of the sheer number of people at the event. The process of interviewing each person and clearing them or putting them into a suspect file and trying to make any connections between them had been a painstaking one. Beau had talked to Tollison on a daily basis and had, as promised, been his sounding board, helping him to work through the case day after day.

Helping from halfway around the world had proved to be a challenge. Beau had set up a crime scene board at home, mimicking Tollison's, and they worked through each and every suspect together. Beau found that, just like with the Royal Street heist, their methods of solving cases were very different, which brought two perspectives. And it helped immensely.

In the end, Beau had been the one who made a connection between a member of the domestic staff and her boyfriend, who just happened to drive a truck for the company that catered the event, and voilà, the culprits. As a team, the thieves had taken advantage of the utter chaos surrounding the house in the hours leading up to and after the event, stashed the million-dollar piece of crystal in a rack of dirty glasses on a catering cart, and rolled it right out to the truck under everyone's watchful eyes.

But as Beau had suspected, what had proven to be an even bigger challenge than solving the case had been being away from Tollison. It had truly tested his resolve to talk every day and work so closely without being able to touch him and hold him. Beau had had more phone sex in the last two months than he'd had his entire life and had enjoyed every second of it. Tollison had proven to be a patient and extremely attentive man, even with countries separating them, and Beau thought they would make a great commercial for Skype, except for the sex part. On second thought, maybe that might just turn a few heads. Either way, he was getting the real thing tonight, or probably this afternoon, if he had his way.

With the case now behind them, Tollison was scheduled to land in Atlanta at 1:35 p.m. and Beau slightly ahead of him in the next terminal at 12:57 p.m. Beau rode the escalator down to the trains that took travelers from one terminal to the other, his heart beating rapidly and full of anticipation at the thought of seeing Tollison again.

Reaching Tollison's gate with five minutes to spare, Beau paced back and forth and then took a seat before he wore a rut in the carpet. His blood was flowing through his veins at breakneck speed, and just the thought of seeing Tollison again was sending it all straight to his groin.

Tollison was the first person off the plane, and Beau saw him hastily scanning the crowd. Beau smiled and opened his arms when their eyes met, and Tollison jogged across the gate area and threw himself into Beau's open arms. They kissed right there in front of God and Delta Airlines, and the feeling of Tollison's lips pressed against his was like crack cocaine to an addict.

Beau decided in that very moment, with Tollison's hard body against his, that it didn't matter how long he'd known the man; he wanted Tollison in his life, and he would do whatever it took to get him there.

The drive to Tollison's Buckhead condo was torture. Beau's hands were roaming incessantly. At every red light, he focused his lips on Tollison's neck, face, and mouth. They barely made it into the front door before shoes and clothing were flying across the room. Tollison lead him to the bedroom, and Beau quickly removed whatever clothing he still had on and started on Tollison's. Beau pushed Tollison unceremoniously onto the bed and dove on top of him.

Nearly an hour later, they were tangled in sheets and basking in the afterglow. The rush of seeing each other again was still alive and thundering through their veins, but the urgency was somewhat sated. For now.

"I missed you so much," Beau said, rubbing his hand over Tollison's chest. "My God, that was the longest two months of my life."

"I know how you feel. It was torture for me too, and if it hadn't been for you, I might still be there."

Beau leaned up on one elbow. "I doubt it, man. You would have figured it out, just like you did with Hayes. I just happened to come at it from a different angle and it paid off this time."

"Either way," Tollison said. "I'm just glad it's over. And did I tell you how excited I am about having you all to myself in the mountains for two whole weeks?"

Beau chuckled. "Not half as excited as I am. And that cabin looks great online, by the way."

"Yep, just the two of us at the top of Black Rock Mountain without another cabin for miles. It comes with two horses, a four-wheeler, and most of all, a fully stocked kitchen and bar."

Beau rubbed his hands together. "Sounds amazing. How long is the drive?"

"About two and a half hours, depending on traffic."

"How soon can we leave?" Beau asked with the excitement of a child. "This is going to be so much fun."

"First thing tomorrow," Tollison said through a smile. "But let me assure you, as fun as it's gonna be, it won't be half as much fun as what I'm about to do right now."

"I'll be the judge of that. But go for it, big—" Before Beau could finish his sentence, he sucked in a ragged breath as Tollison covered his nipple and bit gently. "Beginner's luck," Beau teased. "Let me see what else you got."

THE NEXT morning Tollison woke Beau with a kiss and a hot cup of coffee just after five o'clock. Beau felt as happy as a kid on Christmas morning, and his excitement for adventure was building with each minute. They loaded their bags into the car and left just before six o'clock in an attempt to beat the heavy Atlanta morning traffic. Once the October morning warmed up a little, Tollison dropped the top to his convertible and cranked up the music. It didn't take them long to realize they both loved classic rock, and Beau seemed to know the words to most every song on Tollison's playlist.

Forgoing the built-in GPS in Tollison's BMW, Beau had decided he wanted to do things the old-fashioned way, so he brought a map of Georgia and was acting as the navigator with a map spread out on his lap. Tollison headed up GA400, and within forty-five minutes, the mountains appeared in the distance. From there the vistas steadily increased.

As Tollison followed Beau's instructions and started maneuvering through the higher elevations of North Georgia, the greens of the mountaintops were so rich against the brisk, light blue Georgia sky the scene looked like a beautifully vivid oil painting.

When they entered Black Rock Mountain State Park and started up the narrow road to the top of the mountain, the scenery completely opened up, and all you could see for miles and miles were mountaintops shrouded in the fall morning mist. Even though Beau knew they were only a couple of hours outside of Atlanta, it was truly a scene from a wilderness movie and reminded him of the foothills of Colorado. Tollison maneuvered the switchbacks with ease, and before Beau knew it had brought them to a scene right out of a Hallmark movie.

They pulled up to a rail fence that seemed to go on for miles in either direction. They drove down a long and winding road until a log cabin with a weathered cedar roof perched on the highest point came into view. The cabin had a full wraparound porch with an enormous stone fireplace and chimney on one end. There was a barn to the left and a parking area to the right, with an old beat-up pickup truck and a horse trailer parked there, and nothing beyond the cabin but amazing scenery.

When Tollison parked, a silver-haired older gentleman got out of the pickup and walked over to them.

The man leaned on Tollison's door. "Morning, boys. I'm Isaac Templeton, the caretaker here. Which one of you is Tollison?"

"That'd be me," Tollison said, extending his hand. "And this is Beau."

"Welcome to Black Rock Manor. Good to meet you both." Isaac took a step back away from the car. "If you want, I'll show you around."

Isaac handed Tollison a card as he led them to the barn. "You boys experienced riders?"

Beau looked at Tollison and nodded. "Yes, sir," Tollison replied.

"Good. The horses are well trained and at your disposal anytime you want to ride," he explained. "Just give me a thirty minute heads-up, and I'll come right over and saddle them up for you."

"Sounds great," Beau said.

"Also, if you don't mind, I'll come by very early in the morning and later in the day to feed the horses and muck out the stalls, but other than that, this place offers total privacy. If you prefer not to ride and rather me not stop by, I'll just load the horses back into the trailer and you won't see me unless you call."

Beau looked at Tollison. "I don't know about you, but I love to ride, so I say what the hell. Come by whenever you need to."

"Me too," Tollison said.

Isaac nodded. "Great. The four-wheeler is over there and full of gas," he said, pointing over his shoulder. "But if you need more fuel, the gas can is in the barn. Let me show you the cabin, then."

Beau stepped through the front door and froze. The cabin itself was exactly what he'd been expecting. It had a lodge feel to it, with a large, open room with a stone fireplace on one end and a kitchen on the other. Beyond the kitchen was a bedroom and bath. It was furnished in a rustic but comfortable style and was very warm and inviting.

But the mother of all mothers, and what made him freeze, was the view beyond. The entire back of the cabin consisted of multiple sets of double french doors that opened to a porch overlooking nothing but mountains and wilderness for as far as the eye could see. While Tollison looked around the inside, Beau opened the door and stepped out onto a porch that seemed to be suspended in midair.

"Get out here, Tollison," he yelled. "You've got to see this."

Tollison and Isaac joined him on the porch, and they leaned on the railing and looked out over the view in silence.

"Quite the view, huh?" Isaac asked.

"That's an understatement," Tollison said.

"The cabin was built on the edge of a gorge to take advantage of the scenery," Isaac explained.

"It's stunning," Beau whispered, never taking his eyes off the panoramic scene in front of him.

"Should I saddle the horses while I'm here, or do you just want to get acclimated and call me later?" Isaac asked.

"You wanna get settled today and we can ride tomorrow?" Tollison asked, looking at Beau.

Beau heard Tollison talking, but he was still mesmerized. "Sure. Whatever you want," he answered without looking away.

Tollison leaned in closely. "Am I gonna have to compete with this view for the next two weeks?"

Beau finally broke away and looked at Tollison. "Of course not. You'll be part of it."

Tollison smiled, squeezed Beau's shoulder and turned back to Isaac. "I think we're good for today, but we'll let you know about tomorrow."

"Sure enough. I'll be lettin' you boys get settled, but if you need anything, you've got my number."

"Thanks, Isaac," Beau and Tollison said in unison.

THE DAY and nights of the next two weeks all blurred into one fantastic dream filled with four-wheeling, daily hikes, horseback riding, eating, and making love, followed by long naps and simply relaxing on the porch. They'd spent night after night sprawled out in front of a roaring fire, sipping nice wine and simply enjoying each other's company.

On the day before they were to leave, they were lying on the porch in chaise lounges, pushed up against each other, sharing a blanket and waiting for sunset, and Tollison was dozing and snoring lightly. Beau was looking back and forth between the view and the man lying next to him and trying hard to remember the last time he'd been so relaxed and happy.

Over the last two weeks, he and Tollison had always seemed to be in tune and never at odds, and although he knew that wouldn't always be the case, it was a nice change from what his life had become before this man had waltzed into it.

He'd known realistically for a while that he was falling in love with the tall, dark, and handsome Tollison Eduardo Braga Cruz, and he'd also realized he didn't want to be away from him again. But as long as they were in their current jobs, it was surely going to happen. And it was going to happen soon. Tomorrow they were heading back to Atlanta, and he was flying back to New Orleans the following day, neither knowing when they would see each other again or when Tollison would be shipped off somewhere to solve another case.

Since they'd worked so well together on the Royal Street heist and on Tollison's case in Prague, Beau had been tossing an idea around in his head, but he'd wanted to see how this time went before he presented it to Tollison. Everything had been so perfect; he'd almost wished they'd had a disagreement so he could see how they would handle it. But then he remembered how tumultuous things had been when they'd first met, and felt certain that if they could make it from there to where they were now, everything would be just fine.

Now he just needed to find the right time.

Tollison stirred and opened his eyes. "Did I doze off?"

Beau chuckled. "You did."

"I'm sorry."

"What for?"

Tollison rolled over and found Beau's hand under the covers. "Leaving you to fend for yourself."

Beau thought it was time to test the waters. "It gave me a little time to think."

"Uh-oh," Tollison said. "That can't be good."

"It's not good," Beau replied. "It's great."

Tollison sat up a little and inched closer to Beau. "You wanna share?"

"Well, you know how we worked so well together on the Royal Street case and how I helped you in Prague?"

"Yeahhh."

Beau closed his eyes, hesitated, and then just went for it. "What do you think about us going out on our own and opening a company together specializing in private investigations?"

Tollison held Beau's gaze but didn't respond.

This was not the response Beau was expecting, and he started to get nervous. *Did I misread something?* he asked himself, recalling every serious conversation they ever had about their relationship. He stood and starting pacing in front of Tollison's chair. "Tollison," he said softly. "In a couple of days, I go back to New Orleans, and you go God only knows where, and we have no idea when we'll see each other again. I don't want to live like that."

Tollison just continued to stare blankly ahead, and Beau really started to panic. He sat on the foot of Tollison's chair and took his hand. He gave it everything he had. "I'm falling in love with you, and I don't want to be away from you again."

That seemed to get Tollison's attention. His eyes got as big as saucers and he sat up and took Beau's face in his hands. "Yes!"

Beau turned his face into Tollison's hand and kissed his palm. "Yes?"

"Yes," Tollison repeated. "I hoped and hoped, but then I wasn't sure if I was hearing you right. It's been giving me fits for the last couple of days, knowing we were going home and had no real plan. I had already decided I was going to retire and move to New Orleans, if you would have me, but this is even better. I think we'll make a great team."

"Personally or professionally?"

"Both," Tollison said warmly. "I'm pretty sure I'm *already* in love with you."

Beau jumped to his feet, took Tollison by the hands, and pulled him up into his arms. "This is gonna be so much fun."

"Personally or professionally?" Tollison repeated.

"Both" was the last thing Beau said before his lips covered Tollison's.

EPILOGUE

TOLLISON AND Beau spent the rest of the evening, the next morning, and the entire ride back to Atlanta discussing their new venture. They decided that since Beau had so many contacts in New Orleans and most of Tollison's contacts were international, it would make more sense to set up their business in the Big Easy rather than Atlanta. With that decision made, Tollison wasted no time retiring.

As soon as they got back to Atlanta, he called his boss and explained the situation, detailing the part about a new business venture, hoping they might get some business out of his former company and he and Beau might be able to travel together, but mostly focusing on the personal aspect of his reasons for resigning. In an attempt to keep Tollison on the payroll, his boss offered to move him to New Orleans and have him work from there, but Tollison respectfully declined, saying it was time to move on.

It took Tollison a little over a month to tie up loose ends, pack up his condo, and put it on the market. And during that time, he and Beau drove the eight hours back and forth between Atlanta and New Orleans a couple of times a week, not wanting to be apart for more than a few days at a time.

With Lloyd's of London, Tollison's sole job had been to recover lost or stolen items for which the insurance company had paid out claims. When he wasn't on assignment, he was a salaried employee on call and without a current case; it had been relatively easy for him to make a clean break and part ways from his company. But for Beau, it had proven to be a little more difficult. He'd recommended to the captain that Bruce replace him and join Auggie as his new partner, and Trenchard had agreed, but the half-dozen open cases Beau and Auggie had been working on were taking longer to transition than any of them expected.

So while Beau wrapped things up at the station, Tollison focused on their new business and started looking for a location to open their storefront. They'd decided they wanted an old-fashioned "private eye," business, the kind you saw in black-and-white movies, but one with all the latest technology at their fingertips. They wanted to offer their clients a personal touch, and that meant their faces had to be part of the brand. What better way to do that than with an old-fashioned storefront?

On the personal side of things, although it had only been four months, Beau and Tollison's relationship had fallen into a natural rhythm of bliss that worked well. They had both agreed that if things had been different and they had lived in the same town, they would have never moved in together so soon. But that had not been the case, and neither thought it made sense to buy another place or pay rent somewhere when they knew they would be spending all their time together anyway.

One evening over dinner, Beau and Tollison were expressing their frustration about not yet finding the perfect location when Beau's eyes got as big as saucers.

"What?" Tollison asked curiously.

"What about Robinette's place? He *is* dead, you know, and I loved the feel of that place. I'll bet it's available."

"And if we play our cards right," Tollison added. "Iona Ball might still be there and looking for a job."

"Two birds with one stone," Beau said, raising his hand for a high five.

AS USUAL, Beau's hunch was spot-on. Robinette's place was vacant, so Tollison contacted the law firm handling Robinette's estate. They hadn't gotten around to listing the property, which is why it hadn't shown up in any ads.

Beau and Tollison immediately made an offer, which was accepted, and just like that, they had exactly what they were looking for.

And as luck would have it, Iona was also available and happy to come on board. Everything was finally falling into place.

WITH BEAU now totally free of the NOPD, he and Tollison had focused all their energy on the business. They'd shopped the many antique stores of Magazine Street and had found just the right furnishings to enhance their nostalgic vision while meeting their goal of incorporating the very latest technology.

It was a week from Christmas and deliverymen were coming and going with furniture. Phone lines and Internet were being installed, and the sign guy had just finished painting Bissonet & Cruz, Private Investigators on the picture window facing the street. Suddenly, a car came to a screeching halt right in front of their business. Beau, Tollison, and Iona all looked up to see a tall, thin, but not unattractive woman with platinum blonde hair burst through the front door, her stilettos click-clacking on the hardwood floor as she approached Iona's desk, her perfume preceding her.

"May I help you?" Iona asked, with Beau and Tollison looking on from the back of the long, narrow space.

The woman's long fingernails tapped nervously on Iona's desk. "My name is Madeline Rothschild, and I need to see the investigators."

Beau and Tollison looked at each other and quickly walked over to Iona's desk. "I'm Beau Bissonet, and this is Tollison Cruz," Beau said, motioning to his partner. "What can we do for you, Ms. Rothschild?"

"My... my boyfriend's dead," she said frantically, tears now sliding down her cheeks, taking her mascara with them. "And the police won't listen to me."

"Won't listen to you about what?" Tollison asked.

"I think his wife killed him, and she's about to get away with it! Will you please help me before it's too late?"

Tollison gave Beau a knowing glance. "Follow us, Ms. Rothschild," he said, leading the woman to his and Beau's office. "You're our first client."

SCOTTY CADE left Corporate America and twenty-five years of marketing and public relations in 2004 to buy an inn & restaurant on the island of Martha's Vineyard with his husband of nearly twenty years.

He started writing stories as soon as he could read, but only recently for publication. When not at the inn, you can find him on the bow of his boat writing romance novels with his Shetland sheepdog Mavis at his side. Being from the South and a lover of commitment and fidelity, most of his characters find their way to long, healthy relationships, however long it takes them to get there. He believes that, in the end, the boy should always get the boy.

Scotty and his partner are avid boaters and live aboard their boat, spending the summers on Martha's Vineyard and winters in various locations down south.

Visit Scotty at http://www.scottycade.com and Scotty Cade on Facebook @scotty.cade.com and on Twitter @ScottyCade. You can also contact him at scotty@scottycade.com.

Don't miss

Acting Out

By Scotty Cade

After one very long tour of duty in Afghanistan and an honorable discharge from the USMC, Elijah Preston comes home to nothing. He barely scrapes up enough money for a cheap motel in Quantico, Virginia, with no money-making opportunities in sight. A chance encounter in a local Walmart finally gives Eli hope for employment. Elijah is ready to sign on with Royce Mackey's proposition… until he hears what's required. Royce operates a gay military porn site and wants Eli as his next star, never mind that Eli isn't gay. Desperate and broke, Eli grudgingly accepts Royce's offer and soon finds himself immersed in a strange new world.

Hamish Turner's been there before. Taking Eli under his wing, he teaches him everything he can about Royce's operation. The two quickly become friends, easing the way for their first scene together. Awkward at first, they both ease into it and find there is more of a connection between them than either expected. Curious to see where their mutual attraction takes them, they begin a relationship off-screen. But life gets complicated when a crazed fan of Hamish's starts sending threatening letters demanding the scenes between the two men stop. Or else….

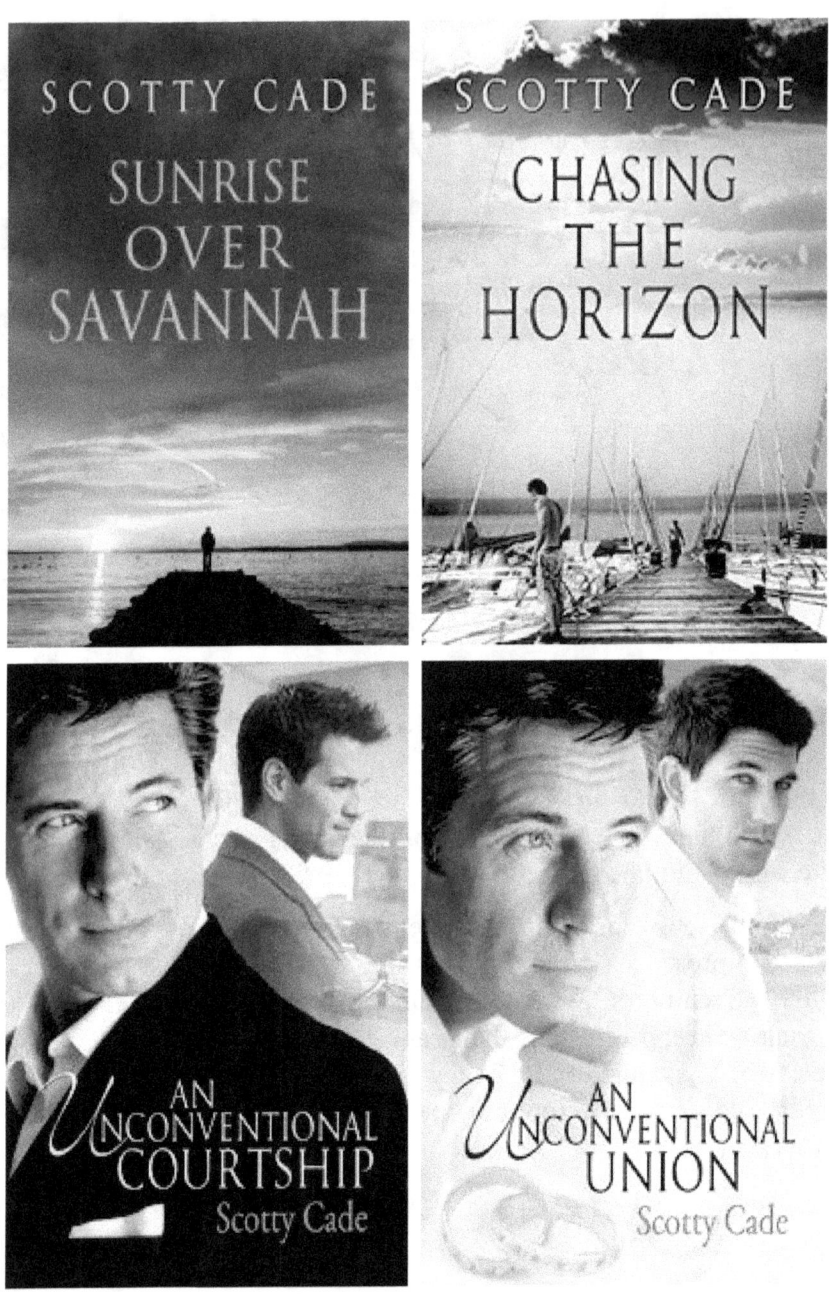

Don't miss

Bounty of Love

By Scotty Cade

The night before his wedding, Zander Walsh, his parents, and his husband-to-be are all shot when they return home and interrupt a mysterious robbery in progress. After three weeks in a coma, Zander wakes up to find out he is the only survivor, and his perfect life falls apart in an instant.

Hunky FBI Agent Jake Elliot is investigating the case, and he eventually apprehends the killer—who soon escapes. Following six months of searching, Zander and Jake realize they're being stonewalled by the FBI… and that they have slowly formed an unbreakable bond that is beginning to turn into much more.

Once they embark on a journey to apprehend the killer for the second time, they'll discover that one terrible night was much more than just an interrupted robbery. Can big business and politics cover up the truth, or will Zander and Jake's quest to unravel the mystery be the end of their newfound love and their lives?

Don't miss

Foundation of Love

By Scotty Cade

Years ago, Wes Stanhope fled his hometown of Charleston to escape the constraints of society and his controlling father, Colonel Robert Lee Stanhope IV. After completing medical school and building a successful practice in pediatric oncology in Seattle, Wes is called home for his mother's funeral and presented with an opportunity to build and run a children's hospital—his mother's legacy—a choice he ultimately makes despite his misgivings about his father's role as chairman of the hospital's board of directors.

When Wes begins to build his team, he is introduced to a young, handsome black architect named Tyler Williams. Sparks begin to fly between the two men, and although Wes doesn't identify as gay, denying his attraction to Ty becomes impossible. But Ty won't be a dirty secret: if Wes wants to build a relationship, he'll have to come out, brave his father's racism and homophobia, and risk his chance to continue as the hospital's CEO and realize his mother's dream.

http://www.dreamspinnerpress.com

Don't miss

Treasure of Love

By Scotty Cade

Hunky Alaskan dive master and charter boat captain Jackson Cameron is absolutely sure he's straight until openly gay treasure hunter Dax Powers calls him and offers him the adventure of a lifetime: Dax and his sister Donatella have found the Anna Wyoming, a ship that went down during the 1889 gold rush on return from Skagway Island—very possibly carrying a fortune in gold.

But real treasure is never free, and this one comes with some heavily armed strings attached. Jack and Dax struggle to keep their small crew safe from a powerful threat while they fight against the attraction they feel for each other. Between the danger of the hunt, the risks in the dive, and the thrill of being lost in passion, Dax and Jack are going to have a hard time holding on to their treasure… and to each other!

http://www.dreamspinnerpress.com

Don't miss

Wings of Love

By Scotty Cade

Devastated after losing his partner of fifteen years to cancer, Dr. Bradford Mitchell tries to escape the emptiness and loss by leaving his life in Seattle behind. Traveling to the Alaskan mountains where he and Jeff often vacationed, Brad reconnects with Mac Cleary, the ruggedly handsome and very straight floatplane pilot who had flown them to Hyline Lake many times in the past. Brad and Mac form an unlikely friendship and buy an old log cabin together, and as he and Mac begin to bring the old cabin back to life, Mac watches Brad come back to life as well, stirring emotions in him he's never felt for a man before.

When fear, confusion, and a near tragedy threaten to force the two men apart, they'll face some tough questions. Can Brad let go of Jeff and the guilt he feels about beginning to care for another man? And can Mac deal with his fears of being gay and accept the fact that he is in love with Brad? It will be a struggle for both men to keep their heads and hearts intact while exploring what life has to offer.

Don't miss

Final Encore

By Scotty Cade

When hunky aspiring country singer Billy Eagan heads to Nashville in search of his big break, a relationship and love are the furthest things from his mind. Taking a foreman's job at the Lazy H ranch and not knowing how he will be accepted, Billy decides to fly under the radar and stay as closeted as he can without denying who he really is. It's immediately confirmed that he made the right decision when he discovers that homophobia is still alive and well in Tennessee.

Then Billy gets his break and meets gorgeous record label executive Ian Dillon. Their worlds collide both professionally and personally, and Billy falls hard. But Ian is still haunted by the mysterious betrayal of his one and only lover, and knowing Billy possesses the power to emotionally destroy him, Ian decides to cut his losses and simply walk away. Determined not to give up on the man he loves, Billy secretly starts to unravel the past and quickly finds that it's not what it appears. Can Billy rescue Ian's heart, or will bigotry and hatred win over love?

http://www.dreamspinnerpress.com

www.ingramcontent.com/pod-product-compliance
Lightning Source LLC
Chambersburg PA
CBHW060049260626
47160CB00005B/1634